WRITER'S BLOCK

Praise for Ali Vali

One More Chance

"This was an amazing book by Vali…complex and multi-layered (both characters and plot)."—*Danielle Kimerer, Librarian (Nevins Memorial Library, Massachusetts)*

Face the Music

"This is a typical Ali Vali romance with strong characters, a beautiful setting (Nashville, Tennessee), and an enemies-to-lovers style tale. The two main characters are beautiful, strong-willed, and easy to fall in love with. The romance between them is steamy, and so are the sex scenes."—*Rainbow Reflections*

The Inheritance

"I love a good story that makes me laugh and cry, and this one did that a lot for me. I would step back into this world any time."—*Kat Adams, Bookseller (QBD Books, Australia)*

Double-Crossed

"[T]here aren't too many lesfic books like *Double-Crossed* and it is refreshing to see an author like Vali continue to churn out books like these. Excellent crime thriller."—*Colleen Corgel, Librarian, Queens Borough Public Library*

"For all of us die-hard Ali Vali/Cain Casey fans, this is the beginning of a great new series…There is violence in this book, and lots of killing, but there is also romance, love, and the beginning of a great new reading adventure. I can't wait to read more of this intriguing story."
—*Rainbow Reflections*

Stormy Seas

Stormy Seas "is one book that adventure lovers must read."—*Rainbow Reflections*

Answering the Call

Answering the Call "is a brilliant cop-and-killer story…The crime story is tight and the love story is fantastic."—*Best Lesbian Erotica*

Lammy Finalist *Calling the Dead*

"So many writers set stories in New Orleans, but Ali Vali's mystery novels have the authenticity that only a real Big Easy resident could bring. Set six months after Hurricane Katrina has devastated the city, a lesbian detective is still battling demons when a body turns up behind one of the city's famous eateries. What follows makes for a classic lesbian murder yarn."—*Curve Magazine*

Beauty and the Boss

"The story gripped me from the first page...Vali's writing style is lovely—it's clean, sharp, no wasted words, and it flows beautifully as a result. Highly recommended!"—*Rainbow Book Reviews*

Balance of Forces: Toujours Ici

"A stunning addition to the vampire legend, *Balance of Forces: Toujours Ici* is one that stands apart from the rest."—*Bibliophilic Book Blog*

Beneath the Waves

"The premise...was brilliantly constructed...skillfully written and the imagination that went into it was fantastic...A wonderful passionate love story with a great mystery."—*Inked Rainbow Reads*

Second Season

"The issues are realistic and center around the universal factors of love, jealousy, betrayal, and doing the right thing and are constantly woven into the fabric of the story. We rated this well written social commentary through the use of fiction our max five hearts."—*Heartland Reviews*

Carly's Sound

"*Carly's Sound* is a great romance, with some wonderfully hot sex, but it is more than that. It is also the tale of a woman rising from the ashes of grief and finding new love and a new life. Vali has surrounded Julia and Poppy with a cast of great supporting characters, making this an extremely satisfying read."—*Just About Write*

Praise for the Cain Casey Saga

The Devil's Due

"A Night Owl Reviews Top Pick: Cain Casey is the kind of person you aspire to be even though some consider her a criminal. She's loyal, very protective of those she loves, honorable, big on preserving her family legacy and loves her family greatly. *The Devil's Due* is a book I highly recommend and well worth the wait we all suffered through. I cannot wait for the next book in the series to come out."
—*Night Owl Reviews*

The Devil Be Damned

"Ali Vali excels at creating strong, romantic characters along with her fast-paced, sophisticated plots. Her setting, New Orleans, provides just the right blend of immigrants from Mexico, South America, and Cuba, along with a city steeped in traditions."—*Just About Write*

Deal with the Devil

"Ali Vali has given her fans another thick, rich thriller...*Deal With the Devil* has wonderful love stories, great sex, and an ample supply of humor. It is an exciting, page-turning read that leaves her readers eagerly awaiting the next book in the series."—*Just About Write*

The Devil Unleashed

"Fast-paced action scenes, intriguing character revelations, and a refreshing approach to the romance thriller genre all make for an enjoyable reading experience in the Big Easy...*The Devil Unleashed* is an engrossing reading experience."—*Midwest Book Review*

The Devil Inside

"*The Devil Inside* is the first of what promises to be a very exciting series...While telling an exciting story that grips the reader, Vali has also fully fleshed out her heroes and villains. *The Devil Inside* is that rarity: a fascinating crime novel which includes a tender love story and leaves the reader with a cliffhanger ending."—*MegaScene*

By the Author

Carly's Sound

Second Season

Love Match

The Dragon Tree Legacy

The Romance Vote

Hell Fire Club in Girls with Guns

Beauty and the Boss

Blue Skies

Stormy Seas

The Inheritance

Face the Music

On the Rocks in Still Not Over You

One More Chance

A Woman to Treasure

Calumet

Writer's Block

The Cain Casey Saga

The Devil Inside

The Devil Unleashed

Deal with the Devil

The Devil Be Damned

The Devil's Orchard

The Devil's Due

Heart of the Devil

The Devil Incarnate

Call Series

Calling the Dead

Answering the Call

Waves Series

Beneath the Waves

Turbulent Waves

Forces Series

Balance of Forces: Toujours Ici

Battle of Forces: Sera Toujours

Force of Fire: Toujours a Vous

Vegas Nights

Double-Crossed

Visit us at www.boldstrokesbooks.com

WRITER'S BLOCK

by

Ali Vali

2022

WRITER'S BLOCK
© 2022 By Ali Vali. All Rights Reserved.

ISBN 13: 978-1-63679-021-3

This Trade Paperback Original Is Published By
Bold Strokes Books, Inc.
P.O. Box 249
Valley Falls, NY 12185

First Edition: May 2022

CREDITS
EDITORS: VICTORIA VILLASEÑOR AND RUTH STERNGLANTZ
PRODUCTION DESIGN: STACIA SEAMAN
COVER DESIGN BY JEANINE HENNING

Acknowledgments

Thank you, Radclyffe, for your support and friendship—I treasure both. Thank you, Sandy, for all you do. You're the best at titles and blurbs and I really do appreciate you and your friendship. As for my BSB family, there are no words adequate enough to let you know how much I care for every single one of you. It's a blessing to go through life knowing there are so many great people who have my back no matter what. Thank you all for your friendship and support in tough times.

Thank you to my awesome editors, Victoria Villaseñor and Ruth Sternglantz. Vic, thank you for all your lessons, and for making me laugh when I explained the premise of this book. I like that you understand me no matter what leaps we're about to take. You and Ruth have taught me so much and given me the courage to try new things. I appreciate both of you. I'd like to thank Jeanine Henning for the awesome cover that sums up this book in one picture.

Thank you to my first readers Lenore Beniot, Cris Perez-Soria, and Kim Rieff. You guys are the best and I appreciate all the help.

A huge thank you to every reader who writes always wanting more. You guys send the best emails, so every word is written with you in mind. This one is a little off my usual path, so I hope you enjoy it. Sometimes all we need is to laugh and forget everything that's happening in the world, and that's what *Writer's Block* is meant to deliver. Another big thank you to all of you for reaching out after the storm. The support, prayers, and good wishes were humbling.

I'm ready to get back to new adventures, so my wish is that we're that much closer to seeing each other in person, telling stories, and sharing a drink or two—an old-fashioned with friends sounds like something to look forward to. For now, I'll lift a glass at home with C. Verdad!

For My Muse
and
To My Fellow Authors and Readers

CHAPTER ONE

Phoned it in and the connection was bad! That's the best way to describe Wyatt Whitlock's latest thriller. Believe me, using the word thriller for this latest work is like trying to squeeze a forty-inch waist into thirty-inch jeans. You can try it, but it's an exercise in futility. Take my advice—skip this one, and try the Yellow Pages instead. It'll be a much more riveting read than *Clifton Heights*.

Wyatt Whitlock read the review, syndicated in dozens of newspapers across the United States, for the fifth time, waiting for the urge to strangle Antonio Skuller with a typewriter ribbon to pass, but no such luck. The slimy asshole took pleasure in other people's pain, especially if they wrote books. The truth, though, was that she couldn't find fault with his review. *Clifton Heights* had started off fine, but then writing it had become like pulling words out of her ass. The problem with pulling anything out of your ass was that it stunk. No matter how fond you were of your crap, it was still crap. You could dress it up, and you could title it, but your shit still stunk. Or was it stank?

"Are you blaming your shit on us?" Her mother's voice popped into her head like it'd been doing for the last three months, as always, uninvited. "I don't need an invitation—I'm your mother. As for the other thing, it's not our fault the gas line in the house shot us into oblivion at two thirty in the morning. Maybe write about *that*. The unfairness of life? That you can complain about, but it's still no one's fault."

"Listen to your mother, kid." Her father's voice hadn't been left out during her slide into a quite humorous but pronounced insanity. She blamed it on the fact that she'd spoken to her parents at least once a day all her life, and in an instant, her sounding boards full of advice and ideas went silent. The quiet some people craved was grating on her nerves and blowing out the creative streak she'd had from age five when she'd written her first two-page book.

She balled up the review and threw it into the fire. The intense but brief fireball gave her a bit of satisfaction. Antonio deserved to get hit, but not necessarily killed, by a city bus. Maybe one of those double-decker numbers always going to Times Square, so the tourists could get pictures and videos of the fucker, moaning as he got gum in his hair. Once the accident made the news, she could write a review about Antonio's pathetic namby-pamby performance.

The white screen with a blinking cursor from hell said otherwise. Her brain had run as dry as the Sahara when it came to the written word. Who would've guessed her creative muses were a contractor and housewife from Brooklyn? Well, that wasn't strictly true—she knew, had always known, her parents' influence. They'd been her biggest cheerleaders and had filled her with the confidence to pursue her passions. That unending support had landed her here.

The brownstone off Central Park was beautiful, according to her mom, and had good bones, according to her father. Now it felt more like a cell than a home, and she had to get out of here or suffocate. She hadn't left it since the funeral, not in the mood to deal with people and their false sympathy. Those insincere voices full of pity were enough to drive her over a cliff. She'd finally ripped the phone out of the wall after some people didn't get the hint when she didn't answer the door. People meant well, but pain was hard to work through. Someone telling her they were sorry didn't mean shit.

Her thoughts ran amok like a mouse who ran a maze in search of cheese but only slammed into wall after wall. She kept slamming into memories of all the opportunities to spend time with her parents she'd missed, times she'd blown them off to work or whatever. Knowing that she'd never have that chance again made her want to go to bed for the next year.

"What the hell are you saying? Are you an idiot?" Her brain had gotten her mother's inflection and word choice down perfectly. "Do you think we want you moping around forever? You spent more than enough time with us. Any more and the world would've demanded you go to therapy for your codependence issues. And you look horrible in sweatpants."

She glanced down at the sweatpants she'd been wearing for five days straight and grimaced at the jelly stain on her knee. Then again, who the hell was going to see her, aside from her dead parents? They dropped in more now than when they were alive.

"We visited plenty despite the crippling traffic into the city. Now, do me a favor, and take those clothes off, take a shower, and go to bed. You're stinking up the place." Her mom would call often with that advice whenever she was battling a deadline. "You're never going to find a wife if you keep acting like personal hygiene is something I never taught you."

One more glance at the laptop confirmed that the screen still hadn't miraculously changed from the blank page, so she slammed it shut and stripped for the shower. The hot water did make her feel more human, and the sheets felt better against her skin as she fell into a dreamless sleep. It was a godsend of oblivion where she didn't have to think about her life and everything that had gone wrong.

As she slept, the blank spaces in her brain started filling with rather vivid pictures, which came with interesting narration by her parents. They supplied a roadmap of what her next steps should be, and their strange plan had nothing to do with writing anything. She woke a few hours later, and the notepad next to her bed held some scribbles, but at the center in her handwriting was: *New Orleans.*

Her dreams came back to her, and she groaned. There had to be some other way to get out of the slump she was in, but her destination was there in big letters. Granted, it appeared like she'd written the words while she was drunk, high, and being chased by killer zombies, yet this wasn't the craziest thing she'd thought about in the last few months.

She opened her laptop, exited the blank page that had mocked her more than Antonio Skuller, and opened Zillow. Scrolling through the houses gave her a sense of purpose, until she stopped her search when her hand momentarily froze, and she shook her head when she glanced at the property. "No. For the love of God and little baby goats, no."

The place didn't look horrible, but she wasn't interested in any real estate in New Orleans. There was a perfectly great luxury hotel downtown. The Piquant had been wonderful the last time she'd been in the city for a book signing. She had no need for an old house that was big enough for a brood of twenty she had no interest in having. Children were like golf and macramé—perfectly lovely pursuits for other people who possessed more patience than she'd have in this lifetime.

That was all true, and yet, she emailed the agent in charge of the property, using more words than she had in weeks. For some ungodly reason, she even made a lowball offer on the place, which for all she knew might just be a pile of rotting boards at this point. According to the listing, the house was last sold in 1913, which seemed strange. Either the owners were a hundred and fifty years old, or the house had been uninhabited for ages.

Fifteen minutes later, her email dinged with a response from Pippa Potts, the agent. Who in the hell named their child *Pippa* if their last name was *Potts*? And if *Potts* was a married name, Pippa should've taken a hard pass on doing that to herself. She'd have to ask if they met, but right now she concentrated on what Pippa had to say. Pippa had contacted the owners, gotten them to accept her offer, and drawn up a bill of sale. In a word, Pippa was impressive.

Buying a house on the internet wasn't wise, but Wyatt suddenly couldn't wait to close the deal. The image of writing on her front porch while she sipped a drink and waved to the neighbors appealed to her recalcitrant muse. After months of looking at a blank page, she figured her muse had packed and taken a slow boat to Tahiti.

"Why the hell not?" She studied the pictures again and printed the documents Pippa had sent. Maybe Realtors in Louisiana had alarms on their email that ensured no customer got away, no matter the time. She filled out the offer page, signed it, and sent it back. She was losing her mind. Should it be concerning that they'd accepted an offer well below the asking price, with no negotiation and within minutes of the offer? Nah. It would be fine.

She scanned and emailed it all back, glad she'd at least written her name and contact information a bunch of times. It counted as actual writing. The excitement gave her the energy to change her sheets, and she fell back into bed. She felt like she could sleep for days, but that wasn't in any way true. She'd gotten really good at lying to herself about a lot, but not that. Still, two hours or so would be better than nothing.

Chapter Two

The weather app showed the temperature outside was eighty, sunny, and humid. That made total sense to Hayley Fox since her plane was taxiing to the terminal in the New Orleans airport. What didn't compute was the next day would be in the forties. That was an epic swing for Mother Nature and might prove there really was such a thing as climate change no matter what the science deniers said.

"Have you been to the city before?" The old lady sitting next to her finally asked a question. Up to now Hayley had listened to the woman talk about her life and family drama as if Hayley was taking copious notes for a biography of the woman's life. "Be careful with your purse."

"Thank you, but I've lived here since August. I just went home to visit my parents for a couple of days." She glanced at her email, hoping their talk was now at an end and they'd never see each other again. This woman was like a walking word salad.

Hayley made it outside with her small bag and was oddly comforted to be back. As a native New Yorker, it'd taken some time to get used to the laid-back attitude most New Orleanians had about pretty much everything. Although her parents were now farmers, they'd lived in the city while Hayley was growing up. After their retirement a few years ago, they'd literally bought a farm, and she'd waved them good-bye, staying on in the city and taking an entry-level job in publishing, right out of college. Two years later, she left New York to move up the publishing ranks. It was like paying her dues in the minor leagues before she got her shot at the big show.

She was now the senior editor and acquisitions manager at Fleur-de-Lis Publishers, working directly with the acting publisher. Once her new boss, Marlo Aiken, knew she could trust her not to burn the business to the ground if left unsupervised, she'd made her responsible for a number of their authors. The move, the job, and her growing list of contacts were all part of her grand plan. Two years in New Orleans would open the doors to big New York publishing houses and a management position. Once she got all that, she could go home and go back to being ignored by everyone she came across on the street. New Orleans, she found, was the capital of Niceville. Everyone said hello.

"Are you back?" Marlo asked. Her boss was great at her job but shit on the phone. It wouldn't matter if she was Attila the Hun, though—the owner, Cornelius Washington, was Marlo's dad. Cornelius had founded Fleur-de-Lis for numerous reasons, the main one being a great city deserved a publishing house, one that would concentrate on the talent prevalent in the South.

"I'm almost to my car," Hayley said. "Did you get the notes I sent yesterday?" Whatever this call was about probably meant a change of plans. Now that she was home, all she could think about was GW Fins and their panko Parmesan crusted grouper. She'd made a reservation for one for tonight.

"I did, but we have a problem with a few of our current projects." Marlo stopped, and it sounded as if she was taking some deep breaths, but Hayley knew better. Marlo was a chain-smoking, coffee-drinking workaholic who loved five o'clock cocktails. Her boss's problems in most cases revolved around stuff she had no desire to do, and not actual problems.

"What projects?" Hayley crossed her fingers, hoping it wasn't one of the resident pain-in-the-ass children. Writers could be temperamental divas when you started editing their work. Cutting a paragraph—God forbid, two—was tantamount to calling their mother a whore. Some of them didn't take it well.

"The anthology you pitched me, for one. We assigned it to Cheryl, but she might not be ready to be thrown into the deep end just yet." Marlo took a few more deep breaths. "That, and there was a false fire alarm, and the NOFD wouldn't let us back in the building for three days. It brought everything to a halt, and we need

to make up some time. Can you run by and pick up the file? I can
have Cheryl bring it to you if you're tired."

So not what she wanted to do on a Saturday night no matter how
pathetic her love life was. Sometimes you had to put your foot down
and narrow people's options if you wanted to get anything done. She
was in no mood for sweet and sincere after the lady from the plane.
Cheryl was a recent hire, and they hadn't gelled. She mostly kept to
herself, which wasn't a problem, but Cheryl was a little…different.
Hayley knew her well enough now, though, to know Cheryl's little
quirks and that she was actually a shy pushover. Which was like
being a vegetarian shark. Cheryl's other problem was her belief God
would strike her down if she worked on certain projects. Sex was at
the top of that list, so Hayley imagined editing a gay sex anthology
had sent her into a tailspin. The word *fucking* in any manuscript
gave Cheryl the vapors, as some old Southern ladies would say.

"Can I connect with her Monday? I promise I'll get us back on
track since it was my idea, but I'm exhausted." It wasn't a lie per
se, but she couldn't handle Cheryl after all the explanations she'd
had to give her mother over the entire weekend about life in New
Orleans.

"You can wait until the end of the week. I just called to make
sure you got back okay." There was more heavy breathing, and then
Marlo hung up.

"Translation, I'm tired of dealing with my father and everyone
in the office, so get back here before I throw my ashtray at someone."
She laughed at Marlo's impatience with people. The written word
was something Marlo loved, but people, not so much.

The late afternoon traffic into downtown was like in any city,
and she was happy to exit into the Quarter after forty-five minutes
of stop-and-go. There was still a logjam of cars, but once she was
on the other side of Esplanade, it was much quieter. The Faubourg
Marigny was the neighborhood next to the French Quarter, and
Hayley had fallen in love with it right off. Tourists flocked to places
like Bourbon Street, but the Marigny was a more laid-back and
eclectic place full of locals.

Her house had been a deal, according to her father. Fred Fox
was a retired trader who'd made enough money to do what he really
wanted, and that was growing organic malt and hops. On Wall Street

her father had the Midas touch, and that luck had followed him into farming. Every self-described brewmaster had him on speed dial. When she'd taken the job with Fleur-de-Lis, her father had pushed her to buy a house. Investment in real estate always trumped paying rent.

"I'm home," she yelled, even though her two cats, Truman and Hugo, were still at the sitter's. Living alone was good because she didn't know if she was ready to share space with anyone, but she did miss conversation. If there was an app that would schedule someone to come over and talk for about twenty minutes and then leave, she'd sign up. And if they replaced conversation with uncomplicated sex, like, every third time, that'd be good too. Right now, she was fine talking to her two rescues.

The house was way too big—and hot, since she'd forgotten to leave the thermostat at some tolerable temperature when she left—yet it also gave her the sense of the history in this place that'd survived. It was a work in progress, and she was enjoying the restoration process in very small doses, but she was taking a break. At the moment her electricity, water, and air-conditioning worked. "I can live with peeling paint and a yellow tiled bathroom."

Her mother wasn't so sure. Esther Fox was a true-crime buff who probably knew more ways to kill someone than six serial killers combined. Hayley found this humorous, but she did worry for her father at times, especially now that her parents were together constantly with the quiet you could only achieve by being surrounded in malt and hops for acres. Their battle of the moment was window coverings, or Hayley's lack of window coverings. According to her mother, she might as well put a sign on the front door that said *Come in and kill me*.

She brought her bag upstairs and glanced out the naked window. The house next door had been vacant for years, according to the other neighbors, and she hoped it stayed that way. The last thing she needed was the place to turn into a crack house for squatters, or to have someone like George St. Germaine move in. George and his wife Karen lived on the other side of her, and the guy was like a friendly stalker if there was such a thing.

"With any luck he won't notice I'm back."

Hayley got naked and headed for the shower. Her talkative

seatmate on the crowded flight home had one of those gagging perfumes that smelled like gardenias, and it clung to her now like bad lint. She had one more day to relax, so she was putting everything off until Monday. If the weather delivered on the promise of rain and cold temps, she'd stay in and finish the book she was reading or cook.

"My life is so full."

CHAPTER THREE

A ll we need is a cashier's check and your signature, Ms.
Whitlock." Pippa Potts sounded way too perky for someone
who'd called Wyatt at six in the morning, which meant it was five
in Louisiana.

After a brief hello from Wyatt, Pippa had taken off like her
commission depended on speed and word count. Ah, word count.
Wyatt missed thinking about those, but right now she concentrated
and added an uh-huh where it seemed appropriate. She was back to
staring at her bedroom ceiling, contemplating if she'd accidentally
taken drugs the night before. But no, she remembered everything
she'd done. There was no way she'd remember her social security
number if she was high or drunk. Today was a new day and along
with that came a new list of things to accomplish. 1) Stare at
computer for hours. *Check.* 2) Carry on mental conversations with
dead parents. *Check.* 3) Buy old house sight unseen because she was
a total git. *Double check.*

She'd always preferred the British *git* to *idiot*. It made her
sound refined. When other people went off the deep end, they bought
things like cocaine or a high-end escort, not real estate.

"They just want to make sure you understand you're buying the
property and contents as is." Pippa lost some of her exuberance with
that comment. "The Fuller house has been empty for about a decade,
and the original owner's great-great-grandchildren are finally ready
to let go of it. The new family home is in the Garden District."

"I understand that, and I'll be driving down, so give me a few
days. I'll hand-deliver the check myself. Anything else I need to

send you in the meantime?" She had to get off the phone and make coffee. There was no food in the house, but the day she ran out of coffee, the apocalypse would be upon them.

"That would be great. I'll let Gator Fuller know your timeline. That's the current owner."

"Their legal name is Gator?"

"Gosh, no. Sam Fuller IV is the head of Fuller and Sons Produce but goes by Gator. Sam's great-grandfather Sam and his wife Lydia purchased the house in the early 1900s when they decided to live in town. The family relocated to Uptown in the eighties, and the last holdout in the house moved after Lydia died at a hundred and two."

"The house has a long history then. Are they sure they want to sell? I'd imagine that much history would be hard to let go of."

"Gator and the siblings agree it's time, so this should be easy peasy."

"Thank you," she said, not giving Pippa the opportunity to add anything else. After using the term *easy peasy*, what more could you add?

"See you in a few days then, Ms. Whitlock." Pippa paused and giggled for some reason. "You aren't *the* Wyatt Whitlock, are you?"

"The writer, you mean? No, there's about twenty of us in the city. We have a support group to help us deal with that question. See you soon." It wasn't a total lie. She hadn't written anything in months. The English language had deserted her so completely that she was shocked she was still able to speak clearly enough to have people understand her.

"Okay then, safe travels."

She hung up and scrubbed her face with her hands. There was no reason to spend another day in this house, wondering what the fuck had happened. The only dilemma now was that she didn't own a car.

"Your father owns a truck. Take that, and remember you still have a life. The old boom-boom happened to us, not you." Her mother's helpful reminders and humor made her sure that if this was insanity, she'd at least laugh her way through it.

The cabbie she waved down talked her ear off all the way to Brooklyn, and she figured it had to do with the boredom of the job. Either that or her face and voice were the human equivalent of truth serum. Either way she now knew the best delis in the city and where not to buy bagels. The other wisdom she was blessed with was if you had children, not to have boys. They were all the spawn of Satan, especially if they were teenagers.

"Thanks, and no need to wait." She pushed some cash through the divider and walked off before the guy gave her any other helpful hints.

Her parents' house had been leveled in the gas line explosion that had damaged another ten homes on the block, so there was no going back there, but their two vehicles had survived. She'd placed them into storage until she decided what to do with them. Of course, if she had to decide right now, they'd stay here gathering dust until she died because she'd never sell them.

She raised the door on the unit. Her mom's Bug had a layer of soot on it, but her dad's truck was just how he'd left it. The old thing cranked right up, and she took a moment to cry for the four hundred sixteen thousandth time since their deaths. Her dad's 1975 Ford F-100 truck was a collectible, but he'd used it for work every day just like his father had done before him. All his tools were in the back, and she left them there as she drove back into the city.

There was packing to do and bad news to break, and she didn't have all day. She made the call to her agent Blanche Peron and held her breath to remind herself to stay calm. Blanche had gotten her job because of her drive and talent for the industry, but also for the name *Blanche*. It reminded Wyatt of *The Golden Girls* and *A Streetcar Named Desire*. Flawed but beautifully written characters were a weakness of hers. She also couldn't help singing "Don't Cry for Me Argentina" whenever she said her last name.

"Hey, I'm down the street from your house," Blanche said. "I picked up all your favorite snacks to power you through those late-night writing sessions. If you're finally calling me, it must mean you have pages."

"That's not the reason for the call." She zipped her duffel and carried it downstairs.

"You're such a kidder. Just wait a few minutes and you can surprise me." Blanche was good at her job because she possessed enough relentlessness for eighteen normal people. She was a human equivalent of a sledgehammer, and she always aimed for the face.

Wyatt was about to say something when she heard the doorbell and hung up to answer it. It was Blanche. If there was a way to schedule a root canal instead of having this conversation, she'd do it. There were times she was convinced Blanche actually worked for the publisher. Her mother had never liked Blanche and hadn't fallen for the cute name. One more bit of advice she should've listened to, but luckily for her, her mother had eternity to remind her of all those mistakes.

"I'm leaving for a while, so there aren't any pages. What I really need is for you to get me out of my remaining obligations." She grabbed the leather messenger bag her mom had given her and packed her laptop and sleeve of pens. Her parents had said they were the tools of a writer, and to do a job well you needed the right tools. They hadn't done much good lately, but she could pretend.

"What exactly does that mean?"

Blanche had that high-pitched tone going, like a warning signal that made dogs bark for a five-mile radius. Instead of a fire, though, that tone marked the unleashing of the mood Wyatt liked to call *I'm going to lose my shit.*

"You said you needed space, Wyatt, and I gave you plenty of it. Virgil's expecting a manuscript next month. He's been screaming for pages, and I've put him off."

"I don't have any pages, and I'm not going to have any." She scribbled a note for her cleaning lady and tried her best to keep the table between them.

"What the hell *have* you been doing, Wyatt?" Blanche had her hands on her hips, and Wyatt was sure she did that to keep from hitting her. "I knew I should've come sooner."

"I've been grieving, Blanche. Remember my parents?" She shut the bag and shouldered it. "They're going to want their advance back, and I need you to take care of that as well." She put her hand up. "Actually, I'll send it back myself."

"That'd be the worst mistake you can make. Virgil"—Virgil Billingsley, the editor in chief of the imprint that published her—"will blackball you," Blanche said. "I know the last book wasn't stellar, but it was a one-time thing. You're still at the top, so giving up is career suicide."

"Are you talking about me or you?" She grabbed a diet drink

and faced Blanche. Maybe she should've held out for a Stella. Flawed characters were often described that way because they were crazy, and sometimes crazy could kill you.

"You know damn well that I want more than a working relationship, so don't give me that." If they'd been standing on a snow-covered mountain, Blanche's shrieking would've caused an avalanche by now. "I love you, and I've given you space and everything else you wanted. All I want is for you to love me back and get back to work. Think of what a marriage between us could accomplish."

She took a moment to do what Blanche asked and thought about it. The possibility of being trapped in a house with Blanche scared her more than kidney pie. There were certain things not meant to be eaten or contemplated. If there was a list, kidneys and any other internal organs should be on it, right there beside marriage to someone like Blanche. "It's not like you're living in squalor, Blanche. Your commissions have made you a rich woman, but now it's time to give it a rest."

She glanced around to see if she'd forgotten anything and noticed, like she always did, the character you never saw in new construction. Her father had spent days working with his crew to restore the house to its original look. She loved this place, and it was the best thing her book royalties had gotten her. Now the writing awards and fame weren't going to change the fact that the part of her mind that'd percolated with so many stories had gone cold. That was a death knell to a writer. Imagination was as important as being a good storyteller. You could write beautifully, but without a good story it was just words.

"You're under contract, Wyatt. Leaving isn't going to be that easy." Blanche had gone from hysterical to venomous as fast as Superman got out of his business suit. Now was the time to wonder if Blanche kept a cattle prod in her purse. "You don't disappoint the publisher and expect to work again on this level."

"I'll be gone at least a month." She was tired, and she could almost feel her mom tugging her by the ear to get her going.

"Wyatt, I need you to listen to me."

She took a few deep breaths, trying to calm the need to run even if it took tackling Blanche to get to the door. That thought actually lightened her mood. "What I need is to get out of here, so move." Damn if Blanche didn't have a way of sucking the life and air out of the room.

"It's a phase, and it'll pass. Virgil will understand, considering your parents. All you need to do is get back in your study and start writing."

Venomous with a side of syrupy was hard to swallow. "Do I have to spell it out for you? There's not one story in my head. That's called writer's block, and if you mention my parents, Virgil, or getting back in the saddle, you're fired." She hadn't strung that many words together in weeks. She'd developed a readership through what the reviewers said was excellent dialogue, but her real-life conversations seldom lived up to the written word. From the look on Blanche's face, her words had made an impact.

"What happens after a month?"

She could tell Blanche was trying to hold back, and she was almost successful. The clenched jaw and fists meant holding her temper in check was like holding a wild stallion with a yo-yo string. "I don't know. We'll see." She pointed to the door and locked it when Blanche made it to the sidewalk.

"We'll see? That's not good enough."

"That's all I got. Take some time and concentrate on your other clients. I'm sure they'd love the attention." She kissed Blanche's cheek and left her standing there. It was time to start over and maybe dedicate herself to something else. She was getting good at staring at ceilings.

CHAPTER FOUR

Hayley woke to pouring rain and a cold room. "So much for my day of exploration and eating out." She'd been too tired the night before to head to the restaurant, so she'd eaten a doughnut and called it a night. The alarm had gone off at six, and she'd come close to beating it to death. It was now after ten, so she threw on an old sweater, mentally bracing herself to sit on the toilet. There was no experience like sitting on an ice-cold seat in an old house first thing in the morning. "Shit," she said loudly.

The freezing bathroom made her consider getting back in bed under a pile of blankets instead of making coffee, but she needed it like she needed peanut butter and books. Those were her three life obsessions, and they really were safer than crack, STDs, and Jack Daniel's. After surviving the toilet horror, she headed down to her Wolf Gourmet coffee maker. It was a splurge that was totally worth it.

She poured her first cup and hit speed dial. "Hey," she said when her friend Lucy Nguyen answered. Lucy had a way of sounding like she'd awoken from death whenever Hayley called her this early. "Want to come over for breakfast?"

"It's raining and I worked until two. Why do you hate me so much?"

"It's ten in the morning, so get up." She'd gone grocery shopping before visiting her parents to save a trip now. Coming home to an empty refrigerator sucked. "It's disgusting outside, so we can eat and watch a movie."

"You expect me to go out in the rain after dealing with drunken bridal parties all night? I swear, I still haven't gotten the smell of vomit out of my nose yet." If there was an Olympics for whining and bad attitude, Lucy would have won her weight in gold medals by now.

"I promise I'm not hiding any bridesmaids in my house, so put on underwear and get over here." She took out everything she needed to make pancakes, hash browns, and bacon.

"If the underwear is a deal breaker, you're going to have to wait until I do laundry."

She laughed so hard she snorted. "You have thirty minutes. After that you tempt fate by leaving me alone with the syrup."

"Is that a proposition for sex?"

Lucy had been her one and only internet date, and they made better friends than lovers. Not that Lucy wasn't sexy, beautiful, and smart, but she was not at all her type. Hayley was a femme in search of the perfect butch who wasn't obnoxious or a total player. She and Lucy had that in common. God only knew why they'd been matched on the dating site in the first place.

"Wait," Lucy said, "you're using me as bait to avoid George, aren't you?"

"George will be too busy trying to keep all his rabbits dry to worry about you."

"All right already, but I have to shower and brush my teeth. Last night really was disgusting, and I was too tired to care when I got home. Can I use your washing machine if I promise to be gentle?"

"Yes. Should I get you an Uber? You can't ride your bike in this."

Lucy's grandparents had immigrated from Vietnam, but Lucy and her parents were true New Orleanians. She lived near Hayley in a small apartment, didn't own a car, and seldom left the Marigny or the French Quarter unless forced to do so. The thing in her profile that'd drawn her to Lucy was that she loved to read, but her job at the Irish pub in the Quarter left her little time for much else. Their only official date had been a long conversation over dinner about their favorite books and lip gloss.

They'd ended up as friends, and Lucy was the sounding board and best friend she'd never had.

"I'll get Larry to drop me off. You can bring me back after you feed me three meals and entertain me."

The batter was done as the sky outside really got dark, and the rain came down hard enough to make it almost impossible to see past three feet. She opened the door to Lucy, who hadn't bothered to change out of her pajamas. "You're soaked."

"Give me your robe, and I'll wash my pj's first." Lucy kissed her cheeks and dropped a large sack of laundry at her feet. "I'd eat my pancakes in the buff, but George is probably watching us through a high-powered telescope, the weirdo."

"That's why I'm glad the kitchen and my bedroom are on this side of the house." She started heating her griddle while Lucy stripped and filled the washer. "How's work?"

"Work is like a revolving door of assholes sometimes, but I love the people I work for and with." Lucy sat at her kitchen island and rested her head in her hand. "I can never convince my mom of that. She wants me to come work for her at the restaurant."

"Wants you to or is insisting?" She flipped the pancakes and glanced back at Lucy. "If she's anything like my mom, it's a barrage of demands."

"You're an editor," Lucy said laughing. "What's the problem? Does she think you'll read yourself to death?"

"She wants me to move closer because New Orleans isn't safe."

"That argument would make sense if you were from a small town with a population of a hundred, where everyone is pasty white and fond of fanny packs. You've spent most of your life in New York." Lucy used her hands a lot when she talked and now was no different as she pointed at her with both index fingers before going back to some sort of sign language only she knew.

"The small town part I understand, but pasty white and fanny packs escape me." She flipped the pancakes again before plating everything.

"Scary white because the weather permits them to be outside for, like, two days before it starts snowing again…duh. They're fond of fanny packs because they've established gathering tendencies like squirrels preparing for winter." Lucy smiled as she poured an unhealthy proportion of syrup on her plate. "You've been in the Quarter when these kinds of tourists descend on us, so you know what I'm talking about. They're usually in big shorts with legs so white you want to give them money to wear pants. That's the exact opposite of what usually happens on Bourbon, when they start to show even more skin after they've decided to give absinthe a try."

"You should work for the tourism bureau. And I'm not sure, but I think you might have insulted me and my pasty-white skin." She joined Lucy in trying to use up all the syrup in the house.

"You've lost the Casper-white thing you had going when you first got here, but we'll have to accept you'll never tan. It makes your blond hair really pop, so it's not a problem you should obsess about." Lucy took a bite of the pancakes. "My point is your mom's crazy in an overprotective kind of way. She's only going to get worse while you're here, and she's got no one but your father and the goats to talk to."

"Mom doesn't have goats." A bolt of lightning lit up her kitchen, followed by a boom strong enough to rattle her dishes. "Don't worry, I'm not going anywhere. I love my job in the city."

"Don't lie, girlfriend." Lucy was now using a fork to make a point. "New Orleans is a pit stop for you. The action you want is in New York."

"Eventually, but being here has changed my mind about my timeline. Besides, there's talent here, and I want to develop it." Fleur-de-Lis had a great group of authors writing mostly romances, but they were expanding into mystery and paranormal. Given they were in New Orleans that made sense, but Hayley wanted to put their fledgling LGBTQ branch on the publishing map. "I got Marlo to go for the anthology."

"That's great. Any good stories you want to share? If I can't find the perfect woman, I can at least read about her."

"I'll let you know this week. Marlo assigned it to Cheryl, and there's been some sort of problem." There'd have to be some reshuffling of her schedule if she took on the project as well as whatever else was wrong.

"Cheryl? Like in Southern Baptist, I-probably-have-a-pet-rattlesnake-for-when-I-praise-the-Lord girl?" Lucy's description was accurate, but she hoped Cheryl was a tad more professional than that.

"That's her, but she does have a unique gift when it comes to finding errors in manuscripts."

"Of course—it's God-given," Lucy said.

The joke made Hayley spit out a mouthful of hash browns. "Today isn't the day to tempt God. I'd miss you if you got hit by lightning." She had a circle of friends in New York she still kept in touch with, but no one made her laugh like Lucy. "I'll give her a pep talk, and I'm sure she'll be fine."

"The girl boycotted Disney because they offered partner benefits. Never mind that she's never been to Disney in her life."

"*Bambi* is her favorite movie, though, and it was a huge sacrifice to vow to never watch it again."

"How'd she get hired, anyway?"

"By not mentioning her questionable views during her interview. There'll be hell to pay now if we fire her because of her devoutness." It really did suck that people couldn't practice what they were supposedly learning on Sunday. Being a devout Christian didn't give you permission to sit in judgment of everyone else, especially on issues like who they loved. "I've always said Cheryl's repression would unravel with the right woman. She gives off that kind of vibe."

"Do Baptists use holy water? Believe me, you'll be swimming in it if you decide to test your theory."

"I'm not sure. I was raised by two Episcopalians who were allergic to going to church, and eww. Don't be disgusting, or it'll ruin my pancakes."

They kept talking until they finished eating what she'd cooked, and then they hit the sofa and Netflix. The storm raged outside, and she watched it sheet down her windows. This was her life, and she was content. Would finding someone who provided what Lucy did as well as sex be welcome? Of course, but she was still young, and that would come in time. It had to. She wasn't built to be alone for the long haul, yet she wasn't one to settle.

CHAPTER FIVE

There's a few things you should remember, Whitlock." Wyatt spoke loudly to hear herself over the wind rushing in from the window. It was freezing, but that and talking to herself kept her awake. This drive was as monotonous as the background of a cartoon. *The Flintstones* had been way before her time, but she'd seen endless reruns. When Fred and Barney drove in their stone car to the bowling alley, the background was all the same. Rock, rock, tree, shrub, repeat. That was it.

"Kind of like this homage to *Children of the Corn*." The radio seemed programmed to only play country-western songs from the sixties. All these ballads of unrequited love and heavy drinking made her sure that she wasn't as mentally unbalanced as she thought if people really did sit in bars, crying into their beers over some woman.

"You were talking about things you should remember," her father said. "Aside from not pushing my baby over sixty-five, that is."

"One thing for sure is that a tropical island would be a good place to go if I'm going mental, or maybe Paris. I could've flown and saved myself all this driving." The only real conversation she'd had aside from with her deceased parents was with Virgil Billingsley. He hadn't been thrilled with her but understood her reasoning. She'd phoned the bank right after and sent the advance back, so now she was free of her obligations. At least her contractual obligations.

The thing about her was she was wired to always have some goal in mind. That made her flip through possible book ideas in her head yet again to see if something came to her. It was like flipping through index cards at the library—back when libraries had such things. Society was trying to eliminate paper, but she loved paper as much as the crooner on the radio loved whiskey and loose women.

"Maybe that'll be my next hobby. Whiskey, women, and romance novels." All this angst and talk of drinking, fantasizing about women, and admiration of horses made her sure she could write a romance. All she had to do was replace her trademark murder, intrigue, and the broody cop with flowers, long beach walks, and goats. Women loved goats. She was sure there'd been studies.

Basically, that kind of book was the exact opposite of what she was known for, and it would kill Blanche if that's what she pitched. Her brain was way off the mark, but hell, she was way off the grid of her normal. All this corn, and where she was going weren't in her norm either, but she figured the only way back was to explore the unknown.

"Good Lord." Getting philosophical before lunch was an invitation to massive heartburn. She took the next exit off the interstate that had signs of life—well, aside from the corn—and filled up. It was her strong opinion Starbucks should venture to places like this if only to show the truckers what they were missing. A good latte could open anyone's horizons and prove there was a God.

"What can I serve you, baby?" The waitress at the truck stop was friendly and chewed gum as if it was a competitive sport.

"Coffee and a burger." With all the corn in the area, she figured the cows were eating well.

The woman screamed her order through the opening to the kitchen and grabbed a mug. She was getting a big tip for dumping the carafe and brewing a fresh cup. "Where you headed?"

"New Orleans." Her characters tended to provide short answers, giving as little information as possible, and at times that trait bled into her life. Hell, if the killer talked right off, the book would be boring.

"That's exciting." The woman popped her gum with impressive loudness.

The judge from New York gives her a ten, giving Mindy the waitress a perfect score in her gum chewing. She smiled at her running mental dialogue as the woman who might or might not be named Mindy poured her coffee. "It's been a while since I've been back, so I'm looking forward to it."

"I'm saving to go one day." It was too late for breakfast and too early for lunch, so her new friend parked in front of her on the other side of the counter and smiled.

"It's a great place if you like to have fun." She added way too much sugar and a little cream to her coffee, wanting the boost for the hours of driving she still had left.

"I'm sure it is, but I'd really like to go and see the Milton H. Latter Library on St. Charles Avenue. My grandma told me about it, and I put it on my list of stuff I want to see."

This was a lesson in assuming stuff about people. "The Latter Library doesn't make any lists of tourist hotspots, but it's a beautiful place." She'd done a reading there, and the mansion-turned-library housed collectible books in the splendor of a bygone era. It was the kind of place that made you want to linger. "You should definitely listen to your grandma and go."

"Thanks." The woman smiled and went to get her burger. She left Wyatt to eat, and she checked her email to make sure Pippa didn't need a blood sample or a kidney. Blanche had stuck to her no-calling demand, but there were fourteen emails in her inbox. Impressive for twenty-four hours, considering how long each message was. There was enough psychobabble in each one to make her gag, so it was satisfying to dump them in the trash. She loved the noise email made when it went into the digital can. After all, she didn't need Blanche to tell her she was going crazy—she'd figured it out on her own.

"Anything else, sugar?" She was never a fan of cutesy nicknames, but the book and library lover deserved some slack. "The pie's good. It's my grandma's recipe."

"A slice of that then. Can I buy you a slice?" After weeks alone with her imaginary friends and family, human interaction wasn't such a bad thing.

"Sure, you don't look like a serial killer ready to go through her death ritual."

The bizarreness of the statement made her laugh. She was actually pen pals with a couple serial killers in maximum security prisons. In her humble opinion their insight gave her characters that little something extra that made readers sleep with their lights on. It was also the reason she didn't give live interviews and didn't put her picture on her book jackets. The world was populated by some sick fucks who shouldn't be able to spot her on sight.

"I promise, no death ritual if the pie's good enough." She smiled, and the woman winked. The short conversation it took to finish the pie was nice, and she welcomed the waitress's embrace when the tip overwhelmed her. She'd left enough for a trip to New Orleans if she really wanted to go.

"And the paper says you're kind of bitchy," her mom said when she got back in the truck. "That was nice."

"I have my moments."

She turned up the radio on George Jones, done with human interaction and her head for the day. The lyrics to "He Stopped Loving Her Today" were depressing as hell, which made her wonder if antidepressants were a necessity if you chose a career in country music. If so, meds would never mix with all the drinking. There should be a public health warning.

❖

Monday came like a body slam in roller derby, only with rain and semiflooded streets. Hayley had already decided on an Uber, not trusting her low-to-the-ground Mini Cooper. The rain hadn't slacked off since the weekend, so Lucy was in her guest room, not wanting to mess up her freshly done laundry.

She stood in the bathroom and held her hair back, trying to decide if that made her appear more mature in case she had to yell at people. It wasn't her go-to option—the yelling, not the hair—but she also wasn't going to spend the next couple of weeks catching everyone up on what they were supposed to be doing without a lot of supervision. She went with a hair-down look to lose the cute cheerleader vibe.

Her bra had to wait when her phone rang, and she smiled at the picture of her father in his coveralls. "Hey, Dad, could you hang on a minute?" She hurried and put on her bra and a blouse since it felt creepy talking to her father half naked. "How are you?"

"Perfect, and your mother sends her love. We checked the national forecasts, so I was calling to make sure you had batteries and emergency supplies." He was totally serious, and by *we*, he meant *I*.

While her mother loved true crime, her father was obsessed with The Weather Channel. Jim Cantore was his kindred spirit, and his preaching about being prepared resonated with her dad. She wanted to answer that she owned a vibrator so of course she had batteries, but saying that out loud would mortify her into a permanent blush, so she went with the standard, "Yes, sir."

"Good, good," her father said, sounding like he was from the 1800s. "What are you wearing?"

There was a question she wished some sexy woman was asking. "I think it's a jeans and galoshes kind of day. Usually I try to look more professional, but I doubt I'll make it outside. It's a catch-up week, I'm afraid."

"Wear something warm, don't work too hard, and thank you for flying out this weekend. We miss you, but we're proud of you." Her father was the sweetest man she knew. "You all set for money?"

"Thank you, and I'm fine. Once I'm through some of these big projects and can spend time showing you around, I'd love for you and Mom to visit."

"Maybe after we plant again. Once you put it in the ground, it's a wait-and-see proposition."

It was weird he'd picked the polar opposite of what he'd done for years as a second career. The life of a farmer was in no way the constant activity beehive of a trader. "Do you ever get bored?"

"I still have some clients I advise, so don't worry about me going raving mad on you."

"I was curious, not worried." She held the phone between her chin and shoulder as she put on mascara. With the weather it was probably a mistake, but her relaxed appearance only went so far. "Love you, and we'll talk soon, but I've got to go."

"Take care, and don't forget the batteries and candles. You can never have enough."

Hayley thought about the closet at the end of the hall, which her father had stocked himself. Clearly you *could* have enough. She could light up downtown if the power ever went out for any significant amount of time. "Thanks, Daddy, and don't forget to kiss Mom for me."

Her Uber blew the horn as she filled her travel mug, and the driver chatted her up until they reached the other side of the Quarter. It was obvious the guy driving thought she'd been waiting for him to show up at her house all her life, and she'd been lucky enough that he had. Some guys were a little out there when it came to flirty behavior.

The building that housed Fleur-de-Lis had once been a coffee processing warehouse, one of three in the Quarter, and she loved that Cornelius had kept some of the old equipment. She was glad to arrive at the office, if only to flee the Uber and make a note to never accept a ride from this guy again.

"Morning, Hay," Fabio Rodrigue said when she ran in, trying to shut her umbrella. Fabio had been hired day one by Marlo to manage who got in to the building and, eventually, to her. That was his story, and his name really was Fabio. His mother had either been a big fan of romance book covers or was wild about butter substitutes. The name suited him. He and his husband Heinrich invited her over often when the mood to cook hit them. "How was your trip to the boonies?"

"Quiet and restful. It was until Marlo started calling. Seems erotica isn't for everyone."

"Girl, Marlo's the spawn of the devil, and Cheryl's an idiot. That girl's got mothballs up all in there." He nodded sagely at her when she laughed.

"Fab…" She laughed harder at his eye roll. "Make sure Marlo can't hear you making comments like those."

"It's our little secret," Fabio said in a stage whisper.

"It is, and while I'd love to talk about it some more, I have to get to work. Do you have anything for me?" She flipped through the stack of messages he handed her. All these people had her cell number, which made her want to toss the messages and just let them try her again, but she'd still have to call them back.

"The best advice I can give you is to run," Fabio said. "This is going to be a shitty day."

"Horoscope?" She picked up the pile of manuscripts on his desk. The last batch only had two worth pursuing, but another three were possibles if the authors were willing to make revisions. "Or was it your granny's Tarot cards?"

"Don't mock the cards, girlfriend, or I'll have Granny cast you a love spell." The bracelets on his right hand jingled as he typed something.

"Good, I can use one."

"I'll make it specifically for your neighbor George." He printed the updated schedule and bowed as he gave it to her. "Go by Marlo's office. She's been waiting for you."

"I'm early." She glanced at her watch to make sure.

"Spawn of the devil, precious. Spawn don't sleep."

"They can burn your hair off, though, and give you something disgusting that involves weeping sores." Marlo walked behind Fabio and made him flinch when she placed her hands on his shoulders. "Stop telling people that. It's supposed to be on the down-low."

"On the down-low?" Fabio asked. "Are you channeling the eighties?"

"Don't throw stones, *Fabio*," Hayley said, following Marlo back to her office on the main floor. It'd been the coffee manager's office once upon a time, and Hayley liked to think she could still smell the coffee beans they used to roast close to here. "Fabio gave me the schedule. We can't be this far behind."

"I was trying to finalize some contracts and lost track. That and the false alarm are everyone's excuse, but Cheryl's in her own category of hot mess. She understands she's got to burn all her inhibitions and hang-ups in the yard and get the job done. Understanding and doing seem to be on different planets when it comes to Cheryl. This isn't kindergarten—you have to do the work or get the fuck out. She's going to do the work if it kills her." Marlo dropped into her chair and lit a cigarette. "If I don't fire her."

"It'll be easier and faster if you just let me edit the collection." She put her stuff on the floor and studied the schedule again. "I can take a month to get all this other stuff going and still get it to print on time."

"Don't let Cheryl off the hook. If she's not comfortable with the books we publish, she needs to go work somewhere else. I'm serious as shit about that." Marlo put her cigarette down on the overflowing ashtray that reminded Hayley of Jenga since the damn thing appeared not to have been emptied since the sixties.

"I might have a solution we can both live with, but that's not my priority until we get started on this schedule." She picked up her pile and got up to leave before Marlo started coughing. "I'll be upstairs if you need anything."

"Welcome back. You were missed."

"Thanks, boss. It's good to be here." She smiled as she went up the back stairs to her little domain. Her office was half the size of Marlo's, but she loved that it overlooked some of the oldest buildings in the French Quarter as well as the manicured garden behind their building. It was the only zen thing she got on most days.

It was still raining when she made it to her desk, and she gave herself a minute to center herself. The weird thought of internet dating of all things came to her again when she saw a romance novel on her schedule, but she laughed it off. Her mother would be the first to warn her that internet dating was an invitation to be chopped into little pieces in someone's bathtub.

"Maybe I should take a page out of Cheryl's book and forget about sex. It's not like I have time for that anyway."

CHAPTER SIX

The outline of New Orleans was visible through the slacking rain when Wyatt reached the top of the I-10 bridge over the Intracoastal Waterway. The mental fog of the last four days cleared. This was going to be her life until she figured out what real life was going to be.

"Damn, that sounds so depressing," she said. Traffic was crawling along, and the woman driving the car next to her waved, giving her a big smile. She paused, not really sure what the protocol was. Waving back got her an even bigger smile before the woman took it as a sign to cut in front of her. New Yorkers weren't often so nice when it came to traffic moves, so this was a first.

The GPS on her phone brought her to the exit that led to Pippa Potts's real estate office. The small but nice house in the Garden District was pink, and that didn't surprise her. She'd bet the house she was about to buy that there was a unicorn somewhere inside. A woman stepped onto the porch and waved while she was thinking about it.

"Good afternoon," the woman said, even though Wyatt's window was rolled up. Between the rain and the damp cold that defined misery, she hadn't rolled it down for hours.

"Good afternoon," she answered after getting out. Despite the rain the woman walked to the gate, carrying an umbrella covered in unicorns, and took her arm. She smiled at the safe bet she'd made in the truck. "Ms. Potts?"

"Yes, but please call me Pippa."

The pink continued throughout the entryway, and it matched

Pippa's outfit perfectly. "Okay, Pippa, and thank you for getting this done so quickly. Did you have any problems?"

Pippa squeezed her bicep and shook her head, making her hair flounce beautifully. It was the first time she'd used the word flounce in her life, but it fit perfectly. "Heavens, no. The problem we have sometimes is clearing the title, but the Fuller house has been in the same family for over a hundred years. We've been waiting for you to arrive."

"We?"

"Sam Fuller IV is the family's representative. I told you about Gator on the phone." They entered a small light lavender conference room, and the middle-aged woman wasn't what she was expecting. "Gator, this is Wyatt Whitlock."

She stared, trying to decipher what all this was without asking any questions. This was supposed to be a house sale and not an episode where she was punked. "Nice to meet you."

"I can see your wheels turning. My great-grandfather was Sam Fuller, and there's been a Sam Fuller in my family ever since, even in generations when it's all girls. My youngest niece is Sam Fuller V. I figured you'd like an explanation since you're buying our family home." Gator Fuller wasn't what she'd call overly friendly but more like a grizzly coach who'd kick your ass if you missed a shot. She was a small but fierce woman you didn't want to turn your back on.

"I'm sure Pippa can find me something else if you're attached to the house. If it's been in the family that long, I can see where it'd be difficult to sell it."

Gator shook her head and laid her hands on the conference table. "No, it's time, and hopefully you understand the stipulations in the contract." Gator appeared ready to punch her if she gave any answer other than yes. "You hand over the check, you get our home. No reneging if you have second thoughts once you've been inside. The contract's been signed."

"Are you in sales?" She took the envelope from her coat pocket and dropped it on the table. "Maybe the hospitality industry?"

"My great-grandmother taught us it's better to get things right straight off." Gator glanced at Pippa and rolled her hand in a get-on-with-it motion. "The house has been in our family for decades, but this new generation is more interested in lofts in the warehouse district than grand old places, and I'm too old to deal with having to keep up the old place. It's pure crazy, but it is what it is. You can't force your kids to see the treasure right in front of them."

"My father used to say the same thing when someone wanted to cover up some great feature in a house he was renovating."

"You get it then."

They signed everywhere Pippa pointed, and Gator took the envelope with her check. Once it was in hand, she stood to leave as if needing to deposit it to make sure it was good. Pippa walked Gator out and laughed nervously when she came back. The interaction was done, but Pippa had a folder in her hands.

"I thought you might appreciate the names of some good contractors." Pippa gave her the bright pink folder and took the keys from her jacket pocket. Wyatt wasn't shocked they were on a unicorn keychain with Pippa's information stamped on it. "Like I've mentioned, the Fuller house isn't in great shape, and I don't want you to be disappointed. You can trust all the names in there for whatever work you have in mind."

"Did they leave a bed, by chance?" Wyatt took the keys and glanced out the window. The weather had cleared somewhat, but the sky was still blanketed with dark clouds, signaling it was only temporary. Even though the weather didn't appear ideal, the area was beautiful with its mature live oaks and beautiful, meticulously kept grand homes. It made her want to write, the same way she sometimes got the urge to run a marathon—in theory it sounded good, but in practice, not so much. Eventually she'd have to try to write again or embrace the jumble her mind was at the moment.

"The family went through and took what they wanted, but I'm sure there's a bed or two still in the house." Pippa clapped her hands together as if she'd told her the house came with a butler and magic beans. "Whatever's still in the house is all yours." The clap came again, and it made her nervous.

"Thank you for your help then." She jiggled the keys and smiled, hoping she didn't seem deranged.

"Call me," Pippa blurted out, then blushed. The color of her face and ears clashed awfully with the walls and suit. "I mean, if you need anything, call me."

"I sure will, thank you again." She had to squeeze by Pippa but didn't make it all the way around.

"Can I ask you a personal question?" Pippa put her hand on her forearm to stop her. If every house sale came with a big hug, this was where Pippa's streak would end.

"*Sure*," she said, drawing out the word. When people asked personal questions, it gave her the willies. At signings, giving someone free rein to ask questions at times led to inquires like the exact date she lost her virginity, or what kind of underwear she was partial to. Why anyone needed to know that to enjoy a mystery novel was beyond her, but the questions usually came from older white guys with facial tics. As if being old, white, and male gave someone the right to ask whatever they wanted.

"Why here?" Pippa asked.

"Why not here?" She moved back a step, hoping the interrogation was over.

"Don't get me wrong—New Orleans is great, but people usually dream about going to New York, not the other way around."

"Sometimes you need to slow down, and you found me the perfect house in which to do that." Compliments always did wonders when she wanted to walk away, and this time was no different. She left Pippa basking in her words and waved when she headed back into the storm. It would have been a good shot if her life was a movie.

❖

She became aware of the intense scrutiny the moment she stopped in front of what could only be described as a dump. Maybe the term fixer-upper meant something different in this town. If the lot contained a yurt full of raccoons smoking hookahs it would've been better than what she was looking at. She wanted to keep her eyes on the house—or the pile of firewood, if she was honest—but the guy next door was staring intently at her, as if he had to remember every freckle on her ass as well as every smudge on her vehicle so he could report it to the police.

"Time enough to sort Mr. Nosy later." She turned her attention back to the house, and it seemed like a sign from the renovating gods when the mailbox clutched its chest and keeled over like someone had poisoned it. "Or maybe it just decided to do itself in to stop the misery. If this is an old home in need of some TLC, then Pippa writes better fiction than I do."

She pulled into the overgrown drive and took a breath before opening the truck door. Getting out felt like making a commitment, and she was still weighing her options. The area outside the truck seemed safe enough, so she took another breath and stood in front of the Fuller place. Her second impression was that this house would never be as popular a tourist's destination as the Leaning Tower of Pisa, so the porch would have to be added to her TLC list of things to do.

The wannabe stalker was still standing in his yard, so she waved, since that's what people did here, and put her foot on the first step of the porch. It was iffy it'd actually hold her weight, but the side yard beyond the drive was way too overgrown to chance it. She went up the stairs slowly as if she was trying to sneak up on someone and made it to the house on boards that bent with every step she took.

She put the key in the lock, and trying to get it to turn was like trying to make a frigid woman come. It took some finesse, but the lock finally gave way, and she waited by the front door to make sure she was alone. There was a quiet when she closed the door that she'd thought only existed in space. The two rooms she could see from where she stood were so cluttered, they still appeared lived in.

Everything was dated, musty, and eerie in a way that Stephen King might find homey. If the Fuller family had really removed anything from the house, then they all would be great candidates for that hoarder show. She watched that on nights when the sandman got caught up somewhere like Poughkeepsie and missed her house. You'd think there would be something better to watch, considering the five thousand channels she had.

"I should've brought a television. If there's one here, it's probably one of those ancient sets trapped in a big piece of furniture."

The dining room had lost some of the plaster in one corner, and the front sitting room had wallpaper nightmares were made of. "And it's all mine." She was glad the electricity was on—she'd gone online and taken care of power and water while she was at a rest stop on her way down.

It took a while to explore the rest of the house, and then she went out for her bag. She sat at the old Formica and chrome table off the kitchen and opened the file Pippa the con woman had given her. The first page was the history of the first couple who owned the house, Sam and Lydia Fuller. There wasn't much about Sam, but Lydia was known for baking, especially for her snickerdoodle cookies, and for mothering every kid in the neighborhood. The couple raised eleven children here, and both Sam and Lydia died here, at ninety-eight and a hundred and two respectively.

"That's a minor miracle," she said, putting the file way. "This house is big, but thirteen people in here must've been a tight squeeze." She had to give the couple credit for their patience and for not killing any of their eleven kids.

"If you're still both here, you should know—I scare easily." She said that loudly as she went upstairs to find a place to sleep. "Let the fun begin."

CHAPTER SEVEN

It took a couple of days for Wyatt to fall into the same rut she'd been digging for herself back home. The sweatpants were cleaner, but she hadn't changed them from that first day. After unpacking the small duffel she'd brought and the bag of groceries from her trip to the Esplanade Mini Mart, she wandered around the house, trying all the bedrooms except the largest. The room she decided on was the closest to the upstairs bathroom and had the firmest mattress. Saying that was in no way an endorsement of the bed she was sleeping on, but it was decent enough to lie on while staring at the ceiling.

Picking that bedroom cut down on the possibility she'd be haunted by the numerous Fullers who'd died in the house, leaving all their shit behind. The only other option was calling a priest over, but she wasn't feeling social, and she also wasn't Catholic. Today was a new day, though, so she listened to her mother's pep talk—since she'd had no choice—and decided to get up and at least look outside.

Baby steps eventually got you to China if you also swam—because you couldn't literally walk to China. A glance at the clock meant an early start wasn't in the cards. After a trip to the bathroom, she stared out the window. It was strange that the place next door gave her a glimpse into every room, the windows bare. Furniture and small touches proved it was occupied, but she hadn't been curious enough to get up and study the house at night.

The same guy who stared her down the first day was standing at the waist-high wrought iron fence that separated the yards, looking up at her. His yard was meticulously kept, and he had what seemed like a permanent expression of annoyance, probably because her yard was *not* meticulously kept. "Maybe you should worry about putting up some curtains, you nosy bastard."

Whoever this guy was walked to the other side of the house when she didn't acknowledge him. "This will either be a funny story I tell at cocktail parties or will make me drive back to New York with some sort of paranoia. Whatever it'll be can't be decided now since I have to have coffee."

She inventoried her groceries as the water for the French press heated. There were still a few frozen dinners and a handful of Slim Jims left from her shopping efforts her first day. Not that she'd been desperate enough to actually eat any frozen dinners or compressed meat sticks, but they were on hand if she felt the need to finally hit rock bottom. For now, she went with her usual of buttered toast and black coffee.

"You're going to get rickets," her mother said.

"I have to remember to google *rickets* later to find out what the hell that is." She ate her toast as the hot water miraculously turned into coffee. Not really miraculous on the scale of the loaves and fishes, but it was to her. Once it was perfectly prepared, she went back upstairs and studied the house closely. She was here, and she wasn't going back to her great house in New York anytime soon because that would be admitting defeat. The room she was pretending to sleep in had light pink wallpaper with big yellow roses. "I wonder if this is original. If it is, Pippa has to be a relative of the Fullers."

She picked a corner of the hideous decorating choice and pulled as she sipped her coffee. An hour later she stood ankle deep in shreds of paper that had been covering numerous holes. It seemed bad wall coverings hid a multitude of sins. The weird thing was that some of the holes were small but uniform. This wasn't from time ravaging the house but someone making them for some reason.

"Not what I planned for the day," she said, wishing the house had a microwave, so she could heat more coffee. The holes were almost perfect squares, making her curious enough to stick her hand inside. "What the hell?" She found something wrapped in a linen towel. Unwrapping it uncovered a few alligator leather journals, and the writing inside was done by someone who had patience with a pen.

She stared at them for a long moment, and everything that had dominated her thoughts for months disappeared. Mysteries were her livelihood, but this was different. Finding someone else's story in a wall, if that's what this was, made the purchase and the drive totally worth it. If the journals held a tragedy, then she wouldn't be the only miserable bastard to exist. She inhaled sharply, realizing she'd been holding her breath.

The find necessitated searching the other holes, and sure enough, they all held journals, all written in the same beautiful handwriting, and she was curious why no one else had found them. By the dates she'd seen on some of the entries, whoever had left them wasn't a recent tenant. Her problem now, though, was that her walls had holes, giving whatever lived in the walls an invitation to crawl in her ear on the off chance she fell asleep.

She knew exactly who to call for help. "Hey," she said when Pippa answered the phone. "Sorry to bother you. Is there a hardware store close by?"

"What do you need?" The enthusiasm in Pippa's voice made her fear a visit. Pippa gave off the same vibe as Blanche—she seemed to want a more personal relationship that'd probably drive Wyatt to commit murder.

"To know if there's a hardware store nearby."

"You'll have to leave the Quarter if you need a lot of supplies, but there's a small place about a mile from you." Pippa gave her the information on all things hardware as if she'd be graded on it. "If you want, we can go to lunch, and I'll help you shop."

"Thank you for the offer." She was beginning to regret the call. "That's all for now, and what a shame, I already have plans for lunch."

"Do you want me to come over and show you where all these places are, then?" Pippa sounded hopeful.

"That's okay. The house isn't up for guests, but you should know that." She hung up and remembered how many times Pippa had used the term *TLC*. TLC, her ass.

She put on her shoes and went down to the truck, to empty the back for everything she needed to get. "And now we know why I got lousy gas mileage down here." Every tool she could think to need was stacked in the back. She teared up when she spotted her dad's leather tool belt close to the tailgate. He'd used this all the time, so it had to be close at hand.

She'd seen the damn thing around her dad's waist all her life and was glad it had survived. It was time to start remembering the good days, like working with him and his crew during the summers. Her father had not only built countless houses around Brooklyn but had a reputation as a man who was fair and a straight shooter. She'd helped him build the house she'd grown up in and knew he would've loved working on this wreck of a house she'd been conned into. Well, maybe not conned. The ad did say it needed love, and she'd seen the pictures, so she'd known it wasn't exactly luxury. Easier to blame peppy Pippa, though.

"Let's see if I can remember some of what you taught me, Dad."

By nightfall she'd emptied the truck, and the holes in the bedroom were larger and ready for repairs. If she ever had something to hide, she'd do it like a normal person and put it under her mattress. The weather was thankfully still on the cold side, but even with that, her clothes were dusty and she'd sweated off a pound by the time she was done. Right now the house's lack of central air-conditioning wasn't a problem, but that would have to be rectified before the summer, or her problems would disappear when she succumbed to heatstroke. A New Orleans summer wasn't for the weak.

She turned off all the lights and headed for the shower. The bathroom setup was bizarre, with a window in the shower, and the damn thing had no covering of any kind. "Why in the world would you put a window in the shower?" She'd gone back to talking to herself as she mentally started a shopping list of the supplies she'd need.

"Crap, that doesn't sound good." The pipes imitated the starting of a muscle car when she turned the knob, but water came out where it was supposed to and was reasonably clear, so she stepped in and put her head under the cold water. If she didn't want pneumonia before tomorrow, she'd have to find a plumber. Hopefully the house actually had a hot water heater, which meant it was plumbed for hot water.

She wiped her face and glanced down at her nipples—they'd never been this hard in her life—and then movement from next door caught her attention. As luck would have it, the two bathrooms lined up perfectly and had one thing in common. No curtains certainly did wonders for friendly neighbor relations.

"This must be Mrs. Nosy." She spoke softly, as if the naked and very attractive woman would hear her. "That makes Mr. Nosy a lucky bastard." She really should look away, but her neighbor was gorgeous. The woman showered in a way that made it impossible not to stare, even though she could only see from the collarbones up. "Okay, I see the allure of having a window in the shower, but why the hell isn't it bigger?"

She turned when she heard the rattle coming from the wall. "What the hell?" The noise got louder right before a stream of putrid rusty water spewed all over her. The water stopped working after that. "Just great. Just fucking great." She turned the knobs, and nothing happened. And now she smelled like week-old trash that had stewed at the bottom of a rusty dumpster, swimming in raw sewage.

"Okay, Karma, I get it. Watching my sexy neighbor shower is a bad thing."

CHAPTER EIGHT

Hayley was finally meeting with Cheryl to discuss her ongoing projects. Her trip to see her parents had put her behind, but with some late nights the piles on her desk were slowly disappearing.

"That brings us to the last thing," Hayley said, and Cheryl's shoulders slumped. That wasn't the body language she was going for.

"The anthology?" Cheryl asked. The poor woman sounded like she was being led to the gallows where someone would flog her for pleasure before hanging her to death.

"That's the one. You do realize that your job is to edit the assignments I give you, right? I'm trying my best to work around your"—she had to pause and think, not wanting to be sued—"objections, but there's only so many cookbooks we publish in a year."

"I realize that, and I tried—I really did, but erotica, Hayley? And lesbian erotica at that. I have no experience with anything like that."

And it definitely shows. The words were dying to come out of her mouth, but she held back because of polite human behavior. Also because of the lawsuit thing. "If I give Joel this book and you the one that he's working on, you'd be ready to work?" Joel was editing the male version of what she'd given Cheryl, and her question was a little out of line, but it made her smile. She figured Cheryl thought gay sex, no matter who was having it, was tantamount to joining a witch's coven.

"No, I'm not saying that. We shouldn't build our brand on sex, Hayley. It's not right."

She was ready for the small cross Cheryl wore around her neck to break off in her hand, Cheryl was fooling with it so much. "So our brand should be built on what, exactly?"

"Good Christian content wouldn't kill us. All this gay stuff is going to turn people off." Cheryl squirmed, but her righteousness had risen and spewed forth like it always did when she felt cornered.

"All the gay stuff sells, Cheryl, and as for turning people off, erotica actually does the exact opposite, so that sells as well. With or without you we'll be releasing three anthologies that deal with sex later this year. It's up to you to decide your involvement."

"I don't want to be involved—that's what I'm trying to tell you."

She sighed. She hated sighing. It seemed clichéd, but sometimes there was just no better response. "Then I'll take your refusal as your resignation. You're a good editor, and we'll be sorry to lose you."

"Wait, I'm not resigning." Cheryl leaned toward her so fast Hayley tensed, thinking she'd have to defend herself. A small gold crucifix sticking out of her forehead would be hard to explain in the emergency room. "I don't want to do that book is all."

"This is the *fifteenth* project you've asked to be excused from. This is the schedule." Hayley handed it over. "There'll be no deviations or excuses from the assignments on there. Either get it done, or tender your resignation—it's that simple. Sex is a part of life, Cheryl, and in this case, all you're doing is editing the work, not performing it."

"I want to talk to Marlo," Cheryl demanded.

"Go ahead." She waved to the door. "Let me know how it turns out, but know that I've already discussed this with her."

"Shit." It was the best description for Cheryl's exit as she stood and slammed the door. Hayley sighed again and rubbed her stomach. Conflict wasn't something she enjoyed or thrived on, and it upset her. A knock at the door signaled her next meeting was there. "Hey, Joel." The door cracked open, and he came in.

Joel was one of her best editors and also knew her pretty well. He handed over a cup of tea and sat. "I couldn't help but overhear the righteous queen of New Orleans. The day she unravels, she's going to take out half the city. Do you want me to pick up the slack?" "I love you, but no. I'll review what we have and do the anthology myself. It might remind me why I should be out looking for a girlfriend." She started packing her stuff, glad she'd scheduled Joel after Cheryl. Like Fabio, Joel was happily married to a guy who was in upper management at a large accounting firm. They were complete opposites, but they fit perfectly.

Joel said, "You're too cute to waste away by your lonesome, and my offer's good. Let me know if you need help, and if you're ready, I'll walk you to your car."

It was almost dark when she made it home, and thankfully it'd stopped raining. The temps had warmed to not-so-freezing, so she poured herself a glass of wine and sat outside to get some reading in. The deep porch that wrapped around to her side door was her favorite part of the house, as were the rockers her mom had insisted she needed. Tonight, though, she chose the porch swing, another of her mother's must-haves.

"Fuck," she said an hour later. The expletive startled Hugo awake, and the cat glared at her for disturbing his nap. Both he and Truman loved sitting out here with her, and they acted as if any grass touching their paws was the equivalent of lava, so she didn't worry about them running off.

"Sorry, Your Majesty." Hugo closed his eyes at her apology, but not before giving her major side-eye shade. "I love to fuck as much as anyone, with maybe the exception of Cheryl, but these are horrible." She'd only read ten anthology submissions so far, and saying they were bad was being kind. "All of these make me want to keep my clothes on and consider celibacy. I'm pretty sure that's not the reaction our readers want when it comes to erotica." It was a running contest as to which one was the worst. "Shit, these are horrible," she repeated in frustration.

"What's horrible?" George St. Germaine asked. He was standing right under her in the yard and scared the hell out of her. Hayley swore he tiptoed over, so he could pop up and catch her doing something like adjusting her bra. This time he'd come close to knocking her off her porch swing. He loved doing that and was a slow learner when it came to stopping bad behavior.

"Just work, George. Nothing that'll interest you." She was praying he hadn't been there long enough to hear the part about her loving to fuck. There was no way to be sure, but she thought George was a secret perv. "What can I do for you?"

"Heard about the Fuller place?" He zipped up the stairs, clearly misinterpreting her question. *What can I do for you* in no way meant *Sit and talk as much as you can before I pass out.* He sat in the closest rocker and sighed. That usually meant he was planning to stay awhile. With any luck he'd do his duty of reporting the gossip and go home. She was never that lucky, but she liked to think of herself as an eternal optimist.

"Aside from it being a dump?" She stared at George, hoping he'd leave once he reported all the gossip he'd gathered. Not that she was anxious to go back to reading bad sex, but George was hard to take in time-consuming doses. "Are they finally tearing it down?"

The Fuller house, as everyone referred to it, looked like someone vomited a rotting monstrosity onto the lot. If she was lucky enough that a demolition crew was headed their way, she prayed the new owner wouldn't build something that'd ruin the charm of their street. She wasn't fully educated on the historical district zoning rules, but there had to be some. The problem was, they weren't considered part of the French Quarter. She knew the Vieux Carré Commission had strict rules in the Quarter, but they might be fair game in the Marigny.

"No, someone bought it." George leaned in closer. "I've seen her and have kept an eye on her. She's not real talkative, but according to the guys down at the bar, she's some foreigner. Can you believe it?" George paused and rocked. Rocking was a bad sign because it hinted at a drawn-out visit. "There should be laws against that kind of thing. Hell, maybe one of us wanted to buy it. How were we supposed to know?"

"By reading the For Sale sign that's been up for months, maybe." She pointed to the Potts Realty sign, surprised she'd missed the Sold sticker on it.

"Yeah, but Pippa didn't have to sell to no damn foreigner."

When it came to George, *foreigner* was a term you had to take loosely. It could mean a person from another country, someone from another state, or someone from Louisiana that wasn't from the Quarter or the Marigny. All those were bad in George's world. It'd taken him months before he spoke to her once he found out she was from New York. His wife still wouldn't speak to her, so she supposed she was still considered sketchy. Now she regretted not speaking to him in an Italian accent. He'd still be on his side of the fence.

"It's not right."

"Well, I'll let you know if I hear anything you can report to the guys at the bar. If you'll excuse me, though, I need to finish this, so I'm headed in." She gathered her papers and wineglass, ready to leave him on the porch if necessary. Even Hugo jumped up as if not wanting to be left alone with George. Truman the slut would stay with anyone who petted him long enough. "Good night."

"Okay, be careful. The person I saw looks shifty." George nodded and stood. He wavered as he headed down the stairs. "Call me if you have any problems. I'll come over night or day, and I'll report in as soon as I have any information."

"I appreciate that." She closed and locked the door, watching him descend the stairs from inside, and wondered if he had any idea what a weirdo he was. The little farewell exchanges were George's way of sucking you in. "Well, guys, hopefully we don't end up with another George," she said to the cats. "If we do, we'll have to get blinds and limit our porch time."

All she was in the mood for was a sandwich, but she craved a shower even more. After days of rain it was the only thing that would warm her as well as relax her. Before that, she sent Marlo an email about the submissions she'd just read and how unacceptable they were. Anyone who thought using *honeypot* for female genitalia was sexy should be banned from writing another thing. This wasn't an anthology for bears, dammit.

There appeared to be no signs of life next door, considering there wasn't one light on, but she only took her sweater and jeans off, not willing to chance it. Her T-shirt and underwear she saved to take off in the bathroom as the water heated in the shower. There was nothing better than hot water on your skin on cold damp days, and she turned around after gathering her shoulder length hair so it wouldn't get wet.

She finished her shower and turned off the water, but the sound of cursing made her look out the window before leaving the tub. There was a naked woman in the jumble of weeds in the backyard of the Fuller place hosing herself down. It was getting dark, and it was drizzling, but whoever she was didn't seem to mind being outside, totally naked. From the way she was shaking the water from the hose it had to be freezing, which could account for the cursing. But all Hayley could concentrate on was the woman was crazy good-looking, even from her limited view.

"I take back every bad thing I said about my new neighbor," she whispered. "You've got a body someone should write erotica about."

The strange display didn't last very long, and the woman shook herself like a dog and went back inside. "You're nothing like George." The day George hosed himself naked in his yard was the day she called the cops. She threw on some loose sweats and a T-shirt and headed to the kitchen, ready to eat before reading the rest of the submissions. Her cell rang, and she was almost afraid it was George with more questionable information, but she smiled when she saw it was Lucy.

"How's the grind?" Lucy asked.

"Interesting," she said, putting a chip in her mouth as her bread toasted. "Or I should say I have interesting news. I have a new neighbor, and I think I just saw her naked."

"Did she rip all her curtains down like you?"

She laughed and glanced out her kitchen window but still didn't see any lights. The truck was still there, but there was no sign of life. "No, she was hosing herself off in the yard, cursing more than you do. According to George she's a foreigner, but I can't verify the naked woman is her."

"So she's from the Garden District, then? George's concept of foreigner is sketchy at best. I'm sure he thinks I'm here illegally, stealing someone's job. I always get the impression he has the ICE on speed dial every time I come over."

"George is an idiot, so don't worry about any stupidity spewing out of his mouth. He gets most of his opinion from Fox News, and we both know what a fantasy world that is." She fixed her sandwich and plated it. "If you come over this weekend, maybe we can go over there and introduce ourselves to the new owner." She gathered everything and moved to the sofa. After reading all afternoon, she could afford a few minutes with the Barefoot Contessa.

"That must mean she's hot." Lucy clucked her tongue before laughing. "It'll have to be next weekend, babe. I'm pulling some extra shifts, so I'm working this weekend. I was calling to tell you I can't make dinner this week. If you're not completely exhausted after work, come by and I'll buy you a beer."

"Be careful and at least call me. You know I worry about you." She smiled when Lucy made kissing noises before hanging up. She ate her simple ham sandwich as she watched Ina Garten make a complicated pasta dish. Hugo and Truman sat next to her and watched as she ate, as if her hand movement was the most interesting thing they'd ever seen. They weren't fooling her. "Here." She broke the last bite into two pieces and gave them a treat. When they finished chewing, they were done with her and adjourned to the bed upstairs.

The chair by the bedroom window was her favorite place in the house to read aside from her porch swing, which she used sparingly to avoid George encounters. The old leather club chair, though, had been with her since the beginning of college and had clocked so many books there was no way to count how many. It was like an old friend, and it only fit in this one spot in her bedroom. The view of the house next door was for shit, but maybe she'd get another glimpse of her naked neighbor in the garden while she read.

The next couple hours of reading were better since the stories evoked the kind of response you were supposed to have if you enjoyed erotica. Her nipples were hard enough to make the T-shirt rubbing against them uncomfortable, and she didn't have to touch herself to know she was wet. If she could get about two more stories like these, they'd be ready for some real editing.

"For now," she said, powering down her laptop, "let me continue my love affair with myself." She didn't date much, so masturbation kept her sane.

She pulled the chain on her antique floor lamp and noticed the light on next door. Her new neighbor was unfortunately fully dressed, but the jeans she had on really highlighted her ass. "Good

Lord, she's wearing a tool belt." It occurred to her then that she'd never actually met anyone who owned a tool belt and wore it for jobs around the house.

The woman patiently nailed what appeared to be slats over one of the holes in the bedroom wall. All the hideous wallpaper she'd noticed during the day was gone, and it gave her hope the dump would find new life with the new owner. "You need a name," she said when the woman reached up to nail the next slat. The move pulled her T-shirt tight across her shoulders. "Butch, maybe." That would fit until she went over and introduced herself, since that's what the woman was—a perfect butch complete with leather tool belt and perfect ass-hugging jeans. She had no problem imagining the work boots that would make the outfit complete.

This wasn't helping the mood she was already in from the sexy stories, so she spread her legs and put her hand in her sweats. It was true that what she'd read made her wet, but the view turned her on as she fantasized about Butch pressing her to a wall and touching her. She could imagine her rough hands moving from her breasts to her sex, demanding she spread her legs, so she did. Her fingers were slick as they glided over her hard clit, making her moan and close her eyes when she squeezed it.

She opened them, needing to see Butch, and found she'd stopped hammering and was standing at the window. It was like Butch had heard her, and the thought made Hayley stop. But that was impossible—they had a side yard between them, and she was sitting in the dark. Those two facts gave her the confidence to keep going. She spread her legs wider and braced her feet on the sill, keeping her eyes on Butch, who seemed to be staring a hole through the glass.

It was hard to remember the last time she was this hard, wet, and desperate, but she couldn't stop. The small part of her that feared Butch *could* see what she was doing also thrilled her to keep going. "Oh fuck," she said as she stroked faster. She came way too quickly, but it was fantastic.

"That was different." She opened her eyes, and Butch was gone. It was almost like Butch had never been there at all, but she hadn't been hallucinating. "Someone should've written that story, guys." Truman and Hugo were on the bed staring at her with little judgment. They were the masters of that half-lidded you-should-be-ashamed-of-yourself expression, but she was too lethargic to care. "Time to stop lusting after the neighbor and reading erotica." She went to the bathroom and changed her sweatpants before going to bed. Her last thought was that she'd touched herself in front of a stranger, but she was too tired to worry about it.

CHAPTER NINE

Wyatt woke up the next morning and didn't need her usual pep talk to roll out of bed. She went immediately to the magic window, but it was empty of the beautiful blond exhibitionist she was fortunate enough to score as a neighbor. The night before she'd had the pure luck to turn around and glance at the next door window opposite the bedroom she was using. It would've been much more enjoyable if the lights had been on, but the streetlight below gave her enough of a view to know what was going on.

For that long but brief moment she'd forgotten about her pain, misery, and problems. Who knew all it would take was a beautiful woman, claiming all she desired. "Had I known, I would've started visiting peep shows way before now."

She got dressed and brushed her teeth with bottled water, then got back to fixing the holes she'd made. After watching her little show last night, she'd been too tired to check out the journals, so she stacked them carefully in a corner until she had time to sit and read them properly.

The next thing to tackle was the plumbing, and after some exploration, she found the trapdoor that allowed her to get underneath the house. It wasn't a basement, but the lattice around the raised house did give it that feel. There was a structure toward the back, so she bowed her head and walked over. There on a slab was the hot water heater and some pipes that snaked along the bottom of the house—all galvanized, meaning they were all crap.

The folder Pippa had given her included a recommended

plumber. Her dad's motto had always been, if it could flood or burn your house down, hire a professional. "That's right, kid. It's why God invented electricians and plumbers," her father said, on the off chance she'd forgotten.

She called the number and had to pull the phone away from her ear when a very enthusiastic guy answered, announcing, "DJ's Plumbing, and I'm DJ. What can I do for you?"

"Hey, I'm having issues with my pipes." She described what had happened in the shower and when she used the toilet that morning. With any luck, once he'd fixed things, it wouldn't sound like she was landing a jumbo jet every time she turned on a faucet.

"What's your address?" DJ asked after saying *uh-huh* a dozen times. When she gave it to him, he gave her one more *uh-huh*, and then, "Figures. I'll see you in ten minutes."

"You can come now?" Two things occurred to her. Either DJ was fucking with her, or he was Pippa's father and didn't know squat about plumbing. In her experience, it usually took some finagling to get workmen to show up, and that was a month later.

"Ten minutes." DJ hung up, acting like phone time was part of the short window he'd given himself, and he didn't want to be late.

"Fuck me." She was shocked when she opened the door eight minutes later to a short, older, balding guy with his clipboard in hand.

"Hey, I'm DJ of DJ's Plumbing."

He offered his hand, and she didn't know whether or not to be insulted that he perhaps thought she'd forgotten their conversation a mere eight minutes ago. It was also interesting that he repeated the company name, but then she remembered passing a DJ's Auto Repair when she went to the hardware store.

"You want to show me what you got?"

"Thanks, DJ, I'm—" She had to think about it for a moment. Wyatt wasn't a common name for a woman, and she wanted to be someone else for a while. He wouldn't necessarily recognize her name, but she didn't want to chance it. "I'm Joe." She gave him her father's name.

He followed her around the house mostly shaking his head and making notes on the antique wooden clipboard that must've belonged to his grandfather. They finished in the main bedroom en suite, where he removed his DJ's Plumbing ballcap and scratched his head as if his brain hurt.

"Think you can handle it?"

"Sure 'nuff. Can we sit, and I'll write something out for you." He stopped at the head of the stairs and pointed to an old picture in a really nice frame. "I'm surprised Gator didn't take this one. That's Mr. and Mrs. Fuller, but I guess they stay with the house."

From the clothes they were wearing, the picture must've been taken on their wedding day. "Sounds like they made a lot of memories here."

"Yeah, I remember Miss Lydia from when I was a boy. Saw her sitting on the porch when I did some work for George." DJ pointed to the house next door.

If George was Mr. Nosy, he had to be lousy in bed if Mrs. Nosy was touching herself in front of windows. This was her chance to get the lay of the land, considering DJ sounded full of information.

"She was real old by then and wasn't making no more cookies. She did that when we were kids and playing with her grandkids. She was real nice."

"Is George the guy next door? We haven't had a chance to meet." She started a fresh pot of coffee while DJ wrote.

"Oh no, George's house is one over from Miss Hayley, your neighbor. I fixed her toilet when she moved in, but the rest was good to go. Nothing like what you got." It was a good thing DJ wasn't a lawyer or doctor, the way he could dish.

That was good news, though. She had a cushion between her and George, who she could tell was an asshole. It wasn't much of a buffer, but she'd take it. With that settled, she wanted to know more about Miss Hayley. That wasn't a name she'd give a character in the romance she was still contemplating if only to fuck with Blanche, but not all girls could be named Magnolia.

"So," she said, sounding the least slick ever. "Is Hayley married? Are she and George an item?" It was hard to miss how much DJ's belly shook when he laughed, given the way his shirt rode up.

"In George's fantasies, maybe. No, he's married to Karen, who you should avoid accepting any pies from. My excuse is that I'm allergic to most fruits and custards. Trust me on that." He accepted the mug of coffee and kept writing. "Now your neighbor, Miss Hayley, according to George, is one of those *ho-mo-sexuals*."

She loved people who pronounced homosexual like it was three separate and distinct words. It was hard not to smile when she saw DJ's expression after his big revelation. He didn't appear to be really upset about the news, and she had her theories about that too. Old DJ probably had some girl-on-girl porn back at the plumbing store and was sure Hayley would invite him over one day when she had company. You know, for a plumbing issue, quote-unquote.

The day that happened, Hayley and her girlfriend would be naked except for the spike heels no real woman ever wore to bed because they were murder on the sheets. After they went down on each other for DJ's entertainment, they'd invite him to join in because all they'd been missing all their lives was DJ.

"That's interesting." It was all she could think to say to stop her mental monologue. "What does Hayley do?"

"Something with books, I think, but I'm not entirely sure what. I'll ask George at bowling on Wednesday. He's over there all the time. Do you bowl?" DJ stopped writing, seeming interested in her answer.

"Bowling isn't a talent of mine, sorry." The question of how DJ charged popped into her head. Considering how much he talked, she hoped it wasn't by the hour.

"Ain't one of mine, either, but the beer helps with the humiliation. Music is good over at the Rockin' Bowl, and it's half off on all the taps if you join a league." He tapped on his notes and put his pencil down. "Mrs. Fuller would be happy you're fixing the place back up. She kept it up nice until she couldn't no more. The Fullers that followed weren't real interested in housework if you catch my meaning."

"I do, and the house does seem to have good bones—it's just a little brittle, maybe." Since he'd finished writing and wasn't getting to the point, he must've felt it to be painful. "So, what's the damage?"

"All the galvanized shit is in poor shape and will have to be ripped out. We're talking total gut job. The gunk you got all over you is cause of them pipes." He took his cap off again and scratched his head as he handed over his list. "I can start today, if you want."

She glanced over at his itemized list and wondered if he'd left stuff off—by New York standards, the bill was cheap. "Think you can retile the bathrooms and refurbish the tubs?" Pink and green tile from the turn of the century were enough to induce hives.

"Yeah, we got you covered on that too. That's a good idea. So we're good?" DJ held his hand out and smiled.

"Go ahead. I have to run out for groceries, so can I leave you a key?"

He was on the phone barking orders at someone before she grabbed her wallet, and he waved as she headed out.

There were four other guys with him when she got back, and they seemed appreciative when she loaded the antique refrigerator with different types of drinks and told them to help themselves. They'd made more holes than she had to get to the shit pipes DJ had mentioned, and she was happy they appeared to know what they were doing. She left them to it, wanting to stay out of the way. The work she could do herself would be better done once they'd finished ripping things apart and putting them back together.

She grabbed one of the journals she'd found and carefully made her way through the jungle out back to the rotting pergola that had one good rocker sitting under it. Once DJ took a break, she'd ask him about a lawn service. She'd never had to worry about that, and she didn't want to start now.

The first twenty pages of the journal were all cookie recipes. Wyatt had no interest in baking a cookie—that's why God invented Oreos—but she read every single one. She was entranced by the beautiful handwriting and how Lydia described each cookie and why baking them was a wonderous thing. It was easy to see why DJ still remembered her and the treats she made for him and his friends.

Things got interesting after that when Lydia gave a detailed account of her eighth year of marriage to Sam, a seemingly incongruous entry after all the recipes. Not that life with a guy who sold produce was an Ian Fleming novel, but Lydia wrote it in a way that made it impossible to put down. Sometimes the mundane was what you needed to unchain your thought process, but in a way Lydia's life with Sam wasn't mundane. Certainly, Lydia hadn't thought so, and her love for Sam was woven through what Wyatt had read so far.

It was a love story, of that she was certain, even if Lydia hadn't written it that way. The short glimpses into their lives opened your heart to the love Lydia had for Sam. This man she'd built a life and a family with was everything to her, and it was reciprocal. Lydia wanted the reader to know that their lives were more than a business and children. At the heart of who they were, to her their love was magical. There was Sam, and he'd made Lydia complete and happy.

Good for them. Wyatt's parents had the same story. They didn't lead exciting action-packed existences, but they knew happiness and fulfillment, and it was enough to sustain them. Defining that in the minutiae of life took the kind of talent that she didn't possess. That was why she wrote mysteries.

She was squinting as dusk painted the sky a beautiful pink that made her think of Pippa, when DJ cleared his throat, startling her. All she had was a blade of grass to mark her place a little less than halfway through, so she snapped the journal closed and took a breath.

"You okay?"

"Sorry, I was afternoon dreaming." She noticed another stack of journals in DJ's hand. They'd found thirteen so far, and she'd try putting them in some kind of order, based on the dates. "Were all those in the walls?" The pages in the ones she'd found were starting to become brittle, so she wanted to get the ones DJ found inside. They'd survived this long without losing any sheets, and she wanted to keep it that way.

"Yeah, in the big bedroom, outside the bathroom in there. Saw you had a stack already, so here you go."

"Thanks."

"We had to keep the water shut off because you got no pipes yet, but I'll try and have that small bathroom downstairs working by tomorrow. We'll be back at six, and if you gotta pee, George said to knock. I'm sure Miss Hayley won't mind either. She's real nice. I'd tell you to try the yard if you're desperate, but baring your ass out there might be an invitation to get you bit by something that's going to require shots and stitches."

She had to laugh—she liked this guy. "I'll keep that in mind, and I'll see you guys in the morning." She locked up and flipped through the new journals. "I wonder if you hid any others? For a housewife with a bunch of kids, Lydia Fuller, you're an interesting woman." If she couldn't find it in herself to write, she'd read all about the life of someone who could.

CHAPTER TEN

Hayley held the phone away from her ear as the woman on the other end raged. The newbie author had never published anything, like, zippo, yet had taken offense at the notes Cheryl had sent on her work. Though this might've not been Cheryl's favorite project, Hayley couldn't find fault with the edits she'd forwarded, but the author had insisted on speaking to Cheryl's supervisor. Hayley agreed to take the call only because if she helped a new author break ground it would be an all-around win.

The author was acting like Hayley had called her a few nasty names while also insulting her mother and entire family. Overall, her behavior was an exercise in what not to do when trying to sell a manuscript. Marlo was sitting in Hayley's office laughing as Hayley held up her middle finger while she rolled her eyes.

"All right, enough!" she said, loud enough to break the woman's stride. "Your submission doesn't meet our needs in its current form. If you feel you don't need editing, that's fine—it's your work."

"I'm glad you understand that. All I need is a contract and a check."

"If you can find someone to publish it, I'm sure they'll provide that—it just won't be us. You might want to reconsider the term *honeypot* for vagina, but what the hell do I know. There might be a lot of people like you out there that find that erotic, but I personally don't know any. Good luck." She slammed the phone down with satisfaction and groaned. "This job would be so much easier without having to deal with writers."

"True, but they're usually more professional than that. You need to train your admin to weed out those types of calls. They're a waste of time." Marlo sipped from her tenth cup of coffee that day and shivered. How she didn't have any major health issues from all the caffeine and nicotine was a miracle. Cornelius was the same way, and he was about eighty by now, so it must be something in the genes that repelled a healthy lifestyle.

"That was the fifth time that woman's called today, and I couldn't do that to Mel, and Cheryl flinches every time the phone rings. Now that I didn't give her a contract and a check, I'm sure you're next on the list of harassing phone calls." She tidied the stack of work she was bringing home.

"That'll be entertaining if she tries. Go home—it's already dark outside." Marlo finished her coffee and pointed to the door. "And relax. I don't pay you enough for all the hours you put in."

"You're getting a bargain then, and I'll see you tomorrow." She went downstairs with Marlo and saw Fabio packing up. "What are you still doing here?"

"End of the month crap, and ordering dinner. Here." He handed her a slip. "That Italian place you like is waiting to hand over your favorite."

"You're the best." She kissed his cheek and then Marlo's. Marlo often got Fabio to order dinner for her as a thank-you for the hard work. It was nice to be appreciated.

The host of the restaurant walked her order out, so she didn't have to park, and the kindness made her consider her new neighbor. Maybe she should cook and invite her over one night. Of course, the brunette might be the new owner's contractor, but even so, Hayley could be friendly. With any luck she'd get to find out if the woman had rough hands or not.

An invitation would also add a voice to the gorgeous package, which would only be a drawback if her neighbor sounded like she was sucking helium. She was more partial to the low burr that didn't come from too much whiskey and cigarettes. Thinking about Butch last night, watching her touch herself, had made her hot enough to almost lose consciousness when she came. That alone had made her curious about who Butch really was.

"Either that or I need to find someone to go out with, so my life isn't all about work and my vivid fantasy world." She laughed about trying internet dating again. With her luck she'd end up with someone like the author who'd sucked up twenty minutes of her time on the telephone today.

Her next stop was the grocery close to the house to get milk for her coffee, and something to cook for Lucy when she came over for dinner, once she got a day's reprieve at work. She grabbed a cart and headed for the small produce section for a salad to go with the fish she was planning. The running list she always had going in her head made her oblivious to her surroundings as she grimaced at the sparse selection.

"Hello," someone said loudly, right behind her. George.

He'd startled her enough to make her jump a step forward, lose her balance, and fall against the bin of oranges. That started an avalanche, so she threw herself on the rest to stop them from rolling off and falling on the ground. One of these days she was going to have to have a talk with George about his questionable behavior. As she slowly got up, she noticed their new neighbor standing at the end of an aisle, watching her strange interaction with George. At least her expression telegraphed in neon red that the interaction was indeed strange. She'd get no argument from her.

"A little warning next time would be good, George." She straightened her clothes, not surprised Butch had moved on. Watching her spread herself over fruit couldn't have been too sexy, so her plan for a dinner invitation might need some more planning while she regained her dignity.

"Sorry, I thought you saw me." George moved his cart to trap her in the sea of oranges. She started picking them up, and he got the message and helped her. The old guy who owned the store had a habit of banning people, and she didn't want to ever be put on that list.

"I didn't see you because you were behind me. Here's a helpful hint—if you keep doing that, I'll never see you." Keeping her voice upbeat when she was being sarcastic took a talent she didn't possess, but one screaming match was enough for the day.

George completely ignored her bad mood. He shrugged, and she expected an *aw, shucks*, but thankfully he refrained. "I'm glad I ran into you. I got a call from DJ today."

"The plumber or the car guy?" One of the neighborhood mysteries was why one of them didn't just use their first name. It'd keep everyone from asking that question every single time.

"Plumber, and we bowl on Wednesdays, but he couldn't wait that long." George followed her once all the oranges had been corralled. "He started redoing the Fuller place. Total gut job, he said."

"That's fascinating." Why the hell was she a magnet for weird people? Not that she didn't love weird people when they were weirdly interesting. George was just weird.

"I thought so because she had a lot of questions about *you*." George reported that in a whisper, making her think he was going to give her a tape that would self-destruct after she listened to it.

A quick stab of panic drilled through the middle of her head when she thought about last night. Had Butch seen her and asked DJ the plumber about her after telling him what she'd been doing? She exhaled when she dropped that thought. Her self-relaxation techniques were still her secret, she was sure. "What kind of questions?" She was sure George was dying to tell her, but he wasn't going to until she asked. Petty but effective.

"She wanted to know what you did for a living."

She stared at him for what seemed like a full minute until she was sure he didn't have anything else to say. "And?" She made a rolling motion to help him along.

"There was more, but he was at the plumbing supply place buying stuff for the job. They start at six tomorrow. He had to get going so he could go to bed." He slowed, and she took a chance and turned down one of the narrow aisles.

"Okay then," she said, waving. "See you soon." She waved again, wanting to make him understand the conversation was over. Saying anything else was chancing the black hole of time that was George.

"I'll keep you updated." He was close to shouting, and she walked faster. Whatever else she needed she'd get tomorrow on her lunch hour. She was done for tonight. She looked around as she checked out, but there was no Butch in sight.

When she got home, she heated the pasta dish Fabio had ordered and stood at her kitchen window to eat it. This wasn't a habit—she ate in front of television like most normal people—but Butch was doing the same thing. Their houses were like mirror images, and Butch's kitchen and bedrooms faced hers. She couldn't take her eyes off Butch, but Butch hadn't really raised her head the entire time. It seemed she was doing something as she ate her sandwich.

They finished together, and as much as Hayley wanted to keep watching, she had some reading to do before bed. She poured a glass of wine and headed upstairs to change and sit in her favorite chair. The light in the bathroom was on, giving her enough illumination to move around and take her shirt off. She got as far as the middle of the room before she stopped, not wanting to move so as not to scare Butch off.

She watched as Butch pulled her shirt off in a brightly lit room, followed by her jeans and underwear. "And we have naked." Unlike the hose incident in the yard, she could see much better now. Butch made her burn.

Naked Butch walked to the wall and started touching it in different spots. She touched, knocked, and seem to caress the walls before stopping to put on sweatpants and a T-shirt. She dropped into a chair facing the window. Hayley stripped her pants off and waited. Maybe she'd get to see Butch's technique, but she was disappointed when the book appeared.

"Still, you did strip for me. It'd be rude not to touch myself now."

CHAPTER ELEVEN

The woman Wyatt now knew was Hayley had been laid out on the navel oranges like some kind of fruit-worshipping nutjob. Wyatt had thought she'd found the perfect opportunity to introduce herself until she'd seen George and decided to take a hard pass. She'd eventually have to formally meet him, she supposed, but certain things in life should be put off as long as possible. Things like setting one's feet on fire and avoiding people who screamed *Danger, I'm a fucking lunatic* without uttering a word.

She'd skipped everything else she'd come for, since the real reason she went shopping was to use the closest available bathroom without having to interact with her neighbors. Hayley's house had been on her list of possibilities, but she wasn't home when the urge to pee hit her. Once she walked home from the grocery, she made a sandwich and noticed Hayley at her kitchen window, eating pasta and watching her. That appeared a much better choice than ham and cheese, though the intense staring was a tad disconcerting, but she didn't move. There was something sexy about being watched by a beautiful woman from afar. She went back to Lydia's journals, not wanting to scare Hayley away.

It was like having dinner with Hayley only without the awkward conversations that always took place on first dates no matter how smooth you thought you were. The only people who always got the witty repartee and subtle flirting right were fictional characters. And that was only true because the author had days of tinkering to make sure they got it right. She finally took a chance when she was done eating and glanced across the way. Hayley smiled and looked skyward. If that was a signal for something, she had no clue what it was. Maybe it was *I'm getting ready to get myself off if you'd care to watch*, and if so, she didn't want to miss it.

She went upstairs and stripped with the light on. It wasn't at all something she'd ever considered doing, but she did owe Hayley a little something for the performance she'd gotten the night before. Hopefully, they'd become friendly if not friends, so she could share how much illumination the streetlight cast into her bedroom. She wasn't psychic, but she had to guess it was more than Hayley realized and would be comfortable with, should the need to masturbate in front of open windows hit her again. The other thing on her to-do list was to figure out when Hayley showered. With workmen around, she wanted to protect Hayley from giving free peep shows.

The lights next door weren't on, so she started knocking on the walls to make sure she hadn't missed any holes that held more journals. She'd managed to start putting them in chronological order, and now, in her sleep clothes, she sat down on the chair she'd placed by the window with the one she thought was the first, dated before the wedding photo in the house. It was the earliest date she'd found so far. As she read, she allowed herself to be transported to another time.

March 1985

The best way to tell a story is from the beginning. It's important not only to the story but also to the history the two people share. I'm sure everyone thinks their life would make a great romance novel, and I'm not any different, I guess. The thing is, Sam Fuller's love for me and mine for him is a story that needs to be told. Ours is more than a romance, but I don't want to be alive when it's told.

All you need to know before I begin is that we've been blessed with children, so there's never been time for writing, but I'm ninety now, and it would seem time is finally limited. I'll try my best to finish before I'm called to the Lord. This tale begins in March of 1913. I'm going to use our real names so you can follow along, and to whoever is reading this, know that sometimes we take secrets to the grave, but they shouldn't stay buried. So here goes.

March 1913

Lydia Blanchard and her sisters took the same path to their father's store outside of New Orleans as they always did. The fields along the way had undergone a transformation from grass to neat rows of different vegetables, and it always made her want to slow and admire the hard work it took to tend this much land. Her father had told them at dinner a few weeks ago that the farm down the way from theirs had a new owner, but she had yet to see him.

Today she stopped, and her sisters glanced back when they noticed she wasn't with them. Lydia's immobility couldn't be helped. She couldn't take her eyes off the young man in the middle of a half-plowed section, having what appeared to be a serious discussion with a mule. The funny part was the mule seemed to be talking back and winning the argument, if the man's frustration was any indication.

"What in the world?" her younger sister Daisy asked.

The new farmer took his hat off and banged it against his thigh, and the mule sounded like he was laughing. That made her sister Millie laugh as well, and the man finally noticed them. She got her sisters walking again but couldn't help looking back. The new farmer was not only young and tall, but the most handsome thing she'd ever seen in her eighteen years. Her job now was to find as much information about this stranger as she could without seeming forward about it. Mama would not look kindly on that. Good Southern girls were supposed to be demure and spend their days thinking about baking and such, not about handsome young men that made their breath catch.

"You girls get all those cans on the shelves," her father said when they joined him behind the counter. Their family had owned the grocery and general store for generations and dealt mostly with the community of day workers and farmers. They didn't go into New Orleans often, and the people in their little town had been here all their lives and recognized everyone on sight. Fishbowls had more privacy.

"I heard he was in the Army and got hurt so he bought the old Hister place." One of her mother's oldest friends seemed to have all the answers as she gossiped with one of the ladies from their church.

"His name's Sam Fuller, and he hired Lester Simmons to work the land with him."

"He seems to be doing a good job," she said, interjecting herself in their conversation. She got the woman's order ready, hoping she had all the information she wanted. At eighteen most people already thought she was an old maid, but she was holding out for someone she loved. Her mama had given her that advice and told her to stop listening to the old biddies who used terms like *old maid* and *spinster*. It was 1913, for God's sake.

"I think so, and I need you to help me carry all this home."

"I can go," Millie said.

"Next time, dear, this time Lydia has to go." The woman winked at her and picked up a bag. "She won't be long."

Lydia could've kissed the older woman, but her walk back was unsuccessful. The mule and Sam weren't there, and he was still missing that afternoon on their walk home. The recently plowed rows were done and planted, so she'd missed him, but there was always tomorrow.

The section ended, and Wyatt took a moment to think about what Lydia had written. Her story wasn't unique. There'd been countless romances through time about couples from kings to common men and the women they fell for. Everyone fell in love, except her. It wasn't that she was incapable of falling in love—she simply hadn't found it and knew all those pie-in-the-sky notions of your one true love only existed in books.

"Don't say anything. I already know you two found that," she said before her mother popped into her head again. The journal was still open, and she used it to covertly study the window across from her. She took a moment to fantasize about whether Hayley wore toenail polish. Not that it would be a total mood killer if she didn't, but she did love that on a woman. Something in the red family would be fantastic.

There was no way to find out—all she could make out were the bottoms of Hayley's feet since she had them on the windowsill again. "What do you think, Lydia?" She closed the journal and tapped it against her knee. "Think she'll hide if I turn out the lights?"

It was worth the gamble, and she snapped off the antique floor lamp she'd found downstairs and gave her eyes time to adjust to the dark. Hayley was moving her hips to the pace she'd set with her hand. The light outside gave her a view of what Hayley was doing but not a clear picture of her face. She'd really only gotten a few glimpses of her neighbor, but she knew the woman was beautiful.

Right now, she wanted to see her since she found nothing sexier than a woman's expression when her orgasm was right there at the edge of her need. Listening to the short gasps and moans turned her on and was a big part of what she missed about sex. All she could do was content herself with what Hayley was willing to share with her. She was turned-on by the time Hayley's feet came off the sill and she sat up.

These were the times she thought about the last woman in her bed. In reality it wasn't the woman but the sex she remembered because none of the women were memorable. With the shock of the loss of her parents, she hadn't had the urge to get out of bed, much less think of sleeping with someone. Hayley was clearly starting to wake her up because she was wet and hard. The problem was she was alone with only a woman in the window across from her.

She took her time and placed her fingers along her clit and squeezed. "Fuck," she said when she moved her fingers and squeezed harder. All her intentions to go slow disappeared when the desire to come became a desperate thing. "Jesus," she said as she dropped her feet and took a breath. A pleasant lethargy overtook her, but it was too early to go to bed, so she clicked a lamp back on and picked up Lydia's journal.

March 1913

Lydia left early for work the next morning, not wanting her sisters to walk with her. She'd thought carefully about her hair and picked a dress that looked the best on her. Her goal was to make an impression on Sam. The field was just up ahead, and she took a breath to calm her nerves. There he was. Sam and his mule were plowing some new rows and continuing what appeared to be a love-hate relationship. Lydia stood at the fence and smiled.

A wave got her no response, but it was most likely Sam hadn't seen her when he turned around to plow in the opposite direction.

It took Mr. Oblivious half an hour to notice her, and Lydia wasn't in the best mood by then. Actually, she was madder than she ever remembered being, and added to that, she was about to be late for work. If her sisters came by and saw her being humiliated, she'd befriend the mule.

Sam appeared confused as he stood motionless staring at her. She crossed her arms over her chest, and he took his hat off and scratched his head. Lydia was mad, but she couldn't deny what watching Sam did to her. The man was infuriating, but he was the most gorgeous thing, and he made her think of things she'd never contemplated.

The way Sam acted, though, made it clear they'd never get anywhere if he didn't change his aggravating ways. He started walking when she motioned him over. His slow gait made his mule bray like he understood Sam was an idiot. He still held his hat, and the way he pressed it to his chest made her think he was using it as a shield to protect himself.

"Can I help you with something?" His gruffness meant the mule probably had better manners and social skills.

"I'm Lydia Blanchard, and I wanted to welcome you." She had to unclench her teeth to say the words and threw her hands up when he glanced back at the mule. "Do you need his help to be sociable?"

"Sorry, I'm not used to visitors." He shifted his weight, and she guessed it might have something to do with the limp she'd seen. "It's usually just me and Lester."

"Is that the mule?"

"Oh no, ma'am, that's Plank. Lester's the only man who agreed to work with me, but he's over by the barn." Sam stared at his shoes, and what Lydia took as dismissiveness was perhaps shyness. Sam wasn't one of those aggressive sorts who'd tried to ask her out.

"Lester Simmons?" she asked, and Sam nodded. "I know his family, and they're real nice people. Is there some reason Lester's the only one who wanted the job?" It was wise to find out early if Sam was some sort of bully or cad before her hormones overtook her brain.

"I'm not from around here, and I'm retired Army, so people aren't sure about me yet, I guess. This leg started my farming career sooner than I expected. Sorry I didn't see you, and thanks for the welcome. I won't keep you." He raised his head and made eye contact. "It's nice meeting you, Miss Lydia." It seemed he could be social but only for short spurts of time.

"My father expects you at Sunday lunch at our house. Do you need directions?"

"I appreciate the offer, but I have a lot of work." The battered hat wasn't going to last that much longer with the manhandling he was subjecting it to. He beat it against his leg and used it to wave toward the fields to show what he was talking about.

"Sundays aren't for work no matter how much you have of it. Be there at eleven, and don't be late. My parents believe in promptness." She pointed to the mule. "And he might be more cooperative if you gave him a nicer name."

"That's the nicest thing we could come up with and be able to say it in mixed company, miss."

She laughed at that. "See you soon." Lydia stopped breathing when Sam smiled. That was enough to convince her she'd made the right decision. Sam Fuller was going to be her husband even if the stubborn man didn't know it yet.

Wyatt ran her finger over the writing and could imagine Lydia sitting somewhere, penning the things she thought important about her life with Sam, turning it into a kind of novel of their romance. The story so far hadn't been riveting, but she did want to finish it. Doing that would honor the woman who poured so much of herself onto the pages.

Putting pen to paper was how she'd started. It was like her brain shut off as the words flowed, and she enjoyed flying on her imagination until the pieces fell into place. She'd been asked about that once at a signing, and it'd been her best explanation. Her brain didn't literally shut off, but giving herself over to the work brought her in directions she never contemplated if she was willing to forgo the outlines and rigid storylines.

She stared at Lydia's handwriting, and an idea started to form. The process of actually writing something down might be the answer she was looking for, and she wanted to go back to the old ways. Tomorrow she'd have to go out and see if she could find the notebooks her father had introduced her to. Her pens were in her bag, so all she needed was ink.

"There's been a lot of days since you stood in that field, waiting for Sam to notice you." She would've liked to have met Lydia. "You were a woman who knew what she wanted and went for it. I can't imagine that was common back then." She placed the journal back on the pile.

The window across the way was empty, and she couldn't make anything out even after she clicked the light off again. One thing she should add to her list of things to do tomorrow would be a trip next door to meet Hayley. It was something she was looking forward to.

"And I thought I'd be bored."

She went to bed wondering what other treasures Lydia had hidden in the walls of this place. The odds of picking a house that came with a story a woman wrote to be found after her death were too infinitesimal to consider, and seeing the stack in the dark made her want to get up and read until she passed out.

Maybe this was the universe's way of paying her back for all she'd been through. It was a piss-poor compensation for losing her parents, but it was a first step in healing what she was convinced would never stop bleeding.

CHAPTER TWELVE

W hat are you working on?" Esther Fox asked. Hayley's mother called her twice a week to check in, but the questions mostly centered around any potential danger she could be in. She really needed to get her mom hooked on rom-coms.

"Hmm," she said, distracted. It was hard to concentrate when the lights next door had started coming on one by one. She'd been in bed when her mom called, and since the sun wasn't up, it was easy to see her neighbor move from room to room. That wasn't strange since it was a new house, and exploring it made sense. What didn't make sense was Butch running her hands over the walls like she had a very unique fetish.

Hayley couldn't make sense of what was happening, and she attributed it to having slept like hell. Last night after relaxing herself to the point of unconsciousness, she stayed in her chair and watched Butch read. And she couldn't be blamed for touching herself after the striptease she'd seen that revealed the most perfect body that was certainly a gift from the gods. Could she?

There'd have to be a quiet moment later to think about the perfect body because right now she had to concentrate on what had happened when Butch flicked the light off. She'd touched herself. Hayley knew that because she'd watched while reality set in. The mortifying truth was that she'd touched herself in front of a possibly deranged person, not once but twice. She hoped Butch hadn't taken that stupid move as an invitation to come over and massage *her* walls before hauling her to the bedroom. Her mother would fly to New Orleans and pack her up before she knew what was happening.

"Did you hear me?" Her mom spoke louder, and it derailed the out-of-control direction her mind was speeding off to.

"Sorry." She closed her eyes and took a breath. When she opened them Butch put her fist through the wall of the bedroom next to the one she seemed to be using. Hayley grimaced when she did it again.

"Did you fall asleep?" Her mom sounded amused, and Hayley could hear her father singing in the background. Her dad's morning serenades were one of her favorite things about him.

"I have a stack of submissions to get through, and I'm editing an erotica anthology." Butch was now pressing herself to the wall, and as strange as it was, she hoped she'd strip again, though there was no logical reason for her to do so.

"Nothing like a little smut to work up the masses." Her mom laughed.

"It's the way to highlight new authors. What the masses do with it is up to them in the privacy of their own homes." She laughed, thinking what she'd done with it. *I read it and touched myself for my strange neighbor's enjoyment.* That would be the number one way to kill her mother on the spot. "How are you?"

"Fine. Nothing happening here that's as exciting as an erotica anthology. Do I get a copy? It might give me new ideas for your father."

That was something you never wanted to talk to your parents about, no matter how open the relationship. "Not unless you leave Dad for your female neighbor."

"Ooh, even better. I'll be happy to help out if you need extra input."

She laughed again. "Is there something you're not telling me?"

"No, your father's still a stud. I thought it'd help me understand what you think is sexy." It sounded like her mom blew a kiss. "Now tell me what George's been up to lately." Her mom used George's ramblings as a way to assess any potential threats.

The real problem was George himself. He rambled, all right, but this time his stream of consciousness hadn't yielded anything useful other than Butch was a foreigner. Big help that was, she thought, as Butch punched through the wall at a different spot. From this angle she could see her rip through the paper and reach inside the hole. This time she pulled something out, but she couldn't tell what it was. Curious.

"We have a new neighbor, and according to the town gossip, she's a foreigner." She watched Butch move to the next spot and use her fist again.

"That's all George knows? I'm disappointed." Her mom paused and hummed. "Hold on while I get a pen."

"For what?" She was going to keep Butch's activities to herself for now. Whatever she was up to made her wonder if Butch knew something about the Fuller house that the heirs didn't. Why else would someone like Butch move into a house that should've been condemned years ago? Maybe there was some great treasure hidden in the walls, and Butch was punching a way to it.

"Does the foreigner have a car?"

"A truck, actually. Again, why?" The hunt was over, and Butch stood with her hands on the wall as if she was tired.

"I need a license plate number. Anyone who moved in next door is either on the run from the police or is planning something that will cause them to be on the run from the police. There's no way I'm going to let anything happen to you."

The passion both her parents had for the lives they chose to lead made her smile. "I think this is more of a case for HGTV's house flip than a serial killer in training." She yawned as the sun started to rise and it got lighter outside. The last glimpse she got of Butch was as she fell into bed. "I've been slammed at work, so I haven't had a chance to go over and introduce myself."

"Don't go in the house, whatever you do. That's how they get you."

"I love you too, Mom, and I've got to start getting ready." Hugo rolled over and stared at her. "I'll call you as soon as I know anything."

"Don't forget the plate number, and be careful."

"I promise, and if George comes up with anything new, I'll report in. He had bowling Wednesday, so he should be dying to tell me something." She hung up and decided perhaps she should make an appointment to have her head examined. Wishing for George to come over, no matter what, and doing highly personal things to herself in front of an odd stranger were surely grounds for a mental health checkup.

❖

The bed squeaked when Wyatt finally fell into it. She might have time for a short nap before her workmen arrived after she'd had another night of staring at the ceiling. That had finally gotten boring, and to have something to do, she'd gone on a Lydia journal hunt. She'd found another thirty-eight to go with the thirteen she already had, which meant Lydia had suffered very little writer's block in her long life. Lydia might've been popular and known for her cookies and child-bearing ability with the eleven she'd brought into the world, but she'd had plenty to write about and had somehow found the time. Either that or she was a freak of nature who never had to sleep.

She read a bit more after destroying more of her walls and found more recipes mixed with the novel Lydia was writing. At least that's what it seemed like she'd been doing. The thought of a small old lady sitting at her desk writing about what was expected of demure Southern girls made Wyatt smile. Yep, Lydia sounded like a woman who'd moved the needle when it came to the women's movement that'd paved the way for everyone else.

She enjoyed putting characters like Lydia in her own books as a reminder that all modern women stood on the shoulders of people like Lydia Fuller. The only reason the feminist needle had moved at all was because the Lydias of the world had enough of the bullshit and had done things to change the status quo. Where some of the recent crop of white supremacist conspiracy theorist women in politics came from was a bigger mystery than the thrillers Wyatt was known for writing. They did prove, though, that women could be bigger assholes than men.

She closed her eyes and managed a good half an hour before sleep became an impossibility, so she got up and thought about coffee. Her problem was water, or rather the lack of it. There were fifteen different choices of things to drink in her refrigerator, but water hadn't made her list. Water was usually something she enjoyed only after it magically turned into something else, like coffee or an old fashioned. There was no chance anyplace would be pouring coffee at this early hour, but she bet she could walk to the Quarter and get a Harvey Wallbanger. New Orleans did have its priorities.

"I have to remember to google how to make those, along with what rickets is." She talked to herself as she dressed to go out and get the last couple of boxes from the back of the truck. She needed to finish unloading her dad's stuff so that she could go get wood to start her own projects on the house. Swinging a hammer and building something might help her sleep problems, she figured, so she was tackling the porch first. Having one of DJ's guys fall through the damn thing might put a crimp in their working relationship.

She eventually pulled the last box out and saw a surprise at the top when she pulled it open. "What'd you use these for?" On the top were five of the notebooks she'd wanted to go shopping for. "Damn, Pop." There was a sticky note on one that had *for Wy* written on it in her father's handwriting. She went into the kitchen to sit and cry. That was something she was getting mighty tired of doing. The other notebooks in the box were filled with her handwriting. Some of them were books she'd published, and others she'd thought were long lost.

"Stop it, kid. It's the kick in the ass I thought you'd eventually need," her father said. It was improbable that she was having conversations with her dead parents, but she hoped this bit of insanity never went away. Losing the sounds of their voices from her memory would only add to her grief.

The main bedroom had a small desk where Lydia probably wrote in her journals, and that's where she dropped her dad's unexpected gift. At the bottom of the box that had held her old journals were a couple of empty journals which actually resembled Lydia's, right down to the linen paper. "Maybe you are on to something, Mom. Write about the unfairness of life and the things you wished you could change but can't." Wyatt's life was unfair due to all she'd lost.

Ballpoint pens weren't her favorite, but she'd have to find a stationery store that sold ink before she could take out her leather sleeve of pens. The ink of a fountain pen penetrated the paper while ballpoint ink glided over it. Penetrating the page made the words permanent, lasting. You were wed to those words you wrote even if

Writer's Block

they eventually went into a word processing app and were edited. Right now, it was her and the page. Time to prove there was still a small part of her soul that housed the stories that hadn't been shredded by grief.

She opened one of the linen paper journals and smoothed her hand over it. She pressed the pen to paper and let her hand begin to flow. "It's nice to know I haven't forgotten how to do this."

An hour later she had a cramp in her hand, she raised her head to sunlight outside, and there was noise coming from downstairs. DJ was a man of his word and a reminder of the fact she had no working toilet. The bathroom at the grocery was a very long time ago, and she was about to use one of the many bushes in her yard, snakes or no. She had to take a few deep breaths to relax her bladder before she embarrassed herself.

"Mornin'," DJ said loudly when she took the stairs like an alpine skier. "Go down two blocks to the Magnolia diner. Maybelle makes great pancakes," DJ yelled as she moved quickly down the street.

The diner was on the corner, and she could see it from here. She hadn't run this fast since her high school track days. If she'd known the need to urinate added this kind of speed, she'd have gotten a scholarship. As quaint as the place was, it was empty, and the bathroom was a thing of beauty. Thankfully, no one was in the one stall, or she'd have had to use the sink. "Sorry about that. It was an emergency," she said to the cute waitress when she came out, close to weak with relief.

"Don't worry about it. DJ called and said you'd be running over. Who knew he was being literal." The young woman pointed to an empty booth. "Thing is, you gotta eat something if you use the bathroom. Maybelle don't play, so don't get on her bad side, or she'll make your life a misery. I speak from extensive experience."

"DJ said something about pancakes. I was frantic, so that might be wrong." She took a booth close to the door and grabbed the menu.

"We already got your pancakes on, so relax. You want coffee?" The woman put her menu back for her as if she didn't have much say in what she got to order.

"That'd be fantastic." Another older woman came out of the kitchen and took the mug and carafe from the woman she'd been talking to. The newcomer picked up another mug and sat across from her before she poured. She reminded Wyatt a little of Pam Grier only with shorter hair. "Good morning."

"Morning." The woman studied her for as long as it took Wyatt to fix her coffee. "Gwen, baby, check on the pancakes, will you."

There were certain people she'd met through the years who spoke in a slow cadence that was mellifluous and relaxed. It was like nothing could rush, spook, or intimidate them to hurry what they had to say. Most of those people lived in this city, as her new friend proved. It didn't appear she was leaving, so maybe this was a service they provided to people they felt sorry for because they were dining alone.

"Do the pancakes come with bacon?" Why did people force conversation on you when it was clear it was the last thing you wanted? Wyatt wondered about that, and it was probably the reason there were serial killers. "You can just add that to my order if not, and that'll do me." She thought that was enough of a hint she'd like to eat alone.

"What, you shy or something?" The woman smiled and held her hand out. "I'm Maybelle Jackson, and I own this place."

"Nice to meet you, Miss Jackson." Maybelle's *miss* days were long gone, but in New Orleans it was an acceptable title. She had to stop herself and remember the name she'd given DJ. "I'm Joe." It might be conceited of her to think she'd be recognized when there were very few photos of her in the public eye, but you never knew when you'd run into a mystery fan. She loved her fans, but right now she didn't want to deal with people, or more people than she had to.

"What *are* you doing here, Joe? Aside from tearing up Lydia's house, that is." Maybelle lifted her right eyebrow to an impressive height.

Some people liked the direct, no beating around the bush type of approach, even if the person being subjected to it was someone they'd just met. Maybelle was that type and wasn't apologetic about it. "Is interrogation one of your sides, like toast? Or are you by chance the sheriff moonlighting as a diner owner?" The woman she now knew was Gwen came out of the kitchen with enough pancakes and bacon to feed her and all the guys at the house, and still have some leftover.

"They don't have diners where you're from? Dishing a little about yourself if you're new is part of the diner rules. Gossip is a must, so I can then add to the story and totally exaggerate it to keep my regulars entertained." Maybelle pushed the syrup in front of her and raised the amazing eyebrow of death again. "You locking yourself in that house like a hermit has already started the rumor mill, so tell Maybelle all about it."

"That's kind of funny. I never thought my life was all that interesting, and I've only been here less than a week." When in doubt shove a wad of pancake in your mouth. The size of the bite bordered on rude and disgusting, but the situation called for drastic measures.

"Girl, you've met George, I'm sure. By tomorrow he should have your DNA and fingerprints, so watch what you throw away." Maybelle refreshed her coffee, adding more cream and sugar for her. "You're new, which means you're nothing but interesting."

"Sort of like an exotic pet, huh?" She cut another too big bite of pancakes, glad they were really good. Using food to shut down uncomfortable conversations was a talent of hers, but when the food was disgusting it was hard to maintain.

Maybelle's demeanor changed, and she dropped her steel magnolia routine. "What kind of exotic pet? There're children here."

"A snake kind of exotic. The Burmese python isn't a lapdog, but they can be left alone if you have plans for the weekend." She shoved in more pancake and bacon, waiting for Maybelle to say something, but she seemed shocked for some reason. "Then there's the satisfaction of the reaction anyone dumb enough to break in has when they run across an eighteen-foot snake that weighs four hundred pounds and can sense fear." She took another large bite and smiled, sure she looked like a deranged squirrel with her cheeks full of pancakes.

"That's not normal, and I hate snakes. You're interesting, Joe, and you haven't told me who you'll be working for here."

"Right now, my job is runaway." She pushed the plate away

and grabbed her wallet. Any more pancake to avoid talking to Maybelle and she'd be sick, and she had no working bathrooms.

"What does that mean?" Maybelle waved off the money. "Explanation please."

"You're going to have to be happy with that explanation for now. A little mystery is good for the soul. And gossip." She pushed the money back. "Thanks for the use of your bathroom and for breakfast. Your pancakes really are good."

"Let me get you some change. If you're going to be a regular, and you *are* going to be a regular, then we don't want to appear to be taking advantage of you by keeping too much money." Maybelle handed the bill to Gwen, studying her again. "Do you cook? You don't look like the type."

"What type do I look like?" She really needed to stop falling into these traps.

"I wouldn't have asked if I knew that. If you don't mind me mentioning it, you do look like you should find some nice girl to take care of you." Maybelle waited, but she stayed quiet. "You got one of those?"

"You sound like my mother." She almost laughed when she thought about how many times her mother really had said those words. "Right now the girl will have to wait."

"So you cook?" Maybelle was persistent.

"No, not really in my skill set." Gwen brought back what seemed like too much change, so she gave her most of it back in a tip. "This was fun, but I have to go. Thanks for the pancakes and the hospitality." The diner was good and close, but she'd only come back if there were other customers for Maybelle to visit with. Gulping down food in large bites gave her indigestion but not as much as talking about herself.

She loved writing because it was a thrill to put the pieces of a good story together, but it was done alone. A solitary sport requiring no chatty teammates except the ones in her head. The only time she interacted with a lot of people was at signings, and she'd enjoyed the conversation and relationships she'd made through the years, but she was always glad to get back to her solitude too. In the ten years after graduate school, she'd written twelve books. It was a blessing to find that she was good and successful at it. She understood and had never taken for granted how lucky she was.

DJ was waiting for her when she got back and gave her directions to a lumberyard on Tchoupitoulas Street, and then he spent five minutes teaching her how to pronounce Tchoupitoulas. She left them ripping out more stuff, and DJ promised he'd have a couple of his guys start pulling up the old porch while she went shopping. She couldn't be sure, but it seemed like there were a lot more people in her house than yesterday.

"And one of my friends has a heavy-duty lawnmower. Once they clear all that crap and find your grass, they can work on it and nurse it back to health." DJ spoke about seventy decibels too loud.

"Great, but try for a toilet today. I don't want to end up with some sort of kidney disease." There was that, and if they mowed the lawn there was a chance her neighbors would see her in the yard if the situation got desperate. "Can they deal with the gardens as well?" Right now she was growing plenty of vines with killer thorns on them and didn't want to touch them herself.

"You got it, and the neighbors will love you for taking those down. You gotten a chance to meet any?"

She shook her head and followed him down the stairs. "Not yet, but soon."

"Just remember what I said about the pies. Karen brings one of those over, and you'll think she's trying to get you to move." DJ's stage whisper needed work, but the little guy meant well.

"Thanks, DJ, I haven't forgotten." She drove to Papier Plume on Royal in the Quarter for an ink bottle, then to the other side of Canal Street, where the old part of the city divided from the newer sections, for her wood. Maybe this would be her life. It was time to let go of the old and embrace the new even if that meant there wouldn't be any more Wyatt Whitlock mysteries.

CHAPTER THIRTEEN

Can you blame her for getting rid of the wallpaper, Hayley? How people didn't go batshit crazy staring at that all day and night is a mystery." Marlo was slouching in one of Hayley's chairs while they talked about their lineup and Butch.

Hayley's house was two blocks from Marlo's. That morning because of street work, Marlo had driven by her house and noticed the freshly mown lawn and the missing porch. She'd also been to Hayley's house more than once and had seen the wallpaper next door.

It'd taken Butch three days to rip the leaning structure out, load a dumpster, and revamp the yard. All that work took place while Hayley wasn't home, so she'd only gotten glimpses of Butch, her tool belt, and her talent for demolishing and fixing walls. There were too many holes now to make sense from their placement, and she tried not to dwell on that, so she concentrated on the overall picture. The house still looked crappy, but she was optimistic.

"Is there some reason you haven't gone over and introduced yourself?" Marlo smiled as she held a cigarette but didn't light it. "I thought I trained you to be a better Southerner than that. Is she weird or doing something you find strange?"

No, she just likes to watch me touch myself until I come hard enough to give me jelly legs because I sit in my bedroom window staring at her. I can't help myself since she's totally hot. She didn't think that was what Marlo was after, so she kept her mental monologue to herself. "She's just redoing the house and doing some of it herself from what I can tell. I haven't wanted to interrupt."

Marlo glanced over the paperwork and nodded. "The anthology is well fleshed out, so thank you for all the extra time you put into that. Why don't you go home early today and introduce yourself to the neighbor. I'm sure she'll welcome the interruption." Marlo seemed to have reached her breaking point on the cigarette and lit it. "If you find anything out, you'll be a big hit at the Magnolia diner tomorrow when we go for lunch. It's Abbott's favorite place." Abbott was one of their paranormal authors who resembled some kind of vampire-slash-ghoul if those people existed and survived on waffles.

"What do you mean?" She made some notes for her admin and emailed them.

"Tippy and I went for pancakes earlier this morning, and the scoop on your neighbor and her massive snake is that they're possibly on the run from the law." Marlo used her coffee cup as an ashtray. "Maybelle told us she needed one more meal with her to get the whole story. Until then pray she keeps her big snake in some sort of enclosure. You don't want it coming over in search of a hug. Hugo and Truman would climb the walls and leave your ass to fend for yourself."

"She's got a snake? Seriously?" That totally creeped her out. Did Butch lock it up somewhere when she touched herself? She didn't think getting distracted to the point of oblivion while a giant killer roamed your house was a good idea. It could be dangerous. She didn't have anything against snakes per se. They were just better on TV or in the movies she never watched because they creeped her out.

"Just keep an eye on the dynamic cat duo, and tell George he might want to inventory the rabbits. I'm no python expert, but I think they love the bunnies." Marlo tossed the butt in her cup and was holding the cigarette she'd put behind her ear. It was her emergency stash.

"I love rabbits too, but those little suckers are always in my yard, eating everything in my herb garden." She was positive George let them loose over the fence so he'd have an excuse to come over and bore her into a conversation coma.

"Get going or we'll never find out anything about…what'd you nickname her?"

"Butch," she said, making Marlo laugh. "Hey, she wears a leather tool belt that has nothing to do with sex"—she held her hand up—"before you comment."

"We'll never find out about Butch and why she's here if you don't go over there and get some answers." Marlo held her cigarette up like a conductor's baton when she stood. "If you're able to breach the front door, make sure to get a picture of the snake. Get that, and there might be free pancakes in our future."

"If that's what it takes to get free food, I'll gladly treat you. Let's hope the zoom on my iPhone is enough because I'm not getting anywhere near it, should the opportunity arise." She shouldered her bag and waved. "Thanks for the short day."

Hayley drove home with the windows down, enjoying the gorgeous afternoon. It was still cold, but the sky was blue, and the Quarter was full of tourists. At least these people had figured out this was a much better time to visit than August with its surface-of-the-sun-worthy temps. She wanted to blame going ten miles under the speed limit on the beautiful afternoon, but truthfully it was her attempt to delay the inevitable. She did want to meet Butch, so that wasn't it. The snake and the holes in the walls gave her pause after hearing that Butch might be a fugitive.

"She could either be getting ready to start hiding bodies the snake killed for her, or they're for the cash she's stolen in the string of bank robberies she's committed." Talking to herself when she was this crazy wasn't helping.

She stared at the Fuller house from the safety of her car, remembering the creepy house on Long Island when she was ten. In her defense, and in defense of her friends, the guy who owned the place practiced taxidermy as a hobby. Why he didn't choose stamp collecting or golf was a good question no one ever had an answer to, and he used his hobby as a way to scare the hell out of all the kids in the neighborhood. He'd posed small animals in different ways and used them as lawn ornaments, which you couldn't help but stare at as you walked by. The place always made her nauseous. Their little bared teeth also fueled the series of nightmares she'd had until she was thirteen.

As for the Fuller house, there'd been some changes since she'd left for work. The lawn had been mowed, two of the gardens had been cleared, and there was a new porch. She couldn't be sure, but she doubted Butch had tackled the yard by herself—she didn't look the type. The porch, though, was probably her handiwork and a missed opportunity to see Butch in the tool belt. At the moment there was no Butch helping DJ and his guys rip off the hideous green shake that covered the side of the house.

"Fantastic," she whispered, still staring. If Butch had gotten this much done in less than a week, by the end of the month Hayley's house would be the dump on the block. She opened her car door and stared at the ground, half expecting to see a coiled snake waiting to borrow a cup of sugar.

"What do you think, little lady?" DJ's booming voice came close to levitating her onto her porch where she'd die of the startled induced heart attack she'd eventually have. What was with the men in this town?

"Hey, DJ, it's great. I thought you only did plumbing. Are there pipes in the wall you needed to get to?" She watched the guys on the ladders standing on the top step and it made her shiver. There was no way in hell she could do that. It wasn't that she was afraid of heights, but she had a fear of falling from a high place. It's why she was glad she was short.

"We usually don't, but your neighbor's damn persuasive. She got most of these off herself, but I pulled the guys out of the house to get the top floor. It's faster with the crew, and we got one of the bathrooms working, so she's good for now. No rush on the ones upstairs." DJ turned and faced the house, scrunching his forehead. "It's weird, though."

"What?" Hopefully, whatever he said wasn't worse than the snake. She still got goose bumps every time she thought about it.

"The other side is a lot worse, but she insisted on starting here." He glanced back at her and smiled, a blush coloring his ears. His face was always red from what she could tell, so his ears were the only way to know he was blushing. "Maybe she's trying to impress you because of…well, you know."

She dropped her head until her chin hit her chest. Of course her sexuality was still a subject of conversation between George and his friends. Ever since she turned George's brother down for a date and told him why, George had informed everyone who'd listen she was a lesbian. Why he felt compelled to do that wasn't something she wanted to talk to him about since it wasn't that important to her. People knowing she was gay wasn't going to make her less gay.

She was sure guys like DJ thought she was only using the *I'm gay* excuse to avoid having to deal with any of them. The thing was, even if she was straight, she'd still take a hard pass on George's brother, Theodore. The guy still owned and wore a leisure suit, which she had to look up because she thought it was some sort of unfortunate uniform he was forced to wear. The baby blue suit along with his polyester shirt with palm trees on it, also baby blue, and puka shell choker were a specific look for sure. To add to all that sexiness, he mixed hair gel and bacon grease for the shine it gave his hair. She was sure Theodore'd be followed by every dog in town trying to lick his head like a lollipop.

"Whatever her reason it certainly is going to turn out nice." She shut her car door when she grabbed all her stuff, not wanting the conversation to slide into something uncomfortable. "It was great seeing you, DJ."

"Yeah, let me get back to it." He tipped his hat and went to lean on something else while he watched his guys work.

She didn't care that Marlo wanted a picture of the snake—her conversation with DJ convinced her she needed more time to build up her courage. If Butch came back and strapped on the tool belt, maybe it would be the push she'd need, but short of that, she was staying inside. The perfect opportunity to replace Butch with the woman's real name had passed her by when she'd run inside, which meant she could forget any type of law-enforcement job should the editing thing not work out. Wheedling the facts out of people was obviously not her strong suit.

The kitchen window had become her new favorite place, and she saw she'd only missed the chance to meet Butch by a few minutes when her truck pulled in, laden with building stuff. DJ's guys unloaded supplies from the back of the truck, and another truck followed Butch that said *insulation* on the side. She was jealous since she was convinced her house had none, which explained the draft in her kitchen. Butch climbed one of the ladders and helped the three young guys rip the last of the shake off.

How could an ass look that good in jeans? She was focused on that when her phone rang. "Hello."

"Are you mad at me that I had to work?" Lucy was always too busy for formalities. "I thought you were coming by?"

"I am, I've been busy." She cringed when Butch leaned over too far for Hayley's comfort.

"When can I see you? You can tell me if you've had sex with the new neighbor."

She laughed and shook her head. "I'm not that slutty, and we haven't met yet."

"Why the hell not?" No one did indignant better than Lucy. "How am I supposed to know if I'm going to steal her away from you if you can't dish about anything? I swear, Hayley, it's like you're falling down on the best friend job."

"My best friend wouldn't steal Butch away from me."

"Wait." Lucy's voice went up a hundred octaves. "Her name is Butch?"

"No, I thought she needed a nickname, and she's been busy with her tool belt strapped on. You're not going to believe the way the house looks when you come over." The siding was all off, and the spray insulation guys got to work. She wasn't sure what connections Butch had, but the work was happening at a rapid pace. "I'm sure she doesn't have time to get to know me."

"We'll cover the tool belt in a minute, but everyone wants to get to know you, girlfriend. You're gorgeous, and you have a body that makes other girls jealous, including me. I should be off Sunday, so buy wine and take out three glasses. We're going over there and offering ourselves up as a harem."

"Yes, we should totally do that." She laughed again and put the phone down when Lucy hung up. When it rang again almost right away, she was expecting the good-bye Lucy forgot. But it was her mother.

"Well, what have you found out?" There was a reason her mother and Lucy loved each other.

"Not a whole lot. I've been slammed since I got back, and my neighbor is doing major renovations. I didn't think it was a good time to put her under a naked bulb and drip water on her head while

I whipped her with a wet noodle." She held her breath when Butch put her hands on her hips and stood with her legs slightly apart. Damn.

"You haven't talked to her at all? She hasn't come over and tried to get into your house, has she?"

"We haven't actually interacted at all. I do see her on occasion." Like right now, and she was sexy as fuck.

"What's wrong with her?"

Hayley took the phone away from her ear and stared at it. Her mother would make a great interrogator—she'd certainly missed her calling. Unlike Hayley, her mother would've grilled Butch for answers, known her whole life story, and would've met the snake by now. "There's nothing wrong with her."

"Uh-huh, tell me what's on your mind. When you only come up with what I like to call white noise, it means you're holding something back. I think we need to come for a visit to reassure me."

"Mom, I already told Dad I'm really busy at work. I want you to come when I have time to take you two around." She did not in any way need her mother grilling Butch. There was a chance Butch would retaliate with a big case of honesty. *Do you have any idea what your daughter does in open windows, lady? It seems like an odd thing to do when you have no blinds.*

"Are you sure? We could be there by tomorrow. It's New Orleans, honey, I'm sure we can find something to entertain us just as soon as I find out all there is to know about the mystery neighbor."

She could hear the eager anticipation she was sure the sheriffs of old felt when they were assembling the posse. "Mom, really, I want you to come when you and Dad can spend time with me. Trying to investigate my neighbor isn't what I had in mind." Once her mother found out about the large snake and possible sordid past, she'd make up Wanted posters and get the FBI involved. There was no way that'd do anything for neighbor relations.

"Okay, but try to get an update, so I won't worry." Her mom's goal in life was to find someone on the most-wanted list of fugitives. She'd die a happy woman if she could check that accomplishment off her bucket list. "Or we might surprise you."

The call ended abruptly after that, which meant her mom had

already bought airline tickets and was waiting for her plane. "Fuck me." She put the phone down and pressed the heel of her hand to her forehead. Butch was still standing in her yard, watching the crew spraying insulation. "Run," she whispered. "Run while you still can."

CHAPTER FOURTEEN

How in the hell are you getting all these supplies so fast?" DJ asked. It was the end of another long day, but Wyatt felt good. The porch was almost done, and they could start putting up the boards she'd had delivered that afternoon. She knew the area had a problem with Formosan termites, so she'd gone with the composite boards that'd last her lifetime anyway. "I grew up with Barney, and the bastard still makes me wait a week when I've got a job waiting."

Wyatt was writing DJ a check for the services he'd already done, as well as giving him a down payment on the rest, so he wouldn't have to be out-of-pocket for supplies. "You should try my method for guys like Barney. It works every time." She wrote the check from her business account and smiled.

"Did you promise to date him or something?" DJ folded the check carefully, matching the edges before pocketing it. "You should know the randy bastard's married and has a bunch of kids."

"No, that's not it. I offered to rip his balls off if he delayed any shipment he had in stock." Her smile widened when DJ's legs came together, and he lowered his hand. "I read it in a book, and it's pretty effective."

"Remind me never to get on your bad side."

DJ's voice was slightly shaky, so she stopped teasing him. The reason Barney was willing to deliver so quickly was because she was willing to pay his exorbitant expedited fee.

"And if you want, I'll bring my nephews tomorrow. They're good carpenters and have experience putting that stuff up."

"That would be great, thanks. Do you need anything for the bathroom upstairs?" she asked.

He shook his head. "I can get an electrician here to rewire the smaller bedroom you're taking in to make the main en suite larger."

"I trust you, DJ, so get someone good. See you in the morning." She shook his hand and walked out with him. "You make a good contractor, so let me know if you and your crew want to help out until I'm done."

"We'd love to, and I'll run anything that's beyond our scope by you."

"Get going then. I have to replenish the drinks and some groceries." She got the keys and her wallet. "Is there a bigger food store than the local market? It's convenient but limited unless you're really into jerky. I keep eating Slim Jims, and my mother says I'll get rickets."

"There's Magnolia Market, but you have to go out of the neighborhood a bit."

She sighed as she locked the door. "Does that mean Maybelle owns it?"

"No, her brother Marty Monty does."

How DJ said that with a straight face amazed her as she listened to him give her directions. They talked a few more minutes, and she hoped Hayley would come out since her car was there, but no luck. Her hermit tendencies were most likely because she realized Wyatt had seen what she'd done, but she did reciprocate. Maybe getting Hayley interested in meeting her would take a sort of bribe, and she needed to get to the grocery to get started on that.

Magnolia Market was about five miles from her house, and it appeared nice enough, but she was withholding judgment, considering she was dealing with Maybelle's family. If pushiness was in their genes, she'd have to find some other place even if it was in another town. She stepped inside, and the people by the registers got really quiet as they all stared. It was so weird she glanced behind her to make sure Beelzebub hadn't followed her in, wearing a funny hat.

She grabbed a cart and noticed everyone followed her with their eyes, making her believe they might think she was the devil because they made an effort to take a step back as if not wanting to be anywhere near her. The waves she gave a couple of people weren't returned, and they all had a piercing stare in common. There was only one logical explanation. Most of these people needed to be on medication and had all decided to collectively skip it.

"Excuse me." She stopped by a young woman putting out milk so slowly she was either weak or bored out of her mind because she appeared ready to keel over. "Could you tell me where the peanut butter is, please?"

"That's on the end of aisle two." The girl spoke at the same speed she stocked shelves. "But, hey," the girl said, stopping her, "heads-up that we don't sell anything *alive*. I thought you should know."

"That's so disappointing." She nodded slowly on the off chance these people were indeed dangerous. They were certainly funny. Aside from DJ and his crew, everyone in this town seemed off the rails.

"Like I said, I thought you'd want to know, so you don't waste time looking. There's not *one* thing in here that's alive except for the people, and they're off-limits." The girl popped her gum and pointed to her. "Need help with anything else?"

Wyatt figured it'd be faster, not to mention safer, walking with a local until she learned the rules of this crazy town. She handed over her list and followed the girl around as she put stuff in her cart. Some of the things weren't on her list, but it must've appeared like she needed the odds and ends since they were on sale. The conversational factor made her ignore the danger part as well as buying canned beans she was never going to eat.

"So, where *can* I buy things that are alive?" If this was code for something, she hoped it didn't include taking illegal substances or running naked through the streets with things that were alive. That this conversation was making it into a book at some point was a given. One of the gifts strange but amazing people gave you was free dialogue, and no writer ever turned that down. She asked the question, hoping to get hit in the head with a clue as to what this was about.

"There's JD's place over close to Jefferson Parish. If you go, though, don't tell him what you're doing with it. He'll run you off with the sawed-off shotgun he keeps behind the counter."

"Why not?" She reviewed every word she said since walking in. Nope, at no time had she given the impression she had sex or did anything else untoward with live animals.

"JD won't like it, and he'll give you hell. I'm not saying that'll happen, but don't take a chance. He's the only one selling live stuff, if you don't count Petco." The young woman kept dropping stuff in her basket and kept up her bizarre conversation. From her inflection, anyone would think they were discussing mundane things like the weather or the price of chicken. It was truly strange, and it seemed to fit with the people she'd met so far. Her new house seemed to be located in some weird vortex, but she was starting to enjoy how off-center they really were.

"Now you mentioned JD. Is he related to DJ?" She had to curse her name. The initials WW didn't make for a cool nickname.

"You talking about the plumber or the car guy?"

"Plumber," she said, trying to stifle a laugh. The answer made her sound like a native.

"JD's related to the car guy. If you need your house painted, then you call the other JD, the plumber's brother. I think he also builds custom cabinets. JD, the brother of the car guy, just runs the feed and seed."

The whole explanation had been delivered in a deadpan voice meaning she was totally serious, which was as surprising as finding an image of the Madonna on a piece of toast—both should be considered a miracle. "Thanks for the information. I'm making repairs to my house, and I'll need a painter. It's not one of my favorite things to do."

"No problem. Anything else you want to know, hit me up."

"Thanks, but this should do it for tonight. You've been a real help." And she was also going to be a character in the new book starting to take root in Wyatt's head.

JD's Feed and Seed was in the next parish, but she made the trip after her personal grocery shopper said he was open until ten and happened to carry a large selection of coffee makers. And JD's in fact sold things that were alive, as well as microwaves. For now she was planning to eat out, most likely at the diner, but being able to reheat coffee and takeout was important.

The car radio was still stuck on old country, and she sang along to the ballad of some cowboy riding the cattle drive, thinking of the woman he loved. For some reason it made her think of her parents, and she was grateful they went together, as sad as it was they'd left her alone. There was no way to imagine the agony one of them would've suffered had one survived.

"You think you're alone, but you aren't," her mom said. "I might not be able to call you, but I'm stuck in your head for eternity. Aren't you lucky?"

She laughed as she wiped her tears away. The new porch gave her a sense of pride she was sure her father would share, and by tomorrow she'd start covering the outside with the piles of HardiePlank siding lined up along the way to the yard. She grabbed some of the bags of her groceries, then had to fumble with the phone as she struggled with the lock. This damn lock had to go.

"What are you doing?"

She closed her eyes at Blanche's irate tone. In a way she was shocked Blanche had held out this long before calling. "Did you not understand the part where I said not to phone?"

"You never said that."

Blanche was used to getting her way, and that was why Wyatt was convinced she was related to Sherman. Her scorched-earth method worked when getting great contracts but was annoying as hell when it came to everything else.

"Let me say it now. When I'm ready to talk to you, I'll call *you*." She went back for the rest of her bags, leaving the small appliances until she got rid of Blanche. "It's not that hard a request."

"It is a hard request, Wyatt. I'm trying my best not to have you committed until you come to your senses. Walking away from a successful writing career to run off somewhere to lick your wounds is crazy." The other thing about Blanche was her ability to spit words out like she was the human equivalent of the tommy gun. They were rapid-fire and just as deadly.

Wyatt didn't respond as she stood at her kitchen window. It was the beginning of the weekend, and Hayley was already in her pajamas. "That's kind of sad," she said softly. The beautiful young woman should be out with someone who'd shower her with devotion. Shower her with devotion? Maybe Blanche was right, and she was cracking up.

"It is sad, Wyatt, not to mention pathetic."

"Blanche, listen to me carefully. Stop talking, or I'm going to fire you." She lost track of Hayley, so she decided to head upstairs to change.

"At least text me your address. I'm worried about you." Syrupy-sweet Blanche was back, making her miss Attila the Hun Blanche.

"No, and stop asking. I've been writing for what seems like a hundred years, and I need a break. If you can't understand that or can't accept it, we'll have to part company." She saw that Hayley was now upstairs and in the shower, and she was missing it because of this fucking call. "Just give it a rest. Jesus H. Christ, you need a life outside of work, Blanche. Try and find one until I get back."

"You know how I feel. You're the one who can't accept it."

"You're in love with the commissions, sweetheart, not me." She leaned on the window frame, wishing she was getting wet too, but in a sense she was. "Remember, call me again, and I'm going to fire your ass."

"Okay, calm down. Promise me it won't be months from now. I'll be out of my mind by then. You're all alone."

"It'll be when it'll be, Blanche. Accept it." She ended the call, and Hayley was out of the shower, so she went back downstairs to carry out the plans she had for the evening. They weren't much more exciting than Hayley's seemed to be, but considering she'd never used an oven, much less an antique one, her night might be exciting after all.

Back in the kitchen she arranged all the ingredients she'd just purchased and opened the first journal she'd found. Blanche was wrong about her being alone. Hayley was back in the kitchen, puttering around and glancing out the window every so often. That was all the company she needed.

It was strange to her that she didn't know Hayley but felt connected to her. Back in New York she'd never taken the time to know her neighbors or anything about them. She was mostly in her study writing and never paying attention to any of the people around her. This time around she'd do better. Well, when it came to Hayley, anyway. She had no desire to know George.

"Time for all new things." She started opening all the ingredients she needed. There was nothing like a little bait to bring all the pretty girls to the yard.

CHAPTER FIFTEEN

Hayley stood in the spray of her shower, thinking about the conversation. Her mother was like an avalanche that buried you under what she wanted. Not that she minded her mom's concern, but she wasn't ready for the inquisition. She put her head under the spray and squirted shampoo in her palm, wondering if Butch could see her in the shower. She lathered her hair and remembered her mom's opinion about her total lack of modesty. She washed a little more slowly.

She and her mom got along, but that didn't mean they didn't butt heads. When her parents had visited last time, their fight, like a couple of times before, was about the windows. She lathered her hair a second time and remembered her mom's opinion about her inviting the world to objectify her. That wasn't it. She simply enjoyed looking out the window when she showered, and it wasn't like anyone could see any actual body parts below the neck. Of course now her daydreaming while in the shower was coming to an end. She wanted to get to know Butch but not give her the impression she was some kind of pervert.

The water started to cool, so she rinsed off and finished. It took some time to blow-dry her hair and get her pajamas back on. She was planning to take it easy for the weekend, doing nothing but reading and getting together with Lucy on Sunday, and they were going out. She didn't want to share Butch, not yet, so working until then wasn't the worst way to spend time.

She glanced next door as she took out some leftovers that were as appetizing as a conversation with George, but that's all there was.

Butch wasn't anywhere around from what she could see, and no matter what happened, she was determined to remain fully clothed. There was something about Butch that made her think they'd met, or at least she should know who she was. No matter how long she thought about it, though, nothing came to her. She couldn't place her, and she couldn't waste any more time trying to figure it out. Work would have to come first tonight before she got a surprise visit from her mother.

Chips would have to do for now since her pasta hadn't aged well, so she grabbed the bag and a soft drink, noticing Butch in the kitchen next door. She was facing away from her, but not far enough away that she couldn't see the jeans. "I can't be sure if you're right in the head, but you do have a nice ass for a weirdo."

She took one more long look before heading up to her chair with the rest of the submissions for the anthology. These were so much better, both in story and writing. The problem with that was the better the story and writing, the better the erotica. That wasn't helping her keep her clothes on. She needed to take her mind out of the sensual gutter and do something else for a minute. If her mother really was making the trip, she didn't want to add clutter to her numerous sins, so she took a break for some housework.

Her phone rang as she put a load of laundry in, and she smiled when her father's face appeared on her screen. "You aren't at the airport waiting for a ride, are you?"

"I explained to your mother that I didn't want to go until we plowed. You've got three months' reprieve, so enjoy it, which means your neighbor is safe now. Your mom has learned the sleeper move, and it would do nothing for neighborhood relations if the new girl next door wakes up with a migraine."

She laughed, trying to narrow down where in upstate New York you learned to choke someone into unconsciousness, since she doubted he was kidding. "Give me a month, and I'll even pay for the tickets."

"You concentrate on what you're doing, and don't forget to have fun. Even when I was in the pit, I was having fun."

"Thank you, Daddy." She thought someone had knocked on her door while her father was talking, but she didn't hear it again. "Make sure you guys stay warm and have plenty of supplies in case you get snowed in." She looked through the peephole, but no one was there. "And call me."

"We will. I'm sure Special Agent Fox will have more questions for you once she's put together a lineup for you to look at."

She pocketed her phone and opened the door, half expecting George to drop from the ceiling. There was no one there, and it took her a minute to see a covered plate with an envelope on top. She carried it inside and discovered what looked like snickerdoodles. She thought of her mother and what she'd say about taking candy from strangers. Granted, if she woke up locked in a closet she'd have to apologize to her.

The cookies were phenomenal, and she finished one as she studied the word *neighbor* written in barely legible script across the envelope. It was a clear D- for penmanship. She waited to open it, wanting to savor more than the cookie since she guessed who the treat was from.

She opened the flap and took out the card inside. It was to the point.

Whenever is convenient, I'd like to finally meet you.

The side yard was empty, and so was the kitchen window. She'd missed another opportunity to get to know Butch, and considering how talented she was at baking cookies, meeting her was a must. No one who baked this well was a serial killer, right? Hopefully, this was going to be the last missed opportunity they'd have. Butch had sparked enough of her curiosity and fantasies that it was time to have a conversation.

Her phone rang again, and it couldn't be her parents, so she expected Lucy.

"Remember the new author we've been after? She's coming in tomorrow at nine, so I'll meet you at the office at eight. Don't worry, I'll make it up to you and promise not to keep you too late." Marlo's habit of starting every phone conversation in the middle was still going strong. It always made her think Marlo had imagined they'd been speaking for at least an hour and she simply hadn't been paying attention. "If we want to diversify, we need this one."

"That's true, and I'll be there." Thankfully, she usually knew what her boss was talking about. "You want me to handle the meeting, or do you want to?" The bedroom light came on next door, which meant Butch wasn't lurking outside waiting for the drugs in the cookies to take effect.

"I'll be there only to remind myself what a great hire you are." Marlo laughed, and Hayley heard Tippy in the background. They were the couple who proved opposites attracted. "Now tell me all about your neighbor. Did you get a picture of the snake?"

"I keep telling you—I'm not getting close enough to the snake to get a picture, and I didn't get a chance to make it over there." She locked up, turned off the lights, and snagged another cookie before going up to her bedroom.

"You chickened out, huh?" Marlo *tsk*ed. "I thought you were braver than that."

"I did not chicken out...Maybe I did, but she dropped off cookies while I was talking to my father." She put her treat down on the small table next to her chair and got her laptop out. "Can you believe she baked me cookies? She doesn't seem the type."

"What's her type?" Marlo sounded interested.

"Butch is talented in home renovation and stays home most nights." She stared at the only room with the lights on but still no Butch.

"She's doing the renovation herself?" Marlo sounded as if that was the most absurd thing she'd ever heard. Most things in life were better if you hired someone. "That is mighty butch of her."

She laughed at Marlo's picking up on her nickname. "It is, and she might or might not be the owner, but she's living there while DJ and a group of guys help her."

"The car guy does home repair?"

"The plumber, actually. She had a plumbing issue when she first got here, and that's who she called." Butch came into view in boxers and a T-shirt with wet hair. That she'd missed her in the shower was a bummer, but there she was with legs that were as sexy as the rest of her. Windows in old houses really were the best if you wanted to visually objectify your neighbor in the nicest way possible. They were tall to accommodate the high ceilings, and when open all the way, someone Hayley's height could walk through them without ducking. That was their function when the houses were first built and were taxed by the door but not the window.

"I'll have to come by and see all the changes. When we drove by all I noticed was the yard." Marlo inhaled deeply, so there had to be a cigarette in her mouth. "And get over there before old Miss Hebert snags it all for herself. She took time to bake you cookies, so that's got to mean something since it's you who should've done that to welcome her to the neighborhood."

"I could've gotten her some at the bakery because I've never baked in my life."

Butch puttered around the room and finally sat with a book and crossed her legs.

"Are you in for the night?" Marlo asked, and Hayley heard Tippy saying dinner was ready. Marlo was truly lucky. Tippy was a tall butch who loved life, cooking, and Marlo—she was the definition of winning the lesbian lottery. Tippy was a great combination Hayley had yet to find for herself.

"Sadly, yes. I'm in my pajamas, so don't ask me to go back to the office."

"Would I do that?" The question was a joke obviously. Marlo was someone who thought everyone worked around the clock because she did. It was great for her that she'd found a kindred spirit. "Kidding, and I'm sending you a story someone submitted today. I realize it's way past the deadline, but you might want to make an exception for this one."

"If you read it and like it, I'll add it to the list. We could use it. Who sent it in?" She smiled when Butch glanced up from her book and smiled back. It was strange to find comfort in Butch's presence after only a few days.

At times she was a stranger in a world that didn't have a place for her. She was different, always had been. In school she'd never been gaga over anyone, hadn't fallen in love every month, had never been devastated when the month-long love affair didn't work out. She watched her parents and their connection, but that part of her that other people had when it came to making relationships work was missing. The thought of being with one person forever made her skin crawl.

But then came Butch. No, she wasn't infatuated—more like she was burning through a lust-fueled crush. Having her close gave her something to look forward to when she got home. She shook her head at that realization. It was new and completely unfamiliar, just like touching herself knowing Butch was watching. That was insane, true, but she also knew it was safe. Butch wasn't waiting to hurt her—she knew that on a deep level like knowing her parents loved her.

"It's most probably one of our authors who isn't used to writing in this genre and turned it in anonymously, so they'd get a fair shot. The other reason might be that they've heard about your biting editorial notes, and that scared them from putting their name on it." Marlo laughed hard enough to send her into a coughing fit.

"Yes, I'm sure the second one is it. Everyone knows how scary I am when they refer to a woman's vagina as her *love cavern*. I know it would totally turn me on if someone uttered those words during sex right after putting on one of those helmets with a light on it. They'd need it to explore my love cavern in search of the elusive G-spot in that big ole space." How some people got laid was a mystery not even Sherlock Holmes could solve.

"Read it, and tell me what you think tomorrow. See you then."

She opened her email and clicked on the story. "Let's see what we've got."

CHAPTER SIXTEEN

It was a total shock to Wyatt when she mixed all the ingredients Lydia listed and took out cookies from the oven that actually tasted good. She tried a few as she waited for all the batches to bake, so she could put them out for the crew tomorrow. The knock thirty minutes later as she was putting the last batch to cool made her stare at the door. It was only six thirty, but it was already dark outside, and she wasn't expecting anyone. If it was Blanche, she was killing her and burying her in the yard. It was big enough that no one would find her, much less miss her.

It was an even bigger shock to see a guy from the cable company smiling on the porch with a clipboard. Those seemed to be popular in these parts. "Hey, sorry I'm running late. My last job was a doozy." He reminded her of a leprechaun if they really existed, and he seemed happier than anyone she'd ever met. "You want cable and internet, right?"

"As well as world peace." She waved him in and turned when he jumped in and immediately went into some kind of combative pose with his hands up as if he was going to chop someone in the throat. "Is everything okay?"

He straightened up after studying everything in the room. "Ah, yeah. Let's see where you'd like your modem. The TV boxes are wireless now, so running cable is unnecessary. You just have to decide where the main box is going to go. That's the only one that has to be wired in."

She pointed to the living room off the foyer and watched him go through the same moves. When she'd made the appointment, she didn't remember mentioning she'd hidden ninjas throughout the house who were trained to kill cable guys, but that's the message this guy had gotten. "Are you sure you're okay?"

New Orleans was, as Tennessee Williams said, one of the great cities in the US, but some parts of it felt like a small town named Eccentricityville. Her experience in the Marigny so far had been good, like having workmen show up on the day she called, and entertaining neighbors. The thing was that some of them seemed to be a tad off center when it came to normal behavior. It wasn't that she minded strange people, but it was hard to imagine there were so many in such a small patch.

"Yeah, I'm good. So here"—the guy pointed to the spot over the fireplace—"is where you're putting the TV?"

"Yes. I thought you could come through the wall before I cover it with siding. For the modem, I thought the office. It's a good spot with a booster upstairs."

"Sure. Is there a way to get under the house?"

It took less than a couple of hours for him to finish. That would've been cut by at least thirty minutes if he'd skipped his commando routine, but having Wi-Fi was worth the extra bit of nuts he needed to go through to get the job done. While he was under the house running cable, she plated a batch of cookies and wrote Hayley a note.

She left the cable guy, which gave her an excuse to cut the visit short if things got uncomfortable with Hayley. Her knock wasn't loud, and she waited a couple of minutes before going back to make sure the guy was okay. It was the coward's way out not to wait for Hayley to come to the door, and she'd try again, just not tonight. Maybe it wasn't a good time for them to become friends, considering all they knew about each other.

Once the guy was done, she gave him some cookies and took a shower downstairs after he'd left. DJ had finished the bathroom as far as the pipes. He'd told her the family had added it for Lydia when she couldn't walk upstairs any longer. When they completed the ones upstairs, she'd have this one with bright yellow and purple tile demolished as well. For now she was grateful to have a working shower that didn't require her to finish in the yard.

She made some coffee to go with her cookie dinner and headed up for more of Lydia's story. The light was on across the way, and she smiled at the way Hayley's laptop softly lit her face. Hayley seemed to be reading and eating a cookie. That made her feel like she was a part of Hayley's night, which was strangely intimate. After tonight she'd make it her goal to meet her.

There was plenty she missed about her parents, but having a simple conversation was at the top of that list. She'd become a writer because she enjoyed solitude, yet human interaction was important even to the biggest introverts. Her parents were her connection to the world, and she needed to find someone who'd be as comfortable in the quiet as in a conversation about anything that came to mind. Across from her she saw so much more than a beautiful woman, but someone who could get lost in the words.

"Is that what you found with Sam?" she asked Lydia as she opened the journal and picked up a cookie.

March 1913

Lydia tried to keep her nervousness down to a minimum, but the moment she opened her eyes that Sunday, she'd had Sam Fuller on her mind. She'd seen him working his fields with Plank and had talked to him more than one time. The reason she never saw him in the afternoons was because of his deliveries to some New Orleans restaurants that bought his produce. He was also busy with the stand he and Lester ran in the French Quarter.

"Do you think he'll try to kiss you?" her younger sister Daisy asked.

"It's lunch, and Sam wouldn't try something like that."

Their father rounded everyone up for church, and she saw Sam in one of the last pews in the back for the first time since meeting him. When her father shook hands with him, she had some idea of his new devotion to religion. Her father respected people who were honest, hardworking, and devoted. If she was interested in Sam, then her father would make sure he possessed all three traits.

"Thank you for inviting me, ma'am," Sam said to Lydia's mother when she invited him to walk home with them. The man was stiff as a post when Lydia fell into step with him, and he didn't relax until it was time to go after an afternoon of stilted conversation.

That same routine went on for three months, and Lydia was

beginning to suspect something was really off. Sam was polite and respectful, and he hadn't tried anything. And nothing meant no holding hands, no kissing, and no sweet-talking. The man sat in church, walked home with them, ate, then left. They'd shared a few conversations when she walked by, and Sam had invited her on some afternoon walks to simply breathe next to her.

Again, during all that time there'd been nothing. Either there was something wrong with her or with him, and Lydia was leaning on it being him. Even the pharmacist's son who was a total bore had tried to steal a kiss after a school dance. Didn't Sam know what he was missing? Heck, she wanted to know what she was missing if Sam would only get off his duff and show her.

"Afternoon, Mr. Blanchard." Sam was in for his monthly supplies, and Lydia noticed he'd come after he'd bathed and changed into fresh clothes. That might be a sign of encouragement if only the man would open his mouth.

"Sam." Her father waved him to the counter. "I'd like to think we're friends, and my friends call me Barney."

"Yes, sir." Sam held his planter's hat in front of him like someone was going to throw eggs at him and he had to protect his best shirt, but he did smile at her.

That smile had started to invade her dreams. "Hello, Sam."

"Miss Lydia." Sam bowed his head slightly. "It's nice to see you."

The same customer who'd tried to help her the first day when she wanted to meet Sam came in and winked at her, then engaged her father in conversation. It was good to have friends. Lydia said, "Sam, could you help me get some feed bags down, please?"

"Sure." Sam followed her to the back, and she made a move that would perhaps scare Sam off for good. She had to, though, since patience wasn't her gift.

She pushed him against a pallet of flour bags and held his face between her hands. "Do you not like me much?"

"No, why would you think that?" The expression about being caught in the crosshairs made perfect sense to her as she studied Sam's face.

"Because you act like I'm your sister." Her parents would be so proud when she pressed herself to Sam and kissed him. He froze for a moment, but he proved human when she didn't let up.

"You don't kiss like you're my sister." Sam's hands ended up on Lydia's hips and didn't move away when she kissed him again.

"I'd say I was sorry, but I got tired of waiting for you."

Sam touched her cheek with a tenderness that made her think she'd break if he wasn't careful. "You're a beautiful girl, Lydia, and you're going to make a man happy one day, but it can't be me."

"How do you know?" Lydia grabbed the front of his shirt and bunched it in her fists. "And don't you dare lie."

"Lydia," she heard her father calling for her.

It killed her, but she stepped away from Sam and put a smile on her face like she was having the best day of her life.

"Everything okay?" her father asked, his eyes narrowing slightly.

"Sam offered to help me get some heavy bags from the high shelf, but the flour's already down. I didn't realize."

"We've got your order ready, and Lester loaded it up for you, Sam." Her father glanced between them but didn't say anything else. "I'll see you on Sunday."

"Yes, sir." Sam smiled as he put his hat back on, but it made him seem sad and miserable. The man didn't say much, but his face said so much that it was like a book of his emotions. "Good day, Miss Lydia."

Sunday was two days away, and Lydia didn't need anyone to tell her Sam wouldn't be in church and wouldn't be at her father's table for lunch. Whatever had happened in the stockroom had spooked him into saying good-bye without saying the words. The loss would leave a scar she had no way of covering up or forgetting.

That night she sat on the padded window seat in the room her parents had given her because she was the oldest. Lydia hadn't been able to stop crying from the moment she'd closed the door. She really didn't know Sam that well, so she shouldn't have let her infatuation get to the point it could cause this kind of pain.

The soft knock made her wipe her face so her mother wouldn't see her crying. "Come in." Seeing her father in the doorway shocked her into silence. "Papa?"

"I know you were expecting your mother, but I thought we should have a talk."

Barney Blanchard was a man blessed with three girls. As the oldest, Lydia knew her father felt that way about her and her sisters, where other men in the same situation did not. He'd encouraged her in school, in working with him to learn the business, and to follow her heart because he loved her mother and had married for that reason. When the time came, he wanted the same for all his girls.

"One of the worst things you'll experience as a parent is to see your child in pain and not be able to do anything about it unless they tell you what's on their mind." He sat next to her and held her hand. "Tell me what happened today."

"Nothing, Papa." She felt the tears fall when she said it, and he sighed.

"If you don't want to tell me, my darling girl, then don't tell me, but please don't lie." He put his arms around her, giving her a safe place to cry.

It took a while for her to tell him the whole story and about the kiss. That part heated her face like nothing ever had, and through it all her father nodded and smiled. Talking about it made her review the words and excuses Sam had given her. None of it made sense. Sam had religiously shown up in church and to lunch, so he had to have had a clue as to why he'd been asked.

"You sound a lot like your mama."

"Mama's a lot luckier than me. He doesn't want me, and I made a fool of myself."

"I need you to forget about all that and get some sleep." He kissed her forehead and hugged her. "It's hard, but I promise it'll be all right."

The next morning Lydia had breakfast with her father alone. Her mother and sisters had left early to open the store, so her father took her for a walk once they were done. She walked next to him and had trouble lifting her feet she was so listless. There was a full day of work ahead, so she tried to shake it off. She stopped when her father walked through the gate that marked Sam's farm and kept going. Her malaise gave way to mortification.

"Papa, no." She tried stopping him before he knocked at the door of a small house that appeared a little ramshackle.

The door opened and Sam appeared worse off than her. "Mr. Blanchard, sir." Sam didn't sound like himself, and his hair was uncombed. Lydia was used to those short, thick, dark locks being neat, as well as Sam being clean-shaven. It didn't make sense that he'd shaved but forgotten his hair unless they'd interrupted his morning routine. "Miss Lydia," he said, softer.

"Explain to me what's wrong with my daughter, Samuel. What kind of man leaves it to his sweetheart to make an overture? If that's who you are, I really misjudged you." It wasn't often Lydia saw her father truly angry, but he was almost sputtering with rage. "Well, what do you have to say for yourself?"

"You can't believe I don't care for Lydia—either of you." Sam glanced at her father before his gaze landed on her. "If you need to hear me say it, I do."

"Then why?" she asked, her tears falling again. How was something that was supposed to make you feel good completely destroy you?

"Please, come in." Sam moved aside and smoothed his hair down as if embarrassed by his appearance. "Sit." There was a table with four chairs in the kitchen and one more comfortable-looking one in front of the fireplace. The table next to it had a stack of books about a foot high, making her wonder what Sam liked to read. "Sorry it's not so nice, but I've been busy with the land. I haven't worried none about this place."

"I'm not judging you for that, son," her father said. "What a man has isn't as important to me as who a man is. How about you tell us who the hell Sam Fuller is? And this would not be the time to clam up like you usually do. I think both Lydia and I are mighty tired of that."

Sam looked from one to the other of them and then took a deep breath. "I'm originally from Illinois where my father farmed a few acres. We didn't have much, and when he died, the bank took the little that was left. To have some kind of decent future, I enlisted and served for three years before an accident left me with this limp." Sam tapped his right leg. "After that the Army didn't have any use for me, and one of the kitchen guys told me about this place. It was Lester's brother, and Lester and me became friends once I got here, and he was glad to come work with me." It was the most Lydia ever heard Sam say in one sitting. "I thought I could build a business and stay at it until I died, but love wasn't in my plans."

"Why not?" Lydia and her father spoke together.

"The accident didn't just leave me a cripple," Sam said, blushing. "I'll never father children, and someone like Miss Lydia deserves a husband who can." Sam focused all his attention on her. "You deserve a full life, and I can't give you that. I thought I'd be honest up front, but it's a tough subject to broach in polite company."

"You're a complete idiot." Her father saved Lydia from having to point that out. "I haven't forced you into church on Sundays for you to think about plowing, planting, and profits while that priest is droning on about God knows what. It's to teach you to have faith in something. Everyone thinks I'm some zealot when it comes to all that, but I go to appease Alice. The woman would be pope if they allowed females behind the pulpit. I don't particularly like it but eventually it does teach you to take some things on faith."

Lydia had to laugh at that. Her mother *was* a zealot when it came to the church. She felt better when Sam smiled as well, and her world righted itself somewhat. There was a chance she was an immature idiot herself for romanticizing a future with Sam, but the man was as easy on the eyes as he was kind.

"Most men pray for sons, but God gave me three beautiful and smart girls who make me proud. My sons will come when they marry. Until that day comes for all three of them, my job is to make sure the men they find are honorable and will treat them like the treasures they are. That's kind of what I thought I was getting in you, or believe me, I'd have shot you the second you stepped into my yard, consequences be damned."

"It's like you said though, sir. God blessed you with children. I can't give Lydia that, and I'd think you'd want that for her as well."

Her father raised his hand before she could speak. "That's not your decision to make, no more than it is mine, numbskull. It's hers, in case you didn't get whose it was." Her father pointed at her. "Lydia knows her mind and what she wants, not you."

"Yes, sir, and I'm sorry," Sam said to her.

"Good, now I trust you to sit at this table, keep your hands to yourself, and talk to my daughter while I go on to work. You're going to be a gentleman while you two decide some things, and once you do, you come and talk to me. Think you can manage that?"

"Yes, sir."

"Good, and make sure you walk her to the store when you're done. Your daddy might not have had much, but I'm sure he taught you some manners." Her father shook Sam's hand and kissed her cheek before leaving. He really was an amazing man, and that's what Lydia thought of Sam as well.

"Tell me what you want," Sam said when it was just them.

"I want you to stop holding back. If you keep me at arm's length, we'll never know if this is real and something we both want." She slid her hands across the table, encouraged when Sam took them.

"Like I said, Lydia, you deserve more and better than me, but you deserve the truth even more." Sam took a breath and gave her just that. One thing was clear when he was done—her life would never be the same.

CHAPTER SEVENTEEN

There were a few things in Hayley's inbox she had to deal with before she got to the story Marlo had sent her. Most of her email correspondence these days had to do with talking Cheryl off the ledge she seemed to climb out onto every day after finishing the edits Hayley assigned. She had to admit she'd been snarky with the constant diet of sex she'd been feeding Cheryl, but her thinking was it'd eventually loosen her up or drive her to the convent. It'd be easier not to have to deal with her, but like other people that annoyed her, it was against the law to kill them. Cheryl's saving grace was that she was as good an editor as she was a complainer.

"And that's what's wrong with organized religion these days. There are way too many people like Cheryl running the show."

She took her glasses off, having traded her contacts for them, but so much time in front of a screen had exhausted her eyes into itchy messes. Butch had sat and read, turning pages at a rapid pace, which made her curious as to what she was engrossed in. It seemed riveting enough that Butch hadn't raised her head since sitting down a while ago. But then she'd snapped the book closed and disappeared somewhere in the house where Hayley couldn't see her.

The sense of loss was ludicrous, but she missed looking at her. She tried to shift her attention to work and forget about her sexy neighbor, but it was near impossible. "I'm getting crazier by the minute. She's probably feeding one of George's precious bunnies to her snake." Hugo and Truman were lying on the bed staring at her with their usual bored but slightly judgmental expressions. The thought of them wandering next door made her shiver.

"You two better behave and stay put. This is not the time to develop an adventurous streak." Neither cat seemed moved by her advice. "If you're not going to listen to me, don't start crying when I can't pry open a python's mouth to save you. Now let's see what Anonymous came up with. If the words *love button, cave,* or *honeypot* appear anywhere in this story, I'm retiring and selling Lucky Dogs in the Quarter to drunks." She opened her mail, already intrigued by the title.

Neighbor

I sit in the dark and wait for her, the anticipation quickening my pulse. Her life seems like a cycle of work, meeting deadlines, and enjoying a good book. It's a different existence from mine, but in a sense also familiar. We're on different sides of the fence, literally, but we have one important thing in common. Our bedroom windows line up to give us a glimpse inside, and we both like to watch.

She's beautiful in that classic girl-next-door kind of way with her blond hair and perfect body. I don't know her, her eye color, personality, fears, hopes, but I'm sure everyone describes her as someone worth knowing. That's perhaps the facade she puts on for the world, but I know a much more intimate side of her that's mine alone. She's the woman who sits at the window and waits only for *me*.

On most nights, I watch as she sheds the armor of the businesswoman who slays the dragons of her domain. Once she's bare, that's when I see her real beauty—it's not her slim hips, pink nipples, and all the soft skin between those two points, but the confidence with which she carries herself. She sits in her favorite chair that faces my window and places her feet on the sill. When she's naked and wet for me, my heartbeat races from the want of touching her, but I can't tear my eyes away from what she does for me. The sight makes me aware of my hard pulsing clit, but I can't turn away until she's done.

She sits in the chair with her feet up and meets my eyes. It's like she's saying, *Here I am, and all this is for you.* The way her hands move up her abdomen to the undersides of her breasts and squeeze them, making me crazy. I know her nipples are hard when she pinches them, and I know it feels good when her head falls back.

Her mouth falls open, and in my mind, I hear the sounds she makes as the ecstasy begins. To me it's the definition of pure pleasure, and my eyes on her make her wet. I don't have to have my hand between her legs to know. She can't wait any longer and moves a hand down her body as she spreads her legs. Now she's truly mine—wet, open, hard, and ready. My wait is over as she touches herself while pinching her nipple. The other truth I know like my own name is it's me on her mind as she rushes toward the peak of pleasure.

It's such an intimate act I'm witnessing, and I stop breathing it's so beautiful. Her hips buck erratically, and she screams her orgasm as her back arches and the pleasure washes over her like waves over a sandcastle. I sense it when she reaches that pinnacle that wipes away everything on her mind. It's like she can almost hang on to bliss for an eternity, but she slumps back to her chair. She's a beauty falling from the heavens of her own creation.

The smile that comes in the aftermath is lazy, and she aims it right at me. I still can't look away. That's who my neighbor is to me, and the sight of her drives my passions until her lights go out and she disappears into the darkness. Perhaps the time has come to bridge the divide between us. I want to follow the path that'll lead me to her room and have it be me who makes her take flight.

Yes, maybe that time has come, but for now I live to stand by my window and enjoy the view of her that's mine alone.

"Oh…My…God." Hayley finished reading and immediately reread it. She peeked over the screen of her laptop at the sensation of being watched. Butch was standing in the window, backlit by the overhead light. She was still in her boxers and T-shirt and seemed to be waiting for something.

The smile Butch wore was almost lazy, if there was such a thing. It felt like a dare, and she came close to going to bed if only to teach her a valuable lesson. Sometimes even good butches had to work for the things they wanted, and standing in a window in anticipation wasn't enough.

Hayley reread the story, concentrating on the words and Butch still standing in the window. The only logical explanation was that Butch had written it, which meant she'd done some research on her.

Considering the gossips around them, including DJ, that hadn't taken much to work out, and one internet search found the publisher's call for submissions for the anthology. That Butch had penned this, if she had, both mortified and turned her on.

All her life she'd been the kid who'd followed the rules and done what was expected of her. Lucy teased her about it. She was no virgin, but something in her shifted at the words Butch had written. The story was proof that her neighbor didn't see her like everyone else, and that made *her* look at herself differently. The main thing was Butch really *saw* her. She'd started this strange relationship they had thanks to the show she'd put on, but having Butch watch her drove her need.

She put the laptop aside and didn't turn off the floor lamp as she placed her hands on her abdomen. That move made Butch lean forward and brace herself with her hands on the frame. Hayley found it easy to imagine Butch between her legs, over her, and sucking on her nipples. She followed the story's direction of sliding her hands up and squeezed her breasts. There was no way she had the guts to strip, so this would have to do. With her luck Butch was recording this, and one of the farmers in her parents' town would find her on Pornhub and show it to her mother who'd immediately have her committed.

She pinched her nipple, and the sensation made her clit pulse. She couldn't wait a second longer. Her pants were loose, and it was easy to slide her hand in and pinch her clit between her fingers. The story hadn't talked about that part, but Butch seemed the type to do that, or who at least wouldn't mind a little improv, and it made her hips lift off the chair.

"Shit." The word came out with a long exhale of air, and she had to let up on the pressure, or this would come to an end too soon. She wanted it to last, needed it to so Butch would stay at the window. Keeping Butch's eyes on her was as important as coming.

She lifted her fingers off her sex, took her hand out of her pants and showed it to Butch, wanting her to know how wet she was. It was too far away to make out the muscles in Butch's arms and shoulders, but she did appear tense. It was empowering to be the center of someone's attention like this. That's all she needed to go back to touching herself with her nipple between her fingers.

She stroked her clit, liking how hard and sensitive it was, and the pressure she added slowly made her crazy. Her orgasm was mind-blowing, and she stopped breathing as she closed her legs on her hand and bucked her hips a few more times.

It was easy to relax after that, and her legs fell limp. This was an interesting exercise in expanding her horizons and courage, not that she'd be doing this in front of anyone else. Eventually she'd give Butch what she wanted and strip herself bare in more ways than taking her clothes off, but not tonight. When that happened, she wanted them in the same room, and any orgasm she was having wasn't going to be self-induced.

She opened her eyes and sat up until her feet were on the floor. Butch didn't move when Hayley stood but did watch as she lifted her hand and pressed it to the glass. The tingle was there when Butch copied the move then bowed her head slightly. She smiled before turning and clicking the lamp off.

One more glance showed Butch was still on post, and she blew her a kiss from the dark. "Good night and thank you for thinking I'm beautiful."

CHAPTER EIGHTEEN

Wyatt liked when Hayley's face was visible or partially visible because she was so caught up in what she was doing.

Hayley had put her laptop down and was staring right at her, her hands on her abdomen. It was Hayley's expression that made her stand up and grip the window frame. She had a hard time breathing when Hayley moved her hands to her breasts. "Fuck me."

The way Hayley touched herself, moved, and kept her eyes on her made her think what Hayley was doing was for her benefit. This time she'd kept the light on, and it was hard to stay in place. She wanted to be the one who put that expression of bliss on Hayley's face. That was a ludicrous notion, but these moments had reminded her she was alive.

She exhaled, and Hayley tensed, stopped, then slumped back. Hayley was gorgeous, and she could only imagine the way her delicate skin was flushed. The lights went out after Hayley put her hand to the glass and smiled at her, making her aware of every inch of skin when it heated up. Sleep would be elusive, but she closed her eyes and tried her best. Tomorrow she was putting up siding and then going over to Hayley's to ask her out on a date.

Thankfully, her dreams weren't about sex since she was already in the kind of pain touching herself wasn't going to quell. Instead, there were vignettes of her family vacations through the years. One of the nice things about having more money than she'd ever need was being able to take her parents all those places they'd wanted to go. They'd traveled together a few times a year, and they explored while she found ways to incorporate great cities like Florence and

Madrid into her books. She didn't do it for the write-off but for the pleasure of giving her readers the chance to explore places they might not be able to visit.

To Wyatt that was the truest talent any writer could possess. The ability to have a reader really visualize a setting like the Great Wall, what it was like to walk it, what the view they peered out on looked like, what the air smelled like, and what they'd hear was as important as who'd done it. She smiled as she looked down at her mother's hand in hers while her dad framed the shot with the Vatican in the background. There were hundreds of people around them acting like the pope came out like a lounge act, but she could still hear her mom's running commentary on the opulence of the place.

"You can't blame me," her mom said when she opened her eyes. "All the artwork and gold everything is not what God had in mind. One room of art could feed a whole country of poor people for a decade. I think *Vatican* means *greed* in Italian."

"You're preaching to a believer in non-opulence, Mom, so no need to convince me." She got dressed before going down and brushing her teeth. It was early but she couldn't be in this house another minute. Every so often the state of being alone morphed into loneliness, and she had to get out where she wasn't hemmed in by walls. That didn't translate into wanting to interact with anyone, but being around people or walking helped.

The diner was open, and if she was lucky, she wouldn't be the only one up at five in the morning. "Are you okay where you are?" she asked the empty foyer, her hand on the knob, hoping her parents could hear her. "Are you happy?"

"Death means your worries die with you, my love. There's no sickness, anxiety, grief, or pain, but there's also no you." Her mom's voice was soft as she said all the things Wyatt herself believed. "Holy fuck, that sounds so depressing, doesn't it? Think about it this way. We're dead and can't sit around all day long learning the harp, so we'll watch over you. Right now, you need a kick in the ass more than you need protecting from anything. I mean, what does the pretty girl next door have to do to get you moving? Taking your clothes off should be a mutual thing, not something you do alone at home. If you want that, there are plenty of places in the Quarter. Start at Rick's Cabaret—they have the prettiest girls."

"Jesus, there's no need to tell me that." Hopefully, her mom's voice really was like having an imaginary friend.

"No such luck, pumpkin. If you're not going to write, then get over there and introduce yourself before she thinks you're a pervert who only likes to watch."

"God help me."

"The man is busy trying to keep the universe intact, so sorry, you're stuck with your father and me."

"Okay, stop talking before everyone in there thinks I'm crazy." She opened the door, hoping Maybelle came in later, but there were some other people sitting and eating to act as a distraction if she was there.

"Well, well, well," Maybelle said as she came out of the kitchen as Wyatt sat down at the counter, put a plate on the table, and slid it toward Maybelle. "I thought you got yourself kidnapped or I'd scared you off." Maybelle pointed to a booth. "You know I can't sit with you at the counter, so go on. I need to be looking at you the whole time to make sure you're not lying to good old Maybelle."

"I was learning to cook." She offered Maybelle a cookie. "Next week I'll try to master pancakes now that I know where you got the recipe for your batter from. You should've given Lydia credit on the menu."

Maybelle took a bite of the cookie and closed her eyes as she chewed. "It's good, and it tastes like hers, but there's something missing."

"She must've taken it to the grave, then." She smiled at Gwen and mouthed *Waffles* in her direction. The bacon was implied.

"You're kind of a smartass, but I see you found her stash of recipes. If you've come across her apple strudel one, promise me you'll give me a copy." Maybelle finished her cookie and poured her a cup of coffee when Gwen delivered the carafe and mugs. "So, how's the house and everything else coming?"

"It's getting there." Why was it coffee tasted better when someone else made it? She took a few sips and smiled at Maybelle.

That seemed to make her suspicious, and she slitted her eyes.

Maybelle appeared to be studying her like she was a serial killer on death row whose brain had to be dissected before that state ordered lethal injection. "From what I hear, the plumbing is almost done, and the outside's getting a facelift. You trying to impress Hayley? You know she's single and looking for love, right? That girl is just cute as a button."

Maybelle sounded like one of the many country songs she'd listened to on the way down here, minus the twang. "Thank you for the heads-up, but I doubt she needs any help on the dating front." She tried to keep her expression neutral. Showing emotion in front of Maybelle didn't feel like the right move. Her life was already an open sieve of information thanks to DJ the plumber. There was no reason to elaborate. "I'm fixing the outside to get my miniature golf course underway. No one's going to want to come if the yard and house are a mess."

"Miniature golf course? You talking about putt-putt golf?" Maybelle put her cup down forcefully, spilling some, and exhaled hard enough to flare her nostrils.

"Thank you," she said to Gwen when she brought out a plate of bacon. "And yes, putt-putt golf. There don't seem to be any children in the neighborhood, but who doesn't love putt-putt golf? I've already ordered the big windmill, and since this is New Orleans, I found a twelve-foot woman with pasties and a thong hanging from a pole. That's going right in the front to attract folks into the yard to play with me."

"Are you a fan of golf?" Maybelle seemed to be trying to figure her out, and her interrogation wasn't going well.

The food here was good enough to deal with Maybelle's grilling, but it didn't mean she couldn't fuck with her a little bit. Life was all about finding small pleasures where you could get them. "Golf is boring as hell, but miniature golf is a lifelong commitment. Have you ever tried to get that little orange ball past the blades of the windmill? And I haven't tried to drop it in the hole through the kicking legs of the twelve-foot Amazon with the light-up pasties, but I can't wait to try."

Maybelle appeared to be digesting what she said, and Gwen delivered her waffles. "Um, you do realize Lydia's house is in a historic district, right? The neighbors aren't going to appreciate becoming a spectacle. What you're planning isn't a good idea at all. That might get folks all riled up, and that don't ever end well."

She poured a river of syrup on her waffles and nodded. "Miss Potts didn't mention any kind of restrictions since we're not in the Quarter, and it's not Lydia's house any longer. It's the house of Joe, and Joe loves miniature golf." She chewed a wad of waffle as Maybelle shook her head. "Think of it as my new castle, and instead of a moat it'll have eighteen holes of fun."

"Don't you think the neighbors might get pissed, you doing that?"

"Once they know I'm not charging them, they'll all be on board." She started eating bacon like it was her job. "This was delicious, and I see meatloaf is the special, so I might see you tonight." She peeled off some money and accepted a coffee to go from Gwen.

"If you like chili, we're having that tomorrow," Maybelle said as she scooted out of the booth. "See you soon."

"Can't wait." She waved to Maybelle and blew Gwen a kiss. Meatloaf gave her heartburn even if she loved it, but not as much as chili and all the questions Maybelle served with her tasty food. The walk back was nice even though the temperature had dropped dramatically, but she decided to enjoy it considering what was to come this summer. She'd only been to Louisiana in the summer once, and she'd been convinced her face would eventually melt off while waiting for a cab.

She got home, and with her new cable service, she saw that New York was frigid by comparison. She didn't miss snow, slush, and congestion, but she also couldn't imagine selling the brownstone. Even if this move was permanent, there were too many memories of her parents tied up there to ever let it go. This place with the pretty neighbor, quirky people, and open spaces appealed to her desire for anonymity. No one was calling offering words of condolence they thought she wanted to hear but didn't really mean.

Loss sucked. She wrote for a living, and that was the best way to describe it. Early morning phone calls to inform you of loss sucked too. It was like an alarm bell ringing, signaling the end of your life as you knew it. There would most likely be no one else, ever, who understood you and accepted you like the two people who made you.

"You know, kid," she heard her father's voice, "the day you were born was the first time I realized how quickly I could fall in love. Even your mother took a couple of months to get me to do that. All those years watching you grow up gave me a sense of pride I couldn't really put into words, but you were something else. No matter what happens, I know you're going to be okay. You're a Whitlock."

"It was easier with you here, Pop."

She found DJ in the kitchen making coffee and reading the paper. In some ways he reminded her of her dad. He was honest, funny, had a great crew—her father had said you had to be a great boss to keep good people. Unfortunately for DJ, he wasn't tall with dark hair and blue eyes, all traits she'd inherited from her father.

"Morning." She grabbed a couple of mugs and waited for the pot to finish. The coffee Gwen had given her had gotten cold as she conversed with her dead parents.

"Good morning, Joe. Went down to Maybelle's, huh?" DJ moved the sugar closer to him for the five tablespoons he put in his coffee.

"I got up early, and unfortunately it's the only place open."

He started with the sugar but appeared confused. "You don't like the food?"

"Love the food, it's the barrage of questions I could do without." She watched the cream go in next, reminding her she needed to replenish her coffee supplies. Keeping everyone caffeinated was an expense she'd gladly shoulder, but they approached coffee more like a vehicle to get their cream and sugar intake for the day.

"You know what you need to do." He stirred his coffee and grinned with mischief. "If you want to confuse Maybelle, that is. That woman thinks of herself as a one-woman neighborhood watch, or perhaps she's writing a gossip rag about all of us in the neighborhood because no one is immune from Maybelle's mouth."

"What do I need to do?" the fly said to the spider, since she'd willingly walked into his web.

"You need to go with a date. Maybe take Hayley from next door. She's awful cute, single, and stays home way too much." He scratched the side of his mouth like it was a slick move. "You're a Southerner now, so show some hospitality and ask her out."

"That's a great idea, DJ. Do you think she'd be interested?"

He laughed and shook his finger at her. "You'd make a cute couple if only you'd listen to a progressive old man."

"It's Saturday, old man, so anything's possible."

CHAPTER NINETEEN

"What'd you think?" Marlo was straightening the piles in her office, which wasn't helping anything. Hayley was convinced there was a manuscript Abraham Lincoln wrote lost in all the crap in Marlo's office, never to be found. Marlo blew her a kiss when she handed over a latte. "That story was hot. Too bad my place doesn't come with a view like that. I'd consider moving for one that did."

Hayley just nodded, not wanting to give away that Butch's place did, in fact, come with that view.

"All we need to do is figure out who wrote it and have them sign a contract. The writing was so good—they should've put their name on it."

Butch had to have written the piece since it described everything happening at her house. Her problem was how to find out if Butch wrote the story. If her only option was knocking on the door and asking, she was screwed. That she'd followed the directions in the story step by step wasn't the problem because she'd done it not only for Butch but for herself. The problem would be if her mother and Marlo found out. There were just certain things your mother and boss shouldn't know about you.

"The writing style seems familiar, but I can't place it. You may be right, that it's one of ours and they're not used to writing this stuff." Marlo kept talking, not concerned Hayley hadn't contributed anything.

"Let me run up and get my notes for the meeting today, and I'll be right back." When she reached her office, there were a few stacks of work on her desk, which meant Fabio had dropped all of it off after she'd left early. None of it was pressing, so she only packed up a few things to bring home. She went down thirty minutes later.

Their meeting with the well-known romance writer went well, and between her and Marlo, they were able to answer all her concerns, signing her to a contract for her next book. That took a couple of hours, so Marlo invited them out to lunch. Hayley liked the new author and was looking forward to working with her. She was familiar with her work and liked the good balance of heat and romance she put into every story. The combination certainly made you want to turn the page.

It was late afternoon by the time they finished, so she walked to the Erin Go Braugh and sat at the bar. There was a crowd, but it wasn't crowded.

"What'll it be, sexy?" Lucy dropped a cocktail napkin in front of her and blew her a kiss.

"Something with whiskey in it. I read somewhere this is the place for whiskey."

Lucy went to work, and Hayley waved to the people she'd met through Lucy.

"What's shaking, sweet pea?" She placed the drink in front of her and told the other bartender she was taking a break. The band started up, so they went through the office to the small patio out back. "What's wrong? You should be much happier to see me, and bonus, I'm coming over tomorrow."

"Nothing's wrong. I'm tired from having my professional face on since nine this morning. We signed a new romance writer, then we had lunch and talked about romance, so of course I thought about you. It's why I'm here." She sipped her drink, coughing at the strength, making this one her limit. All she needed was to go home drunk and do a striptease in her bedroom window. Though that might be like waving a red sweater in front of a bull and make Butch charge right on over. Maybe she'd have a couple more.

"Come on," Lucy said, flicking her on the back of the head. "I know you, and something's not quite right." She lost her smile and tried to appear serious. "Tell Dr. Lucy all about it. I'm listening and I care."

"Shut up." She waved her hand at her. "I would, but it's embarrassing, which means you're going to tease me until I'll want to move back to New York." She covered her face with her hands, not believing she didn't have more willpower to keep her mouth shut. That only meant she'd be naked before ten.

"That's not fair. I've told you every embarrassing thing I've done, and we've only known each other six months. If you're worried about me judging you, remember Kerry Lee."

She'd been horrified for Lucy when she'd told her the story of this woman who'd sweet-talked her into going home with her one night. Lucy wasn't the one-night stand kind of girl, not usually, but Kerry Lee had checked off a lot of her boxes, so she'd agreed. After they'd gotten naked and had gotten intimate, Kerry Lee had puked where no woman ever wanted to be doused in vomit. Hayley had found Lucy's retelling both horrifying and amusing, but really it was a nightmare she never wanted to experience.

"That story took courage to tell, and it gives me the willies every time it pops into my head." She smiled as Lucy nodded. "Okay." She took a breath and blew it out slowly. "You know how I like to read upstairs." Lucy kept nodding, so she told her what had happened—from her touching herself, Butch getting naked then touching *her*self, to the story she received. She opened her email from jdeaux000069 and the attached file and stayed silent as Lucy read.

"I'm no literary expert like you, but this is fucking hot." Lucy fanned herself even though the space was cold. "She wrote this? Wait, she wrote this and submitted it? How is that even possible if you two have never met?"

"My best guess is the Mouth of the South and his posse. George knows what I do and told all his bowling buddies, which includes DJ." It was embarrassing to admit everything she had, but she did feel better since Lucy wasn't on the ground rolling around in laughter. "One Google search later got her to Fleur-de-Lis and the anthology."

"Okay, that's something I'll unpack later, and clearly renovation isn't her only talent." Lucy handed her phone back and put her hand on Hayley's forearm. "Are you okay after reading that?"

"Um…" She would've said more but the heat in her ears was making her uncomfortable.

"That's an interesting reaction. Spill."

"I read that and gave her what she wanted, only I didn't take my clothes off. I do have some standards." The heat in her face was probably warming the entire patio and the building next door.

"Clearly, and if you think I'm going to make fun of you, you're dead wrong. What you should be doing is sitting at home and writing a story for this anthology from your point of view, then emailing it back to her." Lucy got up and hugged her. "Would it be wrong to say I'm jealous?"

"You don't think it's crazy?" She wanted to believe Lucy as much as she'd wanted to believe her parents when they'd tried explaining Santa was real after the class bully had spilled the truth.

"Don't take this the wrong way because I'm not criticizing you, but you're wound a little on the tight side. If Butch loosens you up a bit and makes you consider broadening the borders you've fenced yourself in with, then more power to her." Lucy kissed her cheek followed by giving her a loud raspberry. "You're way more beautiful than you'll ever think you are, Hayley, and Butch clearly thinks so. That makes me believe she's highly intelligent and not planning your untimely demise. Maybe this is who you've been waiting for, even if it's unconventional."

"I still want you to come over tomorrow. I need your opinion on whether or not she's crazy or just all my fantasies rolled into one."

"Don't worry, I'll be there. Now finish your drink and get home. If you try hard enough and put out enough bait, you'll lure the big bear to your yard. Maybe make a trail from her front door to yours with all your sexy underwear."

She'd lucked out finding Lucy, and their talk had unraveled the tension in her stomach. "Why in the hell didn't I think of that. It's genius."

"I know, right?"

They chatted some more until Lucy's break was over, and Lucy got her a ride home, declaring she didn't want her walking home alone. It was after seven by the time she got home, and Butch's house was dark, but that didn't necessarily mean she wasn't there.

Hayley sighed at the kitchen window before going upstairs and changing into her oldest sleep pants. It was too late to start getting ready to go out again and too early to go to bed, so she decided on a few hours of television. Her open laptop was like a siren's song, though, and she was powerless to resist it. Seeing yourself through someone else's lens was interesting. Who ever thought of themselves as beautiful unless they were vain?

She opened the story again, but this time she read it with Butch and herself in mind. The intimacy of the words flowed over her and made a connection from her brain to her clit. Butch had tapped into some fantasy she'd never had, making it impossible not to get turned-on. It wasn't hard to imagine Butch standing across from her, loving her every move, getting hard for her, and waiting to claim her and take everything she wanted to offer her.

The last couple of years had been filled with finishing graduate school, followed by a crappy entry-level publishing job before her move. The crappy job had sucked up all her time, leaving no room for a social life. Now she was ready. She was ready for someone who'd make her wet with just their presence, just a look and, once they had, someone who would enjoy touching her until she came. That made her think of Butch's hands again. She'd never experienced this overwhelming need before, especially for a total stranger. The woman could be a complete jerk, for all she knew.

"I really need to go out on a date or find a hobby. Taxidermy, maybe." She turned so she could drape her legs over the arm of her chair. Her laptop went on the floor so she could put her hands in her pants. Obviously, she'd already found a hobby, and it didn't require the need to procure dead animals.

She was so wet she'd have to shower again after she was done, but her whole world had narrowed to her hard clit. It'd be easy to come fast, but the story made her slow down and enjoy this. Her nipple stiffened when she brought her other hand up and pinched as hard as she could stand. The T-shirt she'd put on felt rough against her chest, but she was too far gone to stop and take it off.

"Fuck, what's happening to me?" She put two fingers over her clit and stroked hard and fast. There was no stopping now, no patience, no control, and no time to think about anything except the orgasm she needed. "God," she yelled as an intense heat seared through her, and she arched into her hand. This would've been better with a partner, better with Butch, but she felt good.

It hadn't occurred to her to glance at Butch's window, and she wasn't surprised to see her standing there when she finally did. Maybe she should've felt bad letting Butch see her yet again, but if she was honest with herself, she wanted Butch to watch. She wanted her to because she was the reason she'd been driven to touch herself.

Butch didn't look away, and neither did she as she stretched before standing up. She kept her eyes on Butch and laughed when Butch wiped her brow and gave her a wide smile. Her plan was to stand there as long as Butch stayed at her window, and she wished she had Butch's phone number. She could be convinced to repeat the whole process, but with Butch's head between her legs this time, if only she had the ability to talk to her without leaving the house. But then…would it mess with the sensuality of what they were enjoying? Words could ruin this thing between them.

There were certain truths everyone had to face about themselves, and her truth was that she was horrible at relationships. One or two dates were fine, but then she started a list of everything that was wrong with the person, from the way they chewed to whatever little tic they had. Going out with someone for more than a short period of time was an invitation to be driven mad, and she wasn't into self-inflicted pain. There was no way of knowing if Butch would find a way to annoy her, so whatever this was between them was safe—for now at least.

"Mom would be so proud," she said and laughed. She'd moved to New Orleans and become an exhibitionist. That made her laugh again, which made Butch smile. She studied everything about Butch that she could see of her. It gave her the urge to walk next door and take Butch to bed, but she waved and stepped back into the darkest part of the room.

Butch appeared disappointed by that move, so Hayley sat and picked up a book after another minute of waiting. She was disappointed Butch didn't touch herself in return but instead went back to the same book she'd seen before, something that looked old and that she handled carefully.

"Maybe I'm not as alluring as I thought." If Butch was reading after everything she'd done, her moves needed work. "I wonder if she'd be forced to make a move if I did all that naked?" They'd eventually find out. But she wanted Butch to make the first move and then so much more.

CHAPTER TWENTY

Wyatt tried reading, wanting to know what Sam was keeping to himself, but all she could think about was the pounding between her legs. Jesus, the woman was driving her slowly mad, and Hayley was beyond sexy. Unlike Lydia and her frustration at Sam not trying anything, she knew exactly what she was missing. Hayley was showing her in vivid detail.

The lights next door were out, so Hayley had probably gone to bed, and she wasn't in the mood to read. To her surprise, she was in the mood to write again. To put words on a page that she'd like someone to read, at least eventually. She went downstairs and made a cup of coffee, which was always the start of her process. A hot cup of coffee was the only companion she had when she wrote, and there was no need to change the formula now.

She'd picked a room on the other side of the house as an office, which she'd figured had been a parlor of some type when the house was built. Since she had no intention of hosting ladies for tea, it was perfect for her needs. Thankfully, she'd found a library desk in the hallway and had moved it in, along with a chair that wasn't the best but would do. There was no point in buying new furnishings until all the renovations were done. She opened one of the notebooks her father had gotten for her and smiled at the crisp white page, a blank canvas she embraced with a pen in her hand. She tapped into the part of her herself where the stories lived and began a new chapter of her career.

Four hours had passed when she glanced at the clock, and she wanted to cry from the joy at not having lost something so vital to her psyche. She started typing what she'd written, something she almost never did because God invented dictation programs. This time she did it to bleed some of the caffeine out of her system, so she could perhaps get a few hours of sleep.

When she was done, she had more than her publisher was waiting on, but this manuscript wasn't going anywhere until it was fully formed, fleshed out, and she was ready to let it go. Tomorrow she'd reread it and see if she'd lost her craft, or if that too had just been in hibernation.

She walked to the kitchen to dump out the remaining coffee in the pot and wash her mug. It was strange to her that all Lydia's dishes and pots were still in the cabinets around her, as were the furniture and other things that made a home for someone. The house was hers now, but nothing in it belonged to her, and she wandered around studying all the things that had been either Lydia's or had belonged to someone in her extended family. All the clutter reminded her of the life she'd had.

Writing wasn't just a career but a way of life for her, and losing that, along with her parents, had stripped away a lot of her identity. Her fans knew her for the mysteries that wove tales that at times turned gruesome, but they were satisfying. A month ago, she would've bet that all that was lost to her, but it was back now, and yet different. This book in her head might not make a difference if the people who'd read her stuff from the very start weren't in the mood for change.

"If this is a test of my mental fortitude," she said, staring at the ceiling in case there was someone in the universe listening, "you could've given me a sudden craving to start doing Sudoku."

It would be the ultimate joke if she became known for a string of romantic intrigue books instead of straight-up mystery. Wherever she ended up as far as her writing, the one thing she was sure of was that it would be different. "It's too late to be this deep." That was true, though, because *she* was different. Her body should be covered in scars to show all the crap she'd been through, but the worst scars were on her heart and in her head.

"Good Lord, I really need to cut down on the coffee."

Hayley's house was still dark, and considering the hour, she wasn't surprised. This house was too quiet, something she'd have to get used to, but it did allow her to think. Silence had a way of laying you bare because there was nowhere to hide from yourself. It had also made it easy to hear her parents and all those conversations they'd shared. She was starting to find her footing and the urge to move forward.

"Is that why you two dragged me out here?" She stripped for bed and punched her pillow a few times before lying down. "Did you figure I'd find my mojo in all this quiet?" She heard both her parents laughing at her.

"You're our kid, and we love you," her mom said. "The secret to a life well-lived and free of regret is to live it every minute. I think you're finally starting to understand that."

"I guess I am, so thanks for planting the idea of this place in my head. The hot neighbor is a happy bonus." She laughed with them this time. If there was a way to send her a gift from the great beyond, with her parents' sense of humor, it'd be a beautiful woman who seemed open to some sort of interesting relationship.

"You're welcome, kid, but it's time to get a move on with the romance part of the equation," her father said. "The lust part I think you both have down perfect. I'd like to think I raised you to respect women, especially the girl next door."

"Got it, Pop, and if you both don't mind, get lost for this next part." She had to do something about her hard clit, or she'd never get to sleep. It seemed it'd only taken a week for her to prove Pavlov's theory since even just the act of looking at Hayley's house got her hard.

Hayley was her last coherent thought before oblivion carried her back to the old memories. There was also the future to dream of, and she planned to blow hers all to hell by making drastic changes. All she was keeping of her old life were the parts essential to who she was. The rest would have to adapt or disappear into the mist.

CHAPTER TWENTY-ONE

Sundays were usually Hayley's catch-up day around the house. She did laundry, cleaned her bathrooms, and paid her bills. It was her penance before taking the rest of her day to either visit Lucy at the bar or walk the Quarter with no agenda in mind.

Today, though, she couldn't motivate herself to get out of bed. If she owned a magic wand, she'd use it to transport Butch to the empty spot next to her. Last night had been something, but she was ready for the real thing. Her orgasm had been intense, but how many more could Butch give her? She craved Butch like she did chocolate, but truthfully it was more than that.

Her one blessing was that she'd slept late, so she wouldn't be stewing for hours in her head about how to get Butch to come over and seduce her. To take her mind off that lovely thought, she made a list of all the things she needed to get done before Lucy came over. That might flip off the part of her brain fixated on sex. When Lucy did arrive, she hoped Butch stayed out of sight because she wasn't ready to share her. Another crazy thought, but it didn't make it any less true.

A knock at her front door propelled her downstairs, thinking Butch had finally cracked. Instead, she opened the door to a very large man holding a bouquet of pink roses. Hayley blinked and stared so long that the guy studied the numbers of her address as if he might have the wrong place.

"Hayley?" For a bear of a man, he had a gentle voice.

"That's me." This was a first. She'd never received flowers in her life. She'd never really dated the flower-giving type of people.

"Great. My name's Daisy, and these are for you. If you don't think it's weird, can I come in and put them down and make sure they're okay?" He held the flowers like he didn't really want to give them to her, but if he had to, they needed a proper farewell.

Her mother would be waving red flags and yelling she was crazy for even contemplating such a thing. Surely, there'd been some show on ID TV about a big burly florist using the excuse of delivering flowers as a way to gain entrance to a victim's kitchen. Once he was in, he'd have the opportunity to use all the knives in the block to cut her into small pieces. She pointed to the center island in the kitchen and stood back while he did his thing. It took him a few minutes of fooling with his creation before he was satisfied it was indeed perfect.

"Thanks for not thinking I was a serial killer. You'd be surprised how often I get that." Daisy headed right for the door as if not wanting to outstay his welcome.

"It's not often I meet a man named Daisy, and you do beautiful work." Her purse was upstairs, so she hoped he didn't mind waiting on her porch. She wasn't that trusting. "Can you hold on?" she asked when he stepped outside.

"Don't worry about a tip—the person who bought you the flowers took care of me. She was very generous. *Very* generous."

"Why pink?" She never really considered herself a flower kind of girl, but she was learning all kinds of things about herself. Turned out, getting flowers made her day.

"Well, I don't know why the person chose pink for you. But the friend who helped me open my shop sent the girl she was interested in pink roses as a way of letting her know how special she thought she was." He smiled as he started his story.

"So it's a sign of *Hi, I think you're special*?" That seemed a little disappointing.

He shook his head. "Let me finish. It took a little more than flowers because her girl had a long list of interesting things she made my pal do, but she'd started to fall in love with her from that very first bouquet."

"Hopefully if you get to come back, you'll tell me about the long list. That sounds interesting." She could've spent a while talking to Daisy. The guy had a soothing voice like a relaxation app.

"I'd like to think the reason my friend's relationship worked out is because of the flowers I still deliver every week." He smiled and stroked his beard. "It's been a few years and a few kids now, but she still smiles when I show up. I hope things work out for you too. After a few deliveries you'll see I can be trusted in every room of the house, so I can put them wherever you want them without you having to jostle them later."

"Thank you for that explanation. Did you happen to tell that story to whoever sent the flowers?"

"I sure did, and I have one more thing for you." The envelope he took out of the chest pocket of his overalls resembled the one she'd received with the cookies. Seeing it made her want to push Daisy off her porch so she could read it.

"Have a great day." He waved over his shoulder and headed for a yellow van with a daisy painted on the side.

Her name was written on the outside, and it seemed Butch had taken her time with it, unlike the first one. Hayley slid her fingers along the underside of the flap and tore it open. She took a breath and closed her eyes for a moment before she pulled the card out.

Hayley,
　　Please do me the honor of having dinner with me this evening. It'll give me a chance to apologize for not offering sooner.
　　Your neighbor,
　　Joe

Joe? Butch's name was Joe? That's the last name she would've picked, but she'd have to adapt. She'd do that right after she freaked out. She looked at the note again and saw the phone number at the top, which was better than having to build a fire and respond with smoke signals.

She stood in the kitchen window, phone in hand. The nerves she was experiencing made her hands shake when she entered the number that was a New York area code. So Joe was a New Yorker, and they'd ended up in the same place. The romantic in her screamed *fate*, while the pragmatist in her declared she might be crazy—in a calm voice, of course.

"Hello." Joe's voice was deep and rich. Thank God for that.

"Hey, it's Hayley." She, on the other hand, sounded like a dork. "Thank you for the flowers. I didn't think florists delivered on Sundays."

"Daisy strikes me as a guy who understands that sometimes nothing but flowers will do."

Surely she'd conjured up Joe and had willed her to life. Like the guy who brought Pinocchio to life. What was his name? *Good God, Hayley, concentrate*, she yelled in her head.

"I'm glad you liked them, and I hope you don't have plans tonight. Or would you rather do lunch? If you need a crowded place to start, I don't mind that at all."

"I'm free whenever." Oh yes, that didn't sound desperate.

"Great. Do you want to choose the place? All I've tried is the diner, and I'd rather order another bouquet of flowers and eat them than go there on a date."

The way Joe said it made her laugh. It was a well-known fact that it took Maybelle about four months to ditch her suspicions of anyone not born in this neighborhood. Even then she still kept an eye on you like you might go bad like week-old fish if she wasn't vigilant.

"I'd rather eat the roses on my couch too than have Maybelle join us for the entire meal. She's not someone who understands boundaries." She smiled when Joe joined her at her kitchen window.

"What do you suggest that doesn't include Maybelle?" Joe stopped to lift a mug to her mouth.

"I'll go wherever you lead." She heated at the comment, but it was the only way to broach the subject of what had transpired between them. "You haven't let me down yet, *neighbor*."

"You're the best thing about this city, and I'll do my best to lead you only to places that make you feel good. I'd invite you over so we can talk about it, but this place is a mess."

"I have coffee and muffins. We can talk here." So, of course, she'd have to be wearing the rattiest thing she owned. In all the erotica people wrote there was sexy lingerie because underwear sounded sexier when it was called lingerie. She owned some—it was just in her underwear drawer filed under *date wear*.

"Let me get dressed."

"No need," she said and loved the laugh Joe gave her. "I'm still in my pajamas." It was amazing how quickly her hormones made her channel a desperately horny woman. "If you own a robe, that'd be fine."

"I don't own a robe or pajamas, but I promise not to take long." Joe smiled and hung up, then disappeared from the window.

Hayley couldn't breathe and turned to go change, but Joe must've raced up for her jeans because there was a knock about a minute later. "Hi," she said, opening the door slowly, trying to sound seductive.

"Hello to you." Lucy stared at her as if she was trying to decide if a call to the mental hospital was in order. "Are you feeling okay? You look flushed."

Would Lucy break up with her if she flung her out the back door? She sighed, not wanting to be that friend. "I'm fine, just surprised. I got flowers."

"You got flowers on a Sunday? Who put out that kind of cash to get into your pants?" Lucy threw her backpack on the sofa and wandered in as if in search of flowers.

The knock that followed was the answer to that question. This time she opened the door to Joe who was wearing jeans and the shirt she'd seen over the boxers the night before. "Good morning," she said, stepping out on the porch and shutting the door behind her.

"That it is." Joe put her hands in her pockets as if she was trying to keep them to herself. That was the last thing Hayley wanted. "Are we swinging?" She jutted her chin toward the porch swing. "I promise I'm house trained if you let me in."

"Please don't hate me right off, but my friend Lucy just got here. I'd invited her and totally lost my mind this morning when I received flowers. You didn't give me a chance to call her and cancel. I don't want to be that friend and blow her off. I mean, I do want to blow her off, but that would be sucky. Do you understand what I'm saying?" Joe nodded and laughed. "I'd made plans to go out to lunch with her, but you have a way of short-circuiting my brain."

"We can reschedule. I'm slightly patient." Joe smiled when Hayley tentatively placed her hands on her stomach. "You have my number. Why don't you call me when you're free?"

"You can come in." Movement in the front window meant Lucy was watching. "I did promise you coffee."

"And a muffin, if I remember right," Joe said and winked.

Okay, now she *slightly* got the cute name for vagina, but it still wouldn't work in erotica.

"You're going to have to settle for an actual muffin right now, big guy—I have a guest." She winked back, angry at herself for not doing this sooner. Joe was as charming as she was good-looking. They stepped inside, and Lucy was leaning against her sofa trying to act nonchalant and failing miserably. "Joe, this is my friend Lucy."

"Hi," Joe said, and Hayley thought for a minute Lucy was mentally orchestrating her plan to steal Joe away before she got a chance to find out anything about her. Not that she could blame her. Joe had the same effect on her.

They sat in the kitchen and engaged in small talk, something she was convinced no one liked doing, and all they covered were the basics. That was great, but not how she wanted to spend her time.

"So…what's your story?" Lucy asked with her *I'm a bull in the china shop of life* bluntness.

"Trying my hand at restoring an old house. It's nothing more exciting than that." Joe smiled and sipped her coffee like it was fine wine. "When I bought the place, I never guessed it'd come with all these interesting people."

"It's an added bonus," Hayley said and smiled. "At least that's what George keeps telling me. You're a New Yorker?"

"I am, but I was in the mood for a change." Joe gave answers like a prisoner trying not to incriminate herself any more than necessary. "Thankfully, I can still watch the Yankees on television."

"You don't like talking about yourself, do you?" Hayley smiled to keep Joe relaxed and in her kitchen.

"I'm not that interesting, so I'm trying to keep from boring you. That's the neighborly thing to do." Joe placed her mug in the sink and excused herself and waited outside for her. "Thanks for the coffee and conversation."

"This isn't what I wanted after waiting so long. And why we waited all this time is just dumb." She noticed the way Joe's biceps pulled at the material of her shirt. "Why did we wait so long?"

"Hayley." Joe slowly raised her hand and pressed it to the side of her neck. "You can think of today as a tester."

"What's that mean?" She leaned into Joe's touch.

"You've probably been thinking plenty of things. What does she sound like? Is she what she seems? Is there something to what I see in the window?" Joe moved her hand until it was in her hair, and she honest-to-goodness wanted to swoon. "Go be a good friend, and I'll be waiting."

She closed her eyes for a moment, trying to memorize the feel of Joe's hand before Joe moved away. What was it about this woman that broke through all her defenses? "What if I don't want to wait?"

"You don't think—"

"Hayley," George said loudly.

Hayley slammed into the door when she jumped back in fright, carrying Joe with her. Not exactly what she had in mind the first time they got this close.

"Are you all right?" he called.

"George," she said just as loud, hoping he heard the frustration in the voice. "I've asked you nicely not to do that. Why do you insist on sneaking up like that?"

"Sorry, but I saw you being manhandled and felt like I had to step in."

George appeared earnest in his concern, but she wanted to knee him in the groin. If she owned a cattle prod, he'd be on the ground right now.

"George, sorry we haven't met before now." Joe stepped away from Hayley and held her hand out. George stared at it as if it was smeared with crap and didn't take it. "Okay," Joe put it back in her pocket and chuckled. "Talk to you soon, Hayley...very soon."

Before Hayley could say anything, Joe descended the stairs and didn't look back. Why the hell were all these people at her house? It was like a conspiracy to keep her from having sex. "What can I do for you, George?"

"Why was she touching you? You have no idea what's happening, and you need to be careful."

George was the kind of guy who screamed he'd seen Bigfoot but always left his camera at home. He also sometimes put out weird vibes when it came to her. She wasn't sure, but George sounded a little jealous.

"I don't know who that woman is, but she's up to no good."

"Has she killed anyone?" She stared him down until he shook his head. "Broken into any house in the neighborhood?" Another shake of his head. "Then I don't want to hear it. What you just did was rude, if you aren't aware of that."

"You don't understand. Let me explain." George appeared ready to stomp his foot.

"Go home, George. I have company, and I'm not in the mood. Joe's from New York, not Mars. She's not here to suck your brains out of your skull when you go to sleep. I suggest you take her up on her offer to get to know her instead of listening to neighborhood gossip." She went back in and laughed at Lucy standing at the kitchen window, peering at Butch's house.

"How can an ass look that good in jeans?" Lucy asked, but Hayley couldn't be sure she was asking her or talking to herself.

"It's a mystery I can't wait to solve."

CHAPTER TWENTY-TWO

Wyatt made herself a sandwich and tried to forget how gorgeous Hayley was up close. Not that seeing her through the window was a hardship, but she wanted to sit and talk to her about anything Hayley chose to tell her. All the people at Hayley's house had to go home eventually.

She took her meal and a fresh cup of coffee into the office and lost herself in her work, figuring best friends needed at least an hour to catch up. The manuscript she was working on reminded her of the first book she wrote. That one had come fast too and had made her fall in love with writing. The first one hadn't sold until her third book had broken through to the top of the best seller list, and then people went back to her first two books. After that, her career had taken off.

The mystery genre was a hard market to make it in, but she loved the secrets of the formula it took to write a good story. Well, some people said there was a formula, but she liked to think she had her own style, and every reviewer always mentioned they never knew who did it until the last chapter. Had she not lost her parents, she would've written them forever, but that wasn't the kind of story that was coming to her now. The consequences of forcing herself to go back to the tried and true might be writer's block again.

She stretched a few hours later and fixed a fresh cup of coffee before she cleared her mind and sat at her laptop and wrote something else. This was starting to get fun again. The words came easily, but they always had when she was having fun. She stopped forty minutes later and sent Hayley a text. They decided on dinner since Lucy was still there for whatever reason, and that was fine. DJ and the crew had called and asked if she wanted them to come and work. Bad weather was in the forecast for tomorrow, and DJ didn't want her insulation to get messed up.

She went up, changed, and put her work boots on. The guys were waiting outside when she unlocked the door and started joking around when she joined them, ready to work. She waved to Hayley and Lucy after noticing them in the kitchen window, and she laughed when they waved back.

She held a board in place at the top of the house, waiting for her helper to nail his side before she did the same. A couple of other guys were waiting on some scaffolding they'd set up to hand up the boards they'd need. DJ's nephews really were great carpenters and kept her laughing while they worked.

"Hey, Joe," one of DJ's nephews said, "think later on when we take a break we can go in and see your snake?"

She came close to smashing her thumb with the hammer. "I'm sorry, what did you say?" She finished with the nails and bent to grab her end of the next board. "What snake?" It was hard concentrating on the snake question when she noticed the shower next door going. Thankfully Hayley had placed a towel over the window because she'd realized in the last week that she wasn't fond of sharing. It hadn't mattered before now.

"You know, your snake. We heard about it at Maybelle's." The guys around her were all nodding and appeared eager to see a monster snake. "She told us to be careful cause it was, like, fifty feet long. We kept looking for it when we were doing the pipes, but we figured you'd hid it, so it wouldn't freak out on you. The guys and me really want to check it out if that's okay. We promise, we ain't scared."

"Someone at the diner told you I own a fifty-foot snake?" All of a sudden, the conversation in the grocery about things that were alive, and the cable guy's weird dancing around the house, made perfect sense. She'd been messing with Maybelle, and now it was biting her in the ass, even if it was pretty funny. This was actually worse than the time the *National Enquirer* put her together with Cher. Granted, she loved Cher, but having people hang out around her block chanting to see Cher had made her lose sleep.

"Like I said, bro, it was Maybelle who told us. You think if we run by JD's later and buy something, we can watch it squeeze the shit out of it and swallow it whole?"

The only thing the guy below her didn't do was press his hands together in a sign of pleading. They all seemed to have put a lot of thought into this, and she had to calm them down before they headed to George's place and started stealing rabbits.

She hated curbing their enthusiasm since they all appeared so sincere. It made her wish she really did own a snake even though snakes freaked her the hell out. She didn't hate them any more than she did ravenous hyenas, but they were better observed in an enclosure or in nature from the safety of your vehicle. They still made her skin crawl, but as her mother liked to say, they were all God's creatures. What God was thinking with the creation of pythons and hyenas was a question for another day.

"Gosh, I wish you guys had told me sooner. I didn't realize until we got to New Orleans that it'd be murder on Jedidiah's allergies. That's his name. I had to ship him to a sanctuary in Texas, so he could stop with the Benadryl. Taking so much was wrecking his sleep cycle."

"Snakes get allergies? No shit?" the guy on the same level as her asked. "I never knew that. Huh, you learn something every day."

"Burmese pythons are known for their extreme dust sensitivity, so this house was murder on his sinuses. The poor guy was miserable." They all nodded as she spoke earnestly, somehow managing to keep a straight face. "That, and I heard my neighbor George was nervous about the pet rabbits he keeps caged in the yard." All the guys made disgusted faces at that. She joined them because she didn't understand the attraction of owning animals that never got to hop around hiding Easter eggs. "I didn't want to take a chance that Jedidiah would be blamed, even though he's a vegan."

"He's religious?" one of the younger guys asked. "I didn't think animals would care about stuff like that."

"I'm not sure about his faith, but if he is interested in religion, he's more of a Buddhist because he's pretty chilled and he chants beautifully. What I meant was, he's an extremely disciplined vegetarian. He doesn't eat animals." She shook her head and tried not to laugh. These guys couldn't be that gullible, but there were still mysteries in the world. Not one of them looked like they were doubting her story.

"Man, you should've told George that, but he probably wouldn't give a shit. We did some work over there, and he was the biggest pain in the ass when it came to every little thing." The older guy handed up another board and cursed some more when it came to the subject of George and his seemingly awesome personality. "Bro, that sucks for you if you liked having Jedidiah around. I bet he was a good and quiet companion."

"I'm trying to be a good neighbor, and Jed's not everyone's glass of beer. You get me? George and I will get along if he stays on his side of the fence. He likes to stand there and stare, and I have to admit it freaks me out a little." She brought up her side of the next board, glad to see the other guys working on the first floor. With one guy cutting and everyone putting siding up, they should be done in about five hours. That would give her plenty of time to take Hayley somewhere nice.

She sensed someone's eyes on her and turned and smiled at Hayley upstairs, back in her pajamas after her shower. Hopefully she wasn't getting naked for Lucy.

"Yeah, he does that. The only one he's interested in talking to is Hayley, and that's the true definition of barking up the wrong skirt. Talk about a butthead. The best advice about that asshole is to never accept a pie from his wife. That lady must've burned her taste buds dropping acid or something because she bakes for shit. When we worked over there, we had to cause some accidental leaks," the guy said, making air quotes, "so the rest of us could bury whatever the hell she offered us in the yard. George had the worst time trying to figure out where all the dead spots in his grass were coming from."

"Yeah," the young guy said. "Can you imagine eating that shit if it actually killed grass?"

"DJ gave me the heads-up on that." They continued to joke as they worked, and they made it from the peak to the bottom of the first floor.

On the ground the guys were moving quickly once they no longer needed the ladders. She was pleased with the finished product that would look even better painted. A call to Pippa would be the best way to find out exactly what color the house was painted when it was built because she wanted the house to look like it did when the Fullers had moved in. With the repairs she'd done, the house would last a lot longer than it had been standing.

"Thanks, guys. The place will really pop when JD comes by and starts painting." She gave them each a bonus, so they could enjoy what was left of their weekend. There were about three hours of sunlight left, and they ended up staying to start ripping the shake off the back and other side.

She followed Hayley's lead and placed a towel over her shower window and rushed through what was one of her favorite parts of the day. Hot showers had a way of making her mind wander through different topics and story ideas. She loved them even if water conservationists probably hated her. Her limited wardrobe made it easy to decide on jeans and one of the three white shirts she'd packed. Now all she had to do was decide on where to go since her culinary skills extended only to reheating takeout in the microwave. That would in no way be impressive.

When she was done, she still had an hour to kill before she picked Hayley up. She didn't want to be the date that showed up this early.

While she waited, she worked some more as a way to forget she was hungry. She was thinking about their short exchange that morning and smiled. Hungry might not be all she was feeling.

She stopped to check her email, not surprised to see another bunch from Blanche. Her agent seemed to be chronicling her breakdown with each message. They went from begging to demanding then devolved into insulting. The insulting ones made her wonder what exactly went through Blanche's mind at times. Was calling her a selfish bastard going to make her want to hurry back to New York and propose?

It was easy to delete all of them so she could spend some more time on emails from fans on her public email account. Writing might be a solitary thing, but reading was universal once you shared your work with the world. The thing about devoted readers was they paid attention to the details. *Why* she wrote the stuff she did was something they tried to glean through numerous intelligent questions. There was the odd person, almost always men, who didn't think women had any business writing mystery novels, and who loved to go to online forums to spew their displeasure.

Those all went into the trash because she didn't have time to argue with anyone who cut her work to shreds on the basis of her sex. The others who simply didn't care for the books for whatever reason she engaged with, truly interested in their opinions. There would never come a moment she'd think herself so important that she'd ignore the people who wrote to her because they loved what she did.

"Well, guys," she said to the screen, "I think it's time to go impress the girl."

CHAPTER TWENTY-THREE

Hayley, I swear if you don't get dressed and wear something to make that woman chew through her leash, I'm going to do it and rub it in when I tell you all about it." Lucy was still at the window as if waiting for another Joe sighting. It seemed watching Joe walk back to her house had left Lucy wanting more.

"Maybe I'm trying to build anticipation." As excuses went that was beyond weak, but all Hayley could do was sit at her island and stare at the beautifully arranged flowers. It was such a strange tradition, the giving of flowers—at least she thought so. To her flowers always seemed such a waste of a thing to spend money on. Take this bouquet, for example. She could've bought boots for what Joe had probably spent on it. The strange thing, though, was these made her feel feminine, cherished, wanted—it was a heady combination.

"What you're doing is hiding in here with me, and it's pissing me off. She baked you cookies, wrote you a phenomenal story, and sent these." Lucy pointed to the flowers as if she might have forgotten them. "From what I can tell, she's interested, and you're acting like you're waiting to pass her a note after English class with the *I like you* box checked off." Lucy finally pried herself away from the window and stood across from her and crossed her arms. "She, from what I can tell physically anyway, is everything you've said you were waiting for. The flowers and everything else mean she's not all looks and ego. Get going and call me in a few days once you come up for air only because one more orgasm will kill you."

"You don't think it's a mistake?" She didn't often need

reassurance, but for some reason this time, even after everything she and Joe had watched each other do, she did. This time she wanted a little more than she'd previously had, and she was afraid that she had no idea of how to go about that. What if all she'd ever have was the two dates, then months spent with her cats?

"I don't," Lucy said, moving to pick up her bag. "It's not me who has to be convinced, though." She kissed her cheek and hugged her before leaving. Lucy could become a life coach with her in-your-face *I'll beat you if you don't comply with what I'm telling you* approach.

She and Lucy hadn't gone out for lunch, but the three hours they'd spent together were going to be hard to explain to Joe especially since she hadn't answered her text. She'd heard nailing outside and had seen Joe on the side of her house putting up siding, which explained why Lucy had been glued to the view next door, and at some point they gave up on the movie altogether and just sat beside the window, commenting on Joe's physique and spinning random questions about her, like whether or not she liked pineapple, or if she ever considered being on the bottom. Joe appeared carefree and not obsessing about her in return as she joked with the guys working with her. Had she lost her chance?

She watched some more, cursing herself for her indecisiveness—a blip on the radar of the side of her personality that derailed her at times because it concentrated on only the things that could go wrong. Dark-cloud Hayley never did her any favors. She took her phone out and sent a short text.

What time tonight?

She thought about adding an emoji, but tool-belt Joe didn't seem like the emoji kind of person. Joe was laughing but stopped and read her phone before turning her head to smile at her. God, that smile was almost as nice as that ass in those jeans. When in the hell had she developed such objectifying tendencies?

If I said six would I sound eager or geriatric? I promise I'm not trying to talk you into the early bird special.

She laughed at the response and replied, *I don't mind a little eager.*

"As soon as the nailing stops, I'm going to treat you to something nice. Like me, for instance." She picked an outfit to wear for when

Joe was done. Even if they stayed in, she wanted to look good, and it also gave her an excuse to wear heels. Lucy had mentioned the extra height made her ass look good.

She took her time in the shower and thought about being alone with Joe. That only made her want to touch herself again, and that wasn't going to cut it today. After she dried off and put her pajamas back on so she wouldn't wrinkle her skirt, she sat at the small desk on the other side of the room and powered her laptop on. There was no reason to torture herself any more than she had already.

It was amazing how fast her nipples puckered to the point of uncomfortable when she saw an email from Anonymous right below one from Marlo. Whatever her boss wanted was going to have to wait. The subject line from Anonymous simply said *addition*, and there was a file attached. When she opened it, the story shared the title of the first once Anonymous had sent, and she sat on her bed to read.

Neighbor

The way she looks standing there is getting me so hard I want to take my pants off. She's naked and staring at me with an expression I'm not sure how to decipher, but I can tell she's determined. All I can ask myself is why. Why isn't she touching herself like all the nights before now?

I move closer to the window and raise my hand to the pane, smiling when she repeats the move. Now I know what she wants from me, and it excites me more than the cutest girl in fifth grade kissing me behind our elementary school. To test my theory, I place my hands on my abdomen, and she mirrors the action. This time I not only get to watch but lead the dance. She wants me to touch her, and I want to give her everything she desires.

The intensity of her stare as she watches me strip off my clothes makes me take my time. Once I'm naked, I spread my fingers and stroke my stomach before running my index finger up between my breasts. She watches me as she follows my movements religiously. The way her eyes narrow a bit means she's enjoying this. It was then that it wasn't hard to imagine the feel of her skin, the hardness of her nipples against my palms, and my lips on her neck. I was in that room—they were my hands on her body.

The echo of her voice reverberates in my head when she moans softly as my hands cover her breasts. I'm standing behind her, liking all that soft skin pressed against mine. She falls back against me when I squeeze and suck right where her neck meets her shoulder, making *me* moan this time. I have the whole expanse of her body in front of me, and I pause not only to savor it, but to decide where I want to touch next. There's no reason to rush but she seems impatient as her hands cover mine as if trying to get me to focus.

"Not yet," I say into her ear, and she reaches back and pulls my hair. I move her closer, and she spreads her legs as if ready for me.

She drops her head to the side when I run a line of kisses down to her shoulder. There is nothing more I want than to touch her, so I move the hand she's covering with hers and run my fingers along her pussy. She grips my wrist and moans again, pressing her ass into my groin. I stop, wanting to enjoy how wet she is, and it seems all she's thought about since we were together last was getting fucked. This is what I've been thinking of as well, and having her open like this, wanting, makes *me* want to rush, but I take a breath. I want to touch her until she's ready for me.

"Baby, please," she says, sounding so out of breath as she chases my fingers.

"Please what?" I turn her head and kiss her. "Tell me what you want."

"Fuck me," she says, her breathing coming in gasps as if she can't control herself. "I need you to fuck me."

I stroke her clit, and she turns and wraps her legs around me. She's clinging to me and bucking her hips like she wants to come. There's been enough teasing, enough foreplay, and enough of everything except going inside her until she's done. It won't be long before she climbs the peak I've led her to and she'll be lost in the pleasure. I sit with her straddling my lap, slide my fingers in, and place my thumb over her clit.

She can't hold back now, and I give her everything she's demanded of me. I fuck her like she belongs to no one but me. It's perfect—she's perfect. The feel of her is the most exquisite thing I've ever experienced.

The walls of her sex grip my fingers, and she screams as I sense how close she is to coming. Her breathing picks up, and a steady stream of *Oh God*s sounds like a mantra as I quicken my pace, wanting her to claim her orgasm.

"Harder, baby, harder. I'm almost there," she says, and I gladly give her what she wants.

She yells and squeezes my shoulders as I stop my hand but not my thumb. My fingers are buried deep in her sex, and I stroke her clit until she screams my name. The way she stiffens and then relaxes in my arms makes me complete. She's done, and she opens her eyes and gazes at me like a woman completely sated. With one last kiss she releases my fingers so she can drop to her knees and take me into her mouth until I come.

When I do, the only thing wrong is it breaks the spell, and I'm back in my chair with my hand between my legs. Thinking of her made me touch myself until I was lost at the sight of her. She makes me feel alive, and I've come to want to see her smile. It's my addiction.

"Thank you." I stand and press my hand to the windowpane again. She nods as if she understands me. Just as quickly she walks away and is gone. "Until next time."

Hayley closed her eyes and took deep breaths. She was so turned-on she wanted to lie down and give Joe a call. There were still construction sounds coming from outside, but she walked to the window on surprisingly strong legs. The guys were still working and joking, only she didn't see Joe. Her phone dinged, and she smiled seeing Joe's name on her message readout.

Are you ready? Or do you need more time? The message was like all Joe's so far, direct and short.

Give me five. She deleted that and retyped, *fifteen minutes.* She sent it and her phone rang right after. "Hey."

"Could I come in and wait? I'd rather not give George the chance to shoot a dart into my neck if he thinks I'm about to manhandle you." Joe laughed.

She had to press her hand to her chest. She needed to calm down. "Are you sure it's not so your pals out there won't tease you for having no game?" If Joe had any more game, she'd be pregnant by now.

"I'll leave it up to you to decide about that. I'm here."

She opened the door and leaned against it when she saw Joe standing there with a bottle of wine and a smile. Even if she'd been a writer instead of an editor, she'd have trouble coming up with the words to describe Joe. That smile of hers could turn a nun into a woman in need of sex.

"Hi," Joe said and waited.

"Come in." She accepted the wine and watched Joe stride in. The way she glanced around seemed more about curiosity than nosiness. It was something she hadn't done that morning, and Hayley wondered what made her do it now. "You've been busy over there."

"I didn't want to rush your time with Lucy, and I wanted to improve the view for you." Joe walked to her living room and pointed to the couch. "Can I sit?"

"Please." She liked the look of Joe on her couch. "You've done wonders for my view, and I was wondering if you'd like to stay in so we can discuss it. We could order Chinese or something."

"I'd love that, but I don't mind taking you somewhere." Joe spread her legs slightly. All the stuff in her head about Joe popped right back to the forefront of her thoughts. "That might be the best way to make me behave."

"Oh, you're going to behave. You've made me lose my mind plenty of times, but I don't want to make it that easy for you. You're right, going out is a good idea." She smiled when Joe pouted. "Let me go finish getting dressed, and I'll be right back down." Joe's jeans and suede coat made her change her outfit to leather pants and boots, considering it was getting colder outside. She put on some light makeup and a dark pink lipstick and was pleased with the results.

She stopped halfway down the stairs and listened to Joe talking to someone. It sounded serious and she prayed it didn't mean Joe was going to have to cancel. She couldn't walk back upstairs without giving away her spot on the stairs.

"Then I drove up and saw that the train wreck was not only my station, but I owned it," Joe said, and she had to be talking about the house. "That's a longer conversation for another day, but I do have a question. Can you guys give me any insight on George? Is he as crazy as he seems?"

The dual meowing made her shake her head and laugh. When she made it back down, she was shocked to find Hugo and Truman sitting on the coffee table while Joe held one of their paws in each hand. If she didn't know her cats and their antisocial behavior with practically every human on the planet, she'd swear the two talking to Joe were imposters. They didn't even let *her* touch their paws, but Joe just sat there like she was thinking of dumping her for the two cats.

"Are they warning you off? They should remember who feeds them." She stopped moving, enjoying the way Joe looked her over.

"They're giving me the skinny on the neighbors, and would you be mad if I told you how beautiful you look?" Joe petted each cat before standing and taking her hands. "You're gorgeous."

"Thank you, and women love hearing how beautiful they are, for future reference." She released one of Joe's hands and placed hers on Joe's chest. It was a bold move, and yet it felt right given the amount of sensuality already humming between them. Joe was solid and, from what she saw so far, respectful. Wasting most of the day on nerves made her an idiot, but the way Joe let her work her way through her stuff brought her a level of comfort she'd never experienced around another woman. "You won't lie to me, will you? That's the most important thing to me."

It was an out-of-the-blue question, and probably too serious for what was essentially the second time they'd met. But she couldn't help but ask. There were different people in the world, some who followed the rules and some who made them up to get what they wanted. The latter were the ones who had the power to eviscerate you if you gave them a chance. Of course if Joe was a liar, a good one, she'd do so now without a problem.

Like she had that morning, Joe touched her, drawing her in. "What you should do is take it a day at a time. Hopefully, our shared moments so far should tell you that you can trust me to keep your secrets safe. Now, if you have George waiting in the kitchen to take me down, you're on your own."

She rested her forehead against Joe's and laughed. "George's been a large concession to good manners. He's a pain in the ass, but I'm too nice to mention it." The way Joe held her made her relax farther into her. "He's a strange man, but he's better than the newspaper when it comes to information about the neighborhood. George is a good cub reporter."

"Maybe I'll just manhandle you for answers so I can avoid George altogether." Joe held her hips with a light touch. Her hands warmed the leather she was wearing, and it made her think of the story she'd read earlier. That Joe had a talent for erotica was an understatement.

"Tell me why you decided to finally ask me out." While a relationship based simply on sex was something she might've thought of at first, something like that wouldn't last. It only worked out in erotica, and even those were usually short stories.

"It's something my father told me once." Joe combed Hayley's hair back, leaving her hand on the side of her neck. "Every woman deserves respect, and I didn't want you to think you don't affect me because you do. That's true, and I'm not sure yet what it is you want, but what I need is more than a night. It's not like I'm proposing, but you're someone I want to know."

"I affect you?" Sex might not be the only reason to be with someone, but it should be an important aspect of any relationship. How someone touched her, saw her, and wanted her were priorities.

"You can't think otherwise." Joe took a chance and pulled her closer. She lowered her head with the slowness that'd give Hayley a chance to stop her if that's what she really wanted. There was no way she was doing that, and she encouraged her by placing her hands behind Joe's head.

There were moments Hayley's father said you never forgot, and this kiss was going to be on her list of memorable highlights. Joe was gentle, and there was something passionate in the way she kissed. It was the kind of act that made her feel like they'd been apart for years and had finally gotten together again. She felt cherished and turned-on, a heady combination.

"Wow," she said when Joe pulled back.

"Wow is right," Joe said. "Hi." Joe smiled and kissed her again.

"Hi." She encouraged Joe to lower her head and kissed her again. "Do you want to order in?"

"I do, but I'm taking you out. We're neighbors, so you know I'm not going anywhere, but I want us to be sure. Is that okay?" Her stomach rumbled loudly, making them both laugh.

"It is, so let's get going."

She took Joe's arm and smiled when she helped her up into the old truck. The old country songs on the radio didn't quite fit Joe. "It's stuck on that channel, and the power button is broken, so I can't turn it off. I'd say I hated that, but these songs will show you that no matter how horrible your life is going, it could be so much worse. I mean, your horse could run off with your girl."

"I'll have to remember that." She sat back, waiting to see what Joe came up with. First date in their case was relative, considering their distant enjoyment of one another, yet she was still curious. They stopped at the Coquille d'Huître, one of the best restaurants not only in the city, but in the country. This place wasn't just impressive, but expensive. Hayley had never been, and it was nice her first time was with Joe. It was also romantic, so the night was off to a good start.

Joe hurried around and got her door before the valet could. They were seated at an intimate table by a window, which was perfect. The dinner and conversation they shared for the next couple of hours was wonderful.

She found out that Joe was a voracious reader, which Hayley was putting on her list of wants, should she lose her mind and try internet dating again. Joe was the whole package when it came to stimulating her brain as well as her body. She'd been more successful than Lucy at getting Joe to open up about herself, and she knew which college she'd graduated from and heard about some of the trips she'd taken. Joe was also smart enough to turn it around on her and talk about her favorite subjects, so they'd covered everything from Jane Austen to Stephen King.

"So," Hayley said as they were waiting to share a dessert, "what exactly is it you do?"

It was the only time in the night that Joe didn't meet her gaze directly. "I'm in between jobs right now, but my dad had a contracting firm before he suddenly retired. The Fuller house was a good opportunity to use all the skills I've learned through the years." Joe stirred cream and sugar into her coffee, a process she appeared to take seriously.

"You're flipping it? Is that why you're moving so fast?" Not seeing Joe next door was something she didn't want to consider just yet.

"No. I bought it to live in it, and I'm moving fast because that's the way I work. I want it done and livable as quickly as possible. The Fuller family was big in size from what I've heard, but none of them were into maintenance."

Joe stopped to take a sip of coffee. The expression on her face and the way she closed her eyes in apparent enjoyment made her want to research perfumes that smelled like coffee.

"What I've done so far were the most pressing things, like the pipes and the outside, so the cold air doesn't come through the walls like I'm living surrounded by cheesecloth."

"You really like coffee, huh?" She placed her hand on the table, happy when Joe threaded their fingers together.

"You can tell a lot about a city from their coffee, don't you think? This place is a coffee lover's paradise. We can discuss the food on our next date."

Joe winked at her and smiled, turning her blood to lava. The urge to go home and strip her clothes off was growing with every sip of the strong brew. Coffee as an aphrodisiac, who knew? "Should we take the dessert to go?" *Please say yes*, she repeated a few times in her head.

"That sounds like a wonderful idea." Joe signaled for the waiter, who brought the check and the chocolate cake they'd ordered. Joe pulled cash from her wallet, so they could get going that much faster.

They stood in the shadows while they waited for the valet to bring their truck and kissed. Their first kiss was good, but tame in comparison to this. Joe held her against the building and possessed her lips as her hands moved right above her ass. She held on, wanting to rush home and get what she'd been waiting for.

"Take me home," she demanded with Joe's shirt bunched in her fists. "Don't make me wait any longer. I need your hands on me—I want you over me until I come."

"Jesus," Joe said, closing her eyes. "You've driven me crazy from the first day I saw you in the shower."

"You watch me in the shower?" She laughed, pinching Joe's side hard. "Perv."

"Don't worry, Karma paid me back by spewing what smelled like raw sewage all over me. The first time I watched, anyway." Joe kissed her neck before biting it gently like the lover in that story. That fucking story that had made her want to combust.

"I was wondering what you were doing in the yard naked." She heard the rumble of the old truck, and Joe practically carried her over and quickly pressed money into the valet's hand. They caught every red light back to the house, but Joe took the opportunities to kiss her. It made her want to start unbuttoning things before they were anywhere near her place. "Right now I'm interested in a closer view of that one glimpse I got."

"Thank God the hose wasn't full of gunk too." Joe walked her to the door but didn't come inside. "And I'm interested in seeing what's under those sweats."

"Please tell me you're not having second thoughts." She clung to Joe, not caring how she perceived it.

"I'm not, but let me run and get my work clothes and lock up, now that the guys are gone. Tomorrow, I don't want them to see me in the same clothes and say shit about you." Joe squeezed her ass as she gave her one last kiss. "I'll be right back."

She watched Joe practically sprint across the yard, clearing the low fence like a hurdler. Joe was worried about people talking about her, which was a good sign. "She's perfect." Joe was that, and she left her door unlocked as she went in and put their chocolate cake in the refrigerator. They could have it as a snack later.

The nightgown she'd taken out just in case was upstairs, and she hurried up to put it on but stopped when she heard a commotion outside. This was New Orleans, the city that could throw a parade for anything from insurance conventions to someone getting married, but this was different. She opened the front door, and her mouth literally dropped open.

"What the hell?"

CHAPTER TWENTY-FOUR

The night had been perfect so far, so all she had to do was release DJ and whoever had stayed. Why they wouldn't just accept a key and come and go like they did in the beginning was mind-boggling, but her supposed giant snake might've influenced that change. Now, except for DJ, they did stuff outside until she came downstairs or waited for her to come home before leaving. DJ and two of his guys had started to tile the shower upstairs when she'd left, so hopefully they were close to done.

"Hey, Joe," DJ said as he stacked up his tools. "Have a nice time?"

"I did, so thanks for the recommendation. You guys finished?" She took a second to admire the work, although in that moment they could've used the hideous green they just ripped out, trimmed it in purple, and she wouldn't have cared.

"Just cleaning up for tomorrow. We'll be ready for grout by then."

There was some noise coming from outside, and Wyatt tried to remember if there was some sort of field or park around. It sounded like cheering for a kids' soccer game or something like that. It was kind of late for a kids' activity, though, but right now, she didn't care. She was interested in getting to Hayley, and that was it. But when she heard DJ's crew saying, "What the shit?" she went downstairs. She wanted to make sure Hayley was okay.

Once she was on the porch, she surmised it wasn't a Little League game or any kind of festive event, but she couldn't quite figure out what she was looking at. There were people, a lot of people, gathered outside her house with picket signs and torches. Not that the picket signs made any sense, but torches in a place where everything for miles was made from old wood seemed insane. And what she thought was cheering was actually booing and hissing. Who the hell knew that happened outside of children's books?

"Is this the antisnake brigade?" she asked DJ when he and the guys joined her outside.

"No, that would be the militant wing of the historical society who are trying to get accredited like the Vieux Carré Commission." DJ took his cap off and scratched his head, appearing as confused as her. "Something's got them in a twist because they sure are pissed."

She glanced at the crowd and their signs and banners, and it dawned on her what the problem was. "Do the people in this neighborhood have any idea what a troublemaker Maybelle is? The woman's a pain in my ass."

Most of the signs had to do with miniature golf and how it must be eradicated from the civilized world.

DOWN WITH PUTT-PUTT! PUTT-PUTT IS OF THE DEVIL! YOU CAN'T RUIN OUR NEIGHBORHOOD, FOREIGNER!

That was the gist of most of the signs, but how anyone could think miniature golf was something evil from Satan needed more explanation on another sign, or they needed to share what they were smoking.

An old woman with a bullhorn called out, chant-like, "If you think you can bring your weird ways here, we say…"

"No way," the mob screamed at the prompt before they went back to booing and hissing. A majority of these people had never been picked to be on the team in school, and it showed.

"Fucking great," she said, knowing there was no way to get back to Hayley now. Torches didn't enhance intimacy. At least, not attached to people wanting to burn you with them.

"*No*, not fucking great, buddy." DJ shook his head as he watched the crowd with wary eyes. "You gotta know these people. They're zealots who are in no way reasonable when someone puts a turd in their shorts."

She laughed despite the major inconvenience. DJ had a way with words she wanted to write down at times, so she could use them in a book. And it couldn't be denied the situation was funny. Or it would be, another day. And because of that, and because she had a true penchant for messing with people who liked stirring the pot, she wouldn't disabuse them of the story they'd been told.

"How charming can you be?" DJ asked.

"Offering to rip their balls off isn't going to work this time, huh?" The guys behind them laughed.

"Not unless you want this to be a permanent thing." He pointed to a bullhorn lady who seemed to be in charge. "That there is their leader, Roberta Sue Walton, and I've always gotten the impression she thinks she's related to the television family of the same name. She's nuttier than a squirrel stash, but that's her posse, and they never get tired of picketing when they think it's warranted. You got to wonder if they have jobs. Who the hell wants to be complaining about shit all the time?"

"Like I said, fucking great." She glanced next door and saw Hayley on her porch with her phone in her hand. Wyatt guessed it had to do with the torches, and she couldn't blame her for appearing concerned.

"The thing about this is it don't make a lick of sense," DJ said. "They got some major problems with putt-putt golf, but what the hell does that have to do with you?"

"I may have been messing with Maybelle." She walked down to her rickety picket fence in the front of the house and waved to the old lady with the bullhorn. "Can I help you?"

"We're here to lay down the law." Roberta Sue spoke in a tone of righteous indignation that was hard to miss, considering she was using the bullhorn even though she was three feet away from her.

"What law are you talking about? What exactly do you think I'm doing wrong? I can tell you I've gotten permits for everything I've done." If she could overcome her fear of snakes, especially big ones, she was seriously thinking of getting one, especially if she could let it loose in the yard. She had to research if Burmese pythons were trainable, right after the rickets search.

"When you break the laws of the historical society, you're breaking all laws." Roberta Sue had probably become a vigilante historical society member only for the use of the bullhorn. Wyatt had no doubts about that. "You need to stop, fall in line, or give the house back to Gator Fuller."

"Gator Fuller accepted a check for this place, so that's not happening." The crowd hissed at that, and it sounded rather creepy when it was done en masse. "How about you show me the written rules for this section of town, which have been ratified by the city council. Once I see that and know I am, in fact, out of compliance, I'll rectify things." She looked at Hayley again and gave her a thumbs-up. This was a major inconvenience, but she didn't have to ruin their evening. "Can you do that?"

"We don't have to write anything down. The rules are the rules, and that's how it is. You're dim if you don't know that."

Everyone applauded Roberta Sue like she'd said something as worthy as the Gettysburg Address instead of the complete craziness she'd shared with half the city because of the damn bullhorn. The man next to her waved his devil and putt-putt golf plaque, coming close to clocking Wyatt with it.

"Okay, so there are no written rules is what you're saying?"

They all quieted to hear her question, then yelled a loud "Yeah" back.

"Then I need you not to block my driveway and stay out of my yard, and I won't tell the police to charge you for trespassing. If you decide to ignore that, all bets are off." She spoke loud enough to be heard by everyone. "And for God's sake, put out the torches before you burn the neighborhood down. This isn't a *Frankenstein* movie."

"You can't tell us what to do." Roberta Sue wasn't one to give up easily. DJ was right about that. The mob agreed with another *yeah*. That was the only acceptable answer to everything Roberta Sue said through her megaphone, loud and proud.

"Ma'am, I'm not telling you not to march. I'm actually a big fan of freedom of expression. What I'm telling you is to keep it on the sidewalk. I'm sure the police will explain it to you when they get here. You might not have written rules, but I'm sure the city has some on open flames. If you're civil, I think we can work something out. If you think differently, then pack a toothbrush so you'll have something to make a shiv out of when you have to protect yourself in prison." She turned and walked back to the porch as she spoke to 911. The threat of police seemed to be the catalyst for Roberta Sue's mob to calm down and head in the direction of the diner and the town crier, Maybelle.

Roberta Sue and her boyfriend with the gigantic sign were another story. They stayed on the sidewalk, walking from one end of her property to the other in their own personal protest, and they weren't going anywhere. Wyatt was just glad the rest of them had left peacefully. What was pissing her off was that she couldn't take a chance and head to Hayley's until all this was resolved. She had no proof but could guess Roberta Sue and Maybelle were the same kind of person. Their talent for gossip led to stuff like this, and Hayley didn't deserve to have that brought to her door.

"How did you do that? I'm impressed." DJ slapped her on the back as he and his guys watched the crowd head down the street.

"I love being the neighborhood entertainment to a point, and I explained that. I was kidding about the miniature golf thing, but now not so much, if only because it will keep their panties in a twist."

"Really?" one of the guys said. "I love that shit. We could build a bar in the back, and it'd be awesome."

"I called the police and told them about the unruly mob, and I promised them I'd have them arrested if they trespassed, and yes really. Your bar idea might be something to think about." She answered both their questions, but DJ's smile was wary and it worried her. "What?"

"The police are going to send over our neighborhood patrolman, Sergeant Walton." DJ pointed to the crazy lady with the bullhorn. "That would be Roberta Sue's grandson, who thinks he's the chief of police. He's also very protective of his grandmother. He's her only grandson, so officially he's her favorite."

"I'm sure they've never considered the semantics of the whole situation and how that would make his sisters feel, and again, fucking great. I guess my golf course is going to be a no, if only so I don't have to get in the middle of their family squabbles. I'll need to think of something equally obnoxious to put in the yard that *will* pass muster with the made-up historical society." This totally sucked. "You guys get going, and I'll see you in the morning."

"Are you sure? Roberta Sue can summon another crowd in nothing flat." DJ appeared hesitant to go. "You might need witnesses."

"If you get here tomorrow and I'm strung up in a tree with a *Down with putt-putt* sign stapled to my head, make sure you tell the chief it was the Waltons. They should be the top suspects at least, and there's going to be some shit these people can't fathom if someone burns my house down. I'm easygoing until someone fucks with me." She shook hands with all three of them and watched them drive off, all the while keeping an eye on Roberta Sue.

She took her phone out and called Hayley. "The universe hates me."

"Not as much as Roberta Sue hates miniature golf," Hayley said, laughing. "Good Lord, what is all that about?"

She watched Hayley on her porch, and it made her almost not care that these idiots could burn the place down. The explanation she gave made Hayley laugh some more. "It was a joke for the love of putt-putt and messing with an old gossip."

"Telling Maybelle that was like poking a hornets' nest, honey. Maybelle and Roberta Sue are rebels looking for a cause. This week it's you and your somewhat warped sense of humor. You can still come over, though."

"I called the police, and now I have to wait." She was truly stuck now.

"You called the police?" Hayley's voice carried enough that she didn't need the phone. "Are you mad? You're never getting rid of Roberta Sue now."

"Can we just call her Roberta?" Why people needed to go by more than one name was time-consumingly baffling to her.

"Only if you want Roberta Sue to mace you." Hayley sighed and said something under her breath. "Okay, wait for the police and then get over here wearing as little clothing as you can get away with."

"Believe me, if I have to wait until tomorrow, I'm going to rupture something important. I'll text you when I'm done in case you're sleeping. I know you have to work tomorrow. I have the crew coming back to finish tiling the upstairs bathroom and put up more siding." She waved when Hayley did before she disappeared into the house. The police had obviously deemed her call a nonemergency, so she went in as well, wanting to be comfortable while she waited.

"Can't you do anything about this?" she asked her parents. "I think you would've found the lightning bolt closet by now if only to visit Blanche."

"Are you kidding? This is better than reality television," her mother said. "I love you to pieces, but not everyone gets your sense of humor, sweetie."

"You're falling down on your guardian angel jobs." She sat in the front room so she could watch for the police and tried to find a comfortable spot on the rocker since she was still hard from Hayley's roaming hands and kisses. "There's only one thing that'll get my mind off all that."

She ran up for the next journal. It was time to find what Sam had been hiding.

June 1913

"You deserve the truth, Lydia," Sam said, taking his hands back. "First off, I love you. Don't ever doubt that even if you end up hating me." He stood and walked to the sink and leaned over it as if he might be sick. He appeared to have picked up a boulder he was having trouble carrying. "All I ask is that you give me at least a day before you tell your father."

"Sam…honey, you're scaring me. I've been trying to get you going, not turn you over to the law." Lydia stood and placed her hands on his back. "I wouldn't be doing that if I didn't care about you."

Sam was stiff but almost vibrating with tension, making Lydia think he'd rather set his hair on fire than tell her he cared and wanted a future with her. "What I said about my father is true. My mother died when I was seven, and it was just me and him after that. I skipped school often to help him in the fields, and we went on like that for years until I turned seventeen."

"And then he died?" Lydia asked softly, and he nodded. She led Sam back to the table and sat next to him. "You said you enlisted."

"I did, and they shipped me to a place in Georgia for training. The work was hard, but I was used to it, and not complaining about it got you promoted." He spoke as if the answers were written on the tabletop and he couldn't break his attention from it.

She stood and put her arms around him from behind. Like before he leaned in to her, seeming to enjoy the feel of her. No matter what he told her, she doubted she'd give him up. "Tell me, sweetheart."

"Three years in one of the guys I served with wasn't paying attention and dumped a pallet of boxes on me, and I ended up with this limp when my leg broke in a couple of places." He put his arms around her when she sat on his lap, and he seemed to find the courage to finish when she pressed her hand to his cheek. "When I came here, Lester and his family took me in since it was his brother who helped me recover in the Army hospital."

"They're a really nice family. Lester and his brother worked for Papa, making deliveries in the summers when we weren't in school."

"They are, and I thought having an adopted family was all I'd have…until I saw you. If you believe I've been indifferent when it comes to you, that's completely wrong. You're the most beautiful woman I've ever had the pleasure of meeting, but you're so much more." The way Sam smiled at her made it impossible not to kiss him, so she did. "You're strong, you aren't afraid to stand your ground, and you've stolen my heart."

"Then why have you pushed me away? That really hurt."

"You don't understand, Lydia. When my father died, had I stayed with my grandparents, they would've forced me into the first marriage they could've arranged. It's what they tried to talk my father into from the minute I turned fifteen because they didn't agree with how he was raising me."

"To be honorable and hardworking? What's wrong with that?" All of this was so confusing, but rushing Sam might make him clam up again.

"Had I been born Samuel Jones Fuller, I'm sure they would've been proud of those traits, but that isn't my given name." Sam closed his eyes and took a deep breath. In a way he looked like he was expecting a blow that would mortally wound him. "I'm Samantha Jane Fuller, and that's not the life I wanted, so I ran. I've been running ever since, trying to find the kind of acceptance I got from my pa even if that meant being alone."

Lydia simply stood in place and stared at him, trying to see what Samantha had hidden in plain sight. Sam stood as well but seemed to know not to come anywhere near her. "Who knows?" Lydia asked, shaking her hands because she didn't know what to do with herself.

"Here?" Lydia nodded. "Lester and his brother were the only two until you." The anxiousness was back, and Sam's posture was ramrod straight. "All I ask is that you give me a day, so I can square things with Lester, and I'll be on my way." The cool facade was firmly in place, and Lydia wanted to scream. "Now it's best if you go."

The shock didn't have the opportunity to set in before Sam walked out. Lydia stood alone and let her tears fall. The man who'd tied her in knots for months, the one she'd fantasized about sharing a life and a family with, was gone, and all that was left was confusion.

She walked home, not in the mood to talk to anyone except Sam, but he'd disappeared somewhere, no doubt to plan his escape before she could divulge his secret. Or was it *her* secret? It was hard to think of Sam as anyone other than Sam, and she had a feeling that's how Sam felt about it as well. He was convincing because he *was* Sam Jones Fuller.

Lydia retreated to her window seat to review everything that had happened and examine her true feelings. Sam was the most aggravating individual she'd ever met no matter what gender Sam was. Sam was who he was, and she could accept that, but he had to accept he was muleheaded. A partner who did all her thinking for her wasn't anyone she was interested in, and that Sam could entertain the possibility that Lydia would run and tell everyone his secret was simply the most insulting thing in the world.

She wiped her face and marched back to the small house prepared to wait Sam out. The suitcase and bags by the door enraged her. Granted, Sam's revelation was shocking and probably a good thing not to have known right off—but now she did. She did, and they'd deal with it because the simple truth was it didn't matter. Whether it was Sam or Samantha, Lydia was in love, and there was no running from that.

"Put all that back where it goes and sit down," she ordered.

Sam stopped short after exiting the bathroom with another small bag. The luggage stayed, but Sam sat, looking both wary and hopeful.

"Here's what's going to happen. You're going to walk me to the store, and then you're going to talk to my father and get his blessing to marry me. The rest we'll deal with together."

"Lydia, think about what you're saying."

"No, you listen." She'd never yelled that loud in her life, but she'd learned a few things from watching Sam deal with Plank, and Sam was nothing if not a stubborn donkey. "You tell me you don't love me, and I'll leave. If I'm not the girl for you, then you can stay and lead whatever life you want here because I'll never tell a soul your secret. To me, though"—she took a step forward—"you're Sam, and I love you."

"Your mama will be the first one to tell you it'd be a sin." Sam actually smiled a little. "All that churchgoing makes me believe that's true."

"And I say denying the love I have for you is the real sin."

"Do you even like women that way?" Sam was consistently stubborn and dead wrong…again.

"Am I going to run off with the first girl who's nice to me, you mean?" That got her the first genuine laugh from Sam since she'd met him. "Maybe I do like women that way because you're the first person in the world who has piqued my interest at the first sight of you. The fact that I've had to do all the chasing up to now is plain ridiculous. It's your job to woo me, so now is your chance to wise up."

"You'd marry me?" Sam asked, not moving when Lydia laced her fingers behind his neck.

"If that's your idea of a proposal, then no. When you do ask, I expect you to have my father's permission and a ring. I'm willing to bend on a lot, but every girl has dreams, Sam Fuller, and I'm no exception." She smiled up at Sam, and any lingering doubt keeled over when Sam made the first move and kissed her. "Ready?" she asked, taking his hands.

Sam didn't let her go until they reached the store, and she sat with her mother and sisters while Sam followed her father to the small office in the back. Lydia hadn't expected it to take over an hour, but the door finally opened, and her father shook Sam's hand. Hopefully, that was a good sign.

"Miss Lydia," Sam said, holding his hat, "would you like to take a walk this evening when I get back from New Orleans?"

"I'd love to." She sighed when Sam took her hand and kissed it.

"Until then."

Chapter Twenty-five

I'll be goddamned." Wyatt reread the last two paragraphs, wondering if Gator and her family knew what rebels their forebears were. Knowing the most crucial part of why Lydia had written their story made her want to finish the other journals. The simplistic tale she started with had taken a definite turn into interesting, and it raised her respect for Lydia that much more. But what about their eleven children? Where had they all come from?

"They haven't shown up yet?" Hayley asked when Wyatt answered her phone.

It was a good thing they were on an even playing field when it came to interest. "I'm still waiting, which makes me glad the mob wasn't carrying pitchforks with their torches. With this kind of response time, I'd be skewered in the yard, burning on a pyre by now."

"Is it wrong to tell you to blow them off and get over here? If you're trying to protect my virtue, I can tell you these people will talk no matter what."

She looked up at Hayley's window and saw her standing in the soft light of her lamp. Their dinner was all the convincing she'd needed to know she wanted to spend time with this intelligent woman. "Let me call back again and tell them the crowd's gone. They told me the first time I called back that they were already on their way and to be patient."

"You called the police twice?" Hayley sounded surprised.

"You aren't the only one anxious for me to get over there, baby. Tonight isn't going at all like I thought it would."

"What'd you think would happen?"

"It wasn't a plan so much as me being hopeful. I don't ever want to be presumptuous when it comes to stuff like this. It's disrespectful." She saw Hayley tap on the glass as she talked and guessed it was a way to bleed off restlessness. "I've been an idiot up to now for not coming over sooner, but I wasn't sure what kind of reception I'd get, given our first introduction of sorts."

"Honey," Hayley said, and Wyatt wanted to run out the door at the sexy way that word sounded coming out of Hayley's mouth. "The first time was an accident because I didn't think you could see what I was doing, but the other times were an enticement to get you over here. Our beginning might not fit what publishers call the meet-cute, but I doubt either of us minds how we started. Right?"

"It's where we end up." She enjoyed the way Hayley laughed. "Let me call off the cops even if it's by taping a note to the door, and I'll be right over."

"Good idea. Don't waste time with pajamas. You won't need any."

Hayley hung up and Wyatt was about to dial the NOPD's number when she saw flashing blue lights in the front of the house. "About damn time." Hayley was calling her back, but she silenced her phone wanting to go out and finish so they could get on with the rest of their night. She figured Hayley would understand she wasn't being rude, just efficient.

She opened the door to five police cars with their lights on and she was having trouble deciphering the situation until she noticed her porch. "What the hell?" The question was starting to get repetitive.

It was the last thing she remembered before everything went dark.

❖

Hayley videoed what was happening and then ran down her stairs to her front door when she saw the number of police cars speeding up the street. Joe wasn't answering her phone, so obviously she hadn't noticed Roberta Sue letting an older gentleman handcuff her to one of Joe's porch posts. If Joe opened the door unawares, this wasn't going to end well. She kept her video running and tried to keep it steady even though she was shaking.

"Answer the phone, dammit." Thank God she was still dressed as she ran out the door, but she was too late. The not exactly slim officer had hurdled Joe's fence, which was kind of amazing, then ran to Roberta Sue and hugged her. All that happened in a flash, but Joe opening the door only seemed to ratchet up the tension of the weird tableau. "Joe, wait," she yelled.

She didn't understand why Roberta Sue was wailing, so she quickened her move toward Joe when the officer reached for a weapon. Hayley lost her mind when he pointed it at Joe. "Wait," she yelled louder. She watched Joe, who was simply staring at the cop, clearly confused. "Wait!"

Joe went down like a felled tree and was flopping around the porch as the cop kept his finger on the trigger of his Taser.

"Stop it. What the hell are you doing?" The only one smiling through it all was Roberta Sue since it appeared she'd gotten everything she wanted. "Joe." Hayley put her phone down and knelt next to Joe to make sure she was still breathing. "Don't just sit there hugging Mrs. Walton—call an ambulance."

Joe was out cold, and for some reason the side of her face was covered in blood. Hayley pressed her scarf to the gash over Joe's right eye, her heart pounding like a drum in her chest.

"You might want to back off, lady, until we get a full assessment of what's going on." The guy kissed Roberta Sue's cheek and held her like it was something he did often.

"Yes," Roberta Sue said. "Just because you're carrying on with her isn't going to save her from what she did."

"Maybe you should've done that important assessment before tasing her. And what exactly did she do?" Hayley kept her hand on Joe's chest and picked up her phone, since it was clear the cop wasn't about to call anyone. She quickly gave the address and details to the dispatcher while still listening to the shit Roberta Sue was piling onto the mound.

"She waited for my friends to leave and handcuffed me out here in the cold. I'm sure she was getting her snake ready to finish me off." It was amazing how quickly Roberta Sue conjured up tears.

Broadway actors could learn a few things from her. "I already feel chilled and sick."

Hayley held up her phone. "Are you sure that's the story you want to go with? Do you need me to replay the video to refresh your feeble mind, Roberta?" The question seemed to worry the officer more than Roberta Sue.

"It's Roberta Sue, but *you* can call me Mrs. Walton." Roberta turned her head to the side as if she couldn't look at her.

"Then I'll call an ambulance, and once I know Joe's okay, I'll be calling news outlets." She leaned in and read *W. Walton* on the nameplate of the cop who'd shocked Joe. "A story about a grandson shocking the hell out of a law-abiding citizen on the order of his grandmother will get us on the *Today* show."

"Wait," the cop said. "What video?" He was staring at the still unconscious Joe.

"The one of your grandma and how she got her pal over there with the big sign about putt-putt golf to handcuff her to this post before you got here."

"Oh my God, I mean *oh my God*. You did this, didn't you? Oh my God." Officer Walton was now looking from Joe to Roberta Sue.

"So, Roberta, what's it going to take for you to admit the truth?" Another siren could be heard in the distance, releasing some of Hayley's worry. With any luck it was the ambulance she called for.

"It's Roberta Sue, I said."

"You're ninety years old. I'm dropping the cute middle name to save time after you tried to have my friend killed." She moved her hand to Joe's cheek. "Honey, open your eyes." That got her nothing.

"Oh my God," Officer Walton said again as one of his buddies walked up with a pad in his hands like he was about to open the investigation.

"Now, Wally, there's no harm done. All I was doing was trying to make a point. Our history must be protected at all costs. She got what she deserved when she planned to throw all our values out the window." Roberta Sue stood as if she had to run off to save another house from the evils of golf.

"No harm done? Don't you dare think about leaving once we

uncuff you. Grandma, did it occur to you when you called and said your life was in danger that I'd lose my job when we found out you lied? I'm not only going to lose my job but everything else when this woman sues me for all my worldly possessions including my underwear. Shit, my mother was right about you."

"Your mother could learn some—" Roberta Sue started.

"Grandma, focus and give me the keys to these things. One of you guys clear the way for the ambulance," he said to the other police officers. "Do you know her name?" he asked Hayley.

"It's Joe." It was then that she realized they'd never exchanged last names. "She's new to town, so I'm not sure who to call." She caressed Joe's cheek, wanting her to wake up so she could ask all the questions she wanted answers to. "She'll be okay, right? You really zapped her with that thing."

"She will be, I promise. Right after she gets over the feeling of being hit by a truck that then backs up and hits you again, like a few dozen times." He had the decency to look chagrined.

The scarf was now covered in blood, and all Joe had done was moan. "Remember we have a date," she whispered into Joe's ear. "I know you like to watch me, but tonight it's your turn."

"Hey, are you two really good friends, by any chance? And I'm Wally, by the way. Wally Walton." He'd lost his attitude now that there was a possibility of a lawsuit in the mix. "Could you put in a good word for me? All this"—he waved his hands around—"it was a mistake. Surely, she'll see that and cut me some slack. Everyone's got a grandmother they love and would do anything for."

"Joe's fairly new around here, like I said, but from what I've seen of her, she's reasonable. I'm sure she's willing to listen, but being shot with a Taser the moment she opened her door might be a lot to ask her to get over. How did this happen?" She pointed to the cut on Joe's face. "Everything happened so fast I didn't get a chance to see. You didn't club her, did you?"

"She hit my protest sign on the way down," Roberta Sue said. "Maybe now she'll see we're serious about not having her get her way."

The ambulance arrived, and she had to move to allow them to get to Joe. She still hadn't come to. "And I'm sure Joe will explain that to a judge when she sues you and your little helper." She pointed to the old guy who'd handcuffed Roberta Sue to the porch. "I'm also sure DJ and his guys will be happy to testify that Joe talked to all of you, and everyone else left peacefully. What you did was unconscionable."

"We need to go," the male EMT said after they loaded Joe on the stretcher. The female EMT and Wally shared a strange look, and Hayley wanted to demand to know what it was about but didn't want to waste any more time.

"I want to go with her." Hayley wasn't about to abandon Joe, especially since the only people she'd seen at Joe's house were DJ and his guys. No one wanted to be hurt and alone.

"That's against regulations since you're not related and she's not a minor," the female EMT said. "We're headed to University Medical if you want to follow us."

"Are you sure there isn't anyone we can call?" Wally asked.

"Officer, I'm it. If you want, call DJ and ask him. He's the one aside from me who's spent the most time with her." She followed the stretcher to the ambulance, holding Joe's hand. "Hang in there, baby, I'll be right there."

"We're going to have to take your phone for our report," Wally said.

She looked at him incredulously. "Try it and I'll do everything in my power to make sure you and your grandma never forget this night. I watch the news, so I'm not an idiot." She started to walk away, hoping none of these guys tried to get her phone by Taser. "If you need to ask me anything or need to see my phone, I'll be at University."

"Were you talking about the plumber or the car guy?" one of the officers asked.

"Plumber." That was all the information she'd stop to give. She had to get to Joe and forget how bizarrely the night was going. This kind of weird drama was totally new to her, and she had to take a breath to get her heart to stop racing. She grabbed her purse and keys, taking a moment to email herself the video and texted it to Lucy as well. It didn't surprise her when Lucy called a few minutes later.

"What the actual fuck?" Lucy said loudly. "What happened, and is that the nutjob Roberta?"

"It's Roberta Sue. Don't ever forget it, and I can't talk right now. I'm on my way to University Medical." Her hands were shaking again, but this time it wasn't from being nervous about calling Joe, it was from rage.

"Fuck Roberta, and fuck you going to University alone. Come by and pick me up. I'll be dressed by the time you get here." The way she was breathing made it clear she was already in motion.

"You do realize there isn't a rule about having to use the word *fuck* prominently in every sentence." She was glad Lucy volunteered to go with her, and she quickly detoured slightly. There was no reason to think Joe wouldn't be fine, but she hated spending time in hospitals.

"And you need to leave your editing hat at the office. Besides, you know you'd rather be fucking than driving to the hospital hoping the electric shock didn't wipe Joe's memory of you. That'd be fucking tragic." Hayley pulled up and Lucy jumped in the car.

Fuck. She hadn't thought of that, but that had to be an urban myth. There was no way she wanted to go back to touching herself in windows to entice Joe to come over and play. "I feel horrible this happened to her."

"Just get her naked, put your mouth on her, and she'll get over it."

She laughed, glad Lucy knew how to cheer her up. "Let's hope I get the chance. She's the real deal."

CHAPTER TWENTY-SIX

Wyatt had once gone for a ride in the trunk of a car so she could more accurately describe what her victims were going through. Basically, that's how she felt right now. In this case, though, it made no sense. There was a possibility she'd been kidnapped, but why the fuck would anyone do that? If that was the case, they'd have to torture her to get any money out of her.

The book *Misery* came to mind, but every character she'd killed in every gruesome way possible had it coming, every last one of them. Who cheered for some of the assholes the dark side of her mind conjured up? She wanted to think about it, or at least open her eyes, but she had the worst headache of her life. Once they stopped, she'd worry about whatever this was.

All she could figure out without spraining her brain was that she was strapped down, so moving was impossible, and the vehicle seemed to be aiming for every pothole. That ruled out her dreaming this from the comfort of her hideous mattress, and she also couldn't blame it on a drug-induced hallucination. Her only vices were beer and the occasional overindulgence in vodka, and all that caused was hearing her mother's disapproval in her head.

"Yeah, yeah," her mother said. "You might want to open your eyes and start to unravel your own mystery. I promise this will be hilarious in ten years."

Wyatt took a deep breath and listened to her mother.

"There she is, thank God."

Wyatt turned her head toward the sound of the overly cheery

voice and saw a bleached blonde with her hands pressed together. She was wearing a uniform and smiling like a deranged person. "We were getting a little worried about you. You've been napping for a while."

"Napping? What exactly is happening, and where are you taking me?"

"We're on our way to the best emergency room in the city." The woman smiled and blinked way too much to be considered normal human behavior. FBI profilers had told her it was a sign someone was lying. Maybe she was being kidnapped, and this was their shtick. "You had a teeny-weeny accident."

"I was driving?" She had no recollection of that. None at all.

"Not exactly, dear." The woman leaned in, and between the potholes and the blinking Wyatt was getting carsick. Combine that with the headache, and she was totally miserable.

"What does that mean?"

"It's really funny, actually. My husband zapped you with his Taser numerous times."

The woman's explanation made it seem so matter-of-fact that Wyatt joined her captor in rapid blinking. Perhaps the exercise would clear some of the cobwebs and put the pieces of how she'd ended up strapped to the back of this hell ride together. *Note to self,* she thought, having to shut her eyes again, *rapid eye movement in a moving vehicle while tied down with no open windows will induce nausea.* She couldn't be positive, but she thought vomiting while on her back could be hazardous to her health. No matter what, she didn't want to test that theory.

"Can you run that last bit by me again." She started breathing through her nose and picked a spot on the ceiling to stare at like it was her job. "Who's your husband?"

"Sergeant Wally Walton," she said with the kind of pride you noticed because it was usually reserved for your kids learning to use the potty. "In his defense, he thought you'd handcuffed his grandmother to your porch to die like some cultures do with their old people. You really can't blame Wally for thinking you were dangerous."

"Uh-huh." She had to close her eyes, take deep breaths, and raise her hand as high as she could get it in the strap to get the woman to stop talking. Her chest hurt like hell, but so did the rest of her body. If knowing what it would feel like to have a nonlethal current of electricity run through her body had ever made it to her bucket list, she was putting a check mark next to it. She was also adding a highlighted note and starring it to remind her never to do it again. "Did he press the trigger until I passed out?"

"Actually, you dropped like a sack of sweet potatoes and cracked your head on Roberta Sue's protest sign. She'd leaned it against the pole she'd handcuffed herself to. I'm sure once you get out of the hospital, we'll all come over for drinks and laugh and laugh about all this." The woman patted Wyatt's chest like she was a stray puppy and gave her an example of the laughing. "We just have to make sure you don't have a concussion first. You can't ever mix alcohol with head injuries. It's a bad combination."

"I'm pretty sure that's not going to happen in this lifetime, but then my sense of humor got frazzled with the rest of me." She kept her eyes closed and made shushing noises to keep Mrs. Dumbass from adding anything else.

The ambulance ride ended with a rush into the emergency room that made Wyatt think she was in an episode of *Grey's Anatomy*, and a doctor who reminded her of Methuselah was waiting in the bay they rolled her into. The fact that any medical professional was waiting to see her came close to sending her into shock. Any trip to the emergency room in New York was a test of sanity and patience, it took so long to be treated.

"Let's see here, little lady."

If she had to guess, this doctor was at Abraham Lincoln's inauguration, and his thick glasses would set her clothes on fire if the overhead lights shined through them. The one good thing was the nurses released her from the straps and moved her to a hospital bed.

"I think that's going to need stitches." That took him thirty minutes to say. If she was wearing a watch, she could've confirmed it. "First, let's get pictures of that cute head."

"Um..." She was trying to find a way to ask for someone else with less experience, in other words, someone under a hundred and forty, when the door crashed open, making the pain in her eyebrow spring to life like someone had tased her again.

"My God, Wyatt." Blanche came in with her hands on her head, scaring the hell out of her with the theatrics. The old doctor clutched his chest and fell on her. There was a real chance the mushrooms that had come with her dinner had been of the magic variety. The menu should have mentioned that.

"What exactly are you doing here? How'd you find me?"

A gorgeous nurse came in with the supplies to start an IV, which would be difficult with her old man blanket. Her doctor was like a turtle on its back trying to right itself.

"I came for you, of course. I'm so glad I followed my instincts. Look at you." Blanche pressed her hands together, trying—Wyatt guessed—to appear caring. She'd have better luck with her make-believe python. "You're a mess."

"Hold that thought, sweetie," the doctor said after the nurse got him back on his feet. "Your girlfriend needs some tests."

"No way, Grandpa," Blanche said with enough contempt to insult everyone in a five-mile radius. "I'm taking her back to New York."

"You heard the man, Blanche. Cut it with the attitude, and go to the waiting room. If that wasn't clear enough for you, get out. And don't stick around."

Blanche sent her a death glare and stomped from the room. "I'll be in the waiting room."

Everyone crowded in the small room had gotten deathly quiet during their exchange, which was great for her headache. All she wanted was to do whatever was needed so she could go home. With any luck she could get Hayley to come over and sit quietly until she recovered enough to do all the things on her list. "Go ahead, Doc, so I can take an aspirin and head out of here."

The pretty nurse wheeled her out for a scan of her head. Once she was back in her cubicle, Dr. Methuselah gave her a thorough exam, declaring she did in fact have a concussion, so she'd have to spend the night. Her EKG was normal, so the Taser hadn't messed with her heart, which was a bonus. He also put in stitches, moving so slowly she fell asleep convinced she'd be completely healed when she woke up because so much time had gone by. When he was done, the nurse woke her and asked who the president was, along with a list of other questions. She was happy to say it was Biden, thank God for that, and accepted a mirror from the nurse. "Wow." The wound was much larger than she expected. Maybe the cool scar would help her book sales. That would give new meaning to suffering for your art.

They moved her to a private room for the night, so they could wake her regularly for checks to make sure Roberta Sue and her criminal family hadn't scrambled her brain. The doctor had given her something slightly better than aspirin but not strong enough to knock her out. Once alone, she went back to her hobby of staring at the ceiling. The stillness and quiet helped control her headache when she thought about the day and all the crazy shit it had given her in spades...whatever the hell that meant. Was Hayley still waiting for her to come over? Or had she seen the clusterfuck situation and gone to bed? Wyatt couldn't help but wish she was there beside her, holding her hand.

"Son of a bitch," she said softly.

"Are you okay?" The nurse came in for her slate of questions. "Now that you remember how to curse, do we need to discuss who the mayor is?"

"Actually, is there an attractive woman in the waiting room making everyone miserable?"

"She's at the nurses' station complaining. The waiting room would be an improvement. I'm sorry if she's a friend of yours, but her voice is like nails on a chalkboard." The woman took her temperature and blood pressure before agreeing to go get Blanche.

"Hello, love," Blanche said, moving to hold her hand. "How are you feeling?"

"Where did you grow up?" She brought the head of her bed up a little, so she could look Blanche in the eye. It made her head pound, but she wanted to be able to see Blanche's face. What she was witnessing was nervousness. "Well?"

"Mostly in New York."

"Then not completely in New York." She brought her head up a little more. "Where was the other *mostly* location?"

"It was here in the city." Blanche wasn't running off at the mouth, which meant something was wrong.

"Really?" She pulled her hand out of Blanche's grip. "We've known each other for years, and you've never mentioned that. I find it curious, considering there is nothing you like more in the world than the sound of your own voice."

"That's because it's always about you, Wyatt. You've never been interested in me beyond what I can get and do for you." Blanche's voice rose, and the sharp tone was back. Blanche's tongue could cut through rawhide.

"What you do for me is negotiate writing contracts. You do that because it's your fucking job, so take it down like a hundred notches and sit." She pointed to the only chair in the room and waited. "They tell me it's important to stay awake, so let's hear it. Think of your answers as the most important of your life. In case you're not following—start talking."

"Funny thing." Blanche smiled and lifted her hand to cover her mouth when she laughed. "The female EMT told me where they picked you up. It's so interesting you bought in the Marigny."

"Uh-huh—go on and let me in on the joke."

"Well, you've been here long enough to know this isn't New York, not by a long shot. I ran from this place the first chance I got before I died of boredom. It took a lot of hard work to get to the big leagues, but I got us there."

So she had connections to the city. "How are you able to hold your head up most days with that enormous ego inside it?" She took a deep breath and went back to staring at the ceiling. "Any other time I'd try to work through the meandering trail you like to draw, but my head hurts, and I'm trying to pull the pieces together as fast as I can. I don't understand why you don't like the Marigny, because I do. Its weirdness has helped me heal, and I've met someone. She's incredibly special, and I want to explore that. And now that you understand I'm not available, let's move on. Tell me, what does your family do here in New Orleans? That is, if you have any left."

"Why is that important?" Blanche jumped up and paced, wringing her hands.

Wyatt watched for a moment, thinking that only happened in period romances. "Because I'm a mystery writer, Blanche. You're a complete mystery to *me*, and I want to know all there is to know about you and your family." She lifted her hand when Blanche took a breath to say something. "Let me be clear. If you want to continue our working relationship, you're going to tell me everything I want to know."

"My father left when I was three, so my mom worked in the family grocery to support us, still does. She's the day manager. At night, when I was old enough, I worked for my aunt in the family diner." Blanche spoke so fast Wyatt had to concentrate on what she was saying.

"Wait," she said, gripping the sheet to keep her from strangling Blanche with it. "Wait, Maybelle's your aunt, isn't she?" She laughed at the absurdity. "She is, isn't she?"

"Yes. Magnolia was my grandmother, and all the businesses are named after her." She lifted her chin, as though in defiance.

"Let me get this straight." She cut Blanche off from saying another word. "Maybelle, the person ultimately responsible for bringing Roberta Sue Walton the terrorist to my door, is your aunt. Is that what you're telling me?" It was hysterically ironic that she'd bought her house a few blocks from Blanche's living LoJack. There'd been no escaping Blanche from the first day she stepped into the diner. "So why all the emails? You lied about not knowing where I was. Why?"

"I wanted to give you the chance to come to the right choice on your own. You belong to me, and I explained that to Aunt Maybelle. She told me all about the stranger who'd come into the diner, and when she described her, I knew it was you even though you gave her a false name. All I asked her to do was keep an eye on you and gently push you into coming home." Blanche sat back down like she didn't know what to do with herself.

Wyatt stared at her, trying to figure out how someone so deluded managed to get through life. "Belong to you? How the hell have you come to that conclusion? And things didn't quite go that way—gently, I mean. The good thing is you and your aunt will have plenty of time to go over all your missteps."

"What do you mean?" Blanche gripped the side of the bed.

"Our current contract expires at the end of this month, and even if my parents could rise from the grave and beg me to sign another one with you, it won't happen. That means you can leave. This is good-bye."

"Wyatt, you can't do that."

"Blanche, I'm in the hospital with a concussion and stitches because you sicced your psychotic relative on me. There's really no coming back from that. Besides, you've been a better dealmaker for the publishing house than for me. Call them and beg for a job." She wished she could yell because she wanted to, and the situation called for it. "I need someone I can trust, who's more interested in me and not what's in it for them. I'm tired of your theatrics and frankly stalkerish behavior. I want you out of my life."

"Wyatt, that's insulting. Think about what you're saying because there's no going back from this."

"We finally agree on something. You're right, there isn't, and you're done. Get out." She brought her head back down and closed her eyes. Things could only get better from here. Little Orphan Annie had to be right. Tomorrow would be better.

CHAPTER TWENTY-SEVEN

Hayley and Lucy were getting nowhere with the receptionist, whose only answer was that she had no answers for them. Hayley saw the EMT who'd brought Joe in and moved to intercept her.

"Hey," she said, and the woman smiled. "Where's Joe? Before you tell me you can't say anything because of privacy, think about this. If you want me to put in a good word about Wally tasing someone unarmed, start talking."

"They ran some tests and said she's got a concussion, so she's not going anywhere tonight. She also got stitches before they brought her up to her room." The woman spoke softly since she was throwing HIPAA and all the privacy laws under the bus. "You two can take off if you want—her wife is up there with her. She's one of those homosexuals."

"Her wife?" Hayley dropped back into her seat, her stomach plummeting. "Are you sure?"

"It's not something you hear every day, so I'm positive. Do you want me to sneak you up there?"

"Hell yes," Lucy said. From Lucy's expression it was a good thing Joe was already in the hospital since she'd need more stitches and tests for her new concussion. "Where is she?"

"Who, Joe or her wife?"

The elevator opened and the woman who stepped out was too made-up. That much makeup was never attractive on anyone. Everything about her, from the shoes to the purse, was put together and expensive. For some reason she was staring at them, and it wasn't a happy expression.

"That's her," the EMT said. "Hey, find her?"

"I did, and I'll be taking her back to New York when she's cleared for travel. She does this every so often—running off and pretending she doesn't have a family, I mean. Lucky for her I'm the forgiving type." The woman laughed and took her phone out of the big purse as if that was the only conversation she could waste on the little people. "Thanks for all your help." She patted the EMT's arm like she had rabies and couldn't get any closer, then gave them one of those finger-waggling waves.

Hayley watched her sashay away and wanted to knock her flat off her too high heels, but instead she turned and fled to the parking lot.

"Why can't either of us find a butch who's not an asshole?" Lucy said when she ran to catch up with her.

"Because they're either taken or stupid. In this case a little of both because Joe's brain is wired to be an asshole when it comes to women. I've never met a woman who's such a bastard and pretended so convincingly that she's not." She walked to her car and fought the urge to call Pippa Potts and list her house. "Shit, I'm such an idiot."

"Hey." Lucy put her arms around her and let her cry. "It was the ass, and we both fell for it. Once you married her, I was praying you would both become swingers. It would have given me a shot at getting her into bed."

"Shut up, and she's all yours." She wiped her face and unlocked the car.

"Are you kidding? Did you happen to see who she picked? That's an awful human being right there, even if I would've totally stolen her purse. That dress, though, was something I wouldn't even buy at the Salvation Army's thrift store in the dollar section."

"And they have kids." She beat the steering wheel a few times before starting the car. "That's the lowest form of worm there is, and I can't wait to hear my mother tell me *I told you so.* She's no killer or thief, but asshole is all her."

"There's no need to feed Eliot Ness any information. That would be like me telling my mother I found a doctor who's madly in love with me and wants her mother-in-law to live with us." Lucy held her hand and leaned over to kiss her cheek. "Get driving, and we'll have a platonic sleepover. There's not much night left, but tomorrow morning we'll prank-call Roberta Sue and egg the Fuller house to make ourselves feel better."

They got back to her house, and she fell into bed without changing. She made a to-do list before falling asleep. The first item on it was to stop being so naive, and the second was to get some blinds. Letting anyone into her life via her windows was over.

Her alarm went off three hours later, and if she'd had a gun, she would've shot it. Lucy seemed oblivious to her alarm, so she left her in bed to take a shower.

When she dressed, she noticed the guys next door had started for the day, but there was no Joe or DJ. "Forget about that asshole." She left Lucy a note and left early, keeping her head down so she didn't have to talk to anyone. Of course Marlo was already there and ready to start a lengthy conversation. Nothing happened in the neighborhood Marlo didn't know about.

"You want to explain what in the world happened? Tippy and I got up early and craved some pancakes. Magnolia's was packed even for that time of the morning, and there was plenty of gossip."

"I'll just bet." She reached for her phone when it buzzed, expecting her mother, because why not. It was that kind of day, and it was only the beginning. But the screen said *Joe*. This would be the perfect way to finish this, since she had no desire to see Joe again. Blinds and a tall fence would take care of the rest.

"Hayley?" Joe's deep voice still had the same effect on her.

"Yes? What can I do for you?" She clipped the words, trying to ignore Marlo's raised eyebrow.

"I want to apologize for last night." Joe sounded drained, but she wasn't falling for that. She'd given up naivety last night.

"Is that all you're apologizing for? I'd think forgetting to mention your wife and children should be added to that list. Then end with I'm sorry for playing me for an idiot."

"Hayley, please," Joe said, her voice staying soft and flat. "What exactly are you talking about? What wife and kids?"

"Please. Playing stupid now isn't going to work, so do me a favor and stay the hell away from me."

"I don't know what you mean, but you're wrong. I'm not married, and I sure as hell don't have any kids."

She laughed. "Do you remember me asking you not to lie to me? It's all I asked of you. Just that one thing, goddamn it."

"And I didn't." Joe's tone never changed.

"Honey, I met your charming other half at the hospital. Run on back home so you both can have a good laugh about me." She doubted Joe heard that last part because the line went dead. It should've been her who hung up in a snit. Why did people have to be so horrible?

"You want to tell me what that was about?" Marlo asked.

Maybe the story would get less humiliating the more she told it. She went through what had happened and the date she'd gone on with Joe. "After they rushed her to the hospital, Lucy and I waited and met her *wife*, who told us about their family. I'm such a moron."

Marlo contemplatively tapped her cigarette on the table. "The thing about Maybelle and all the people in that diner is they're all about the gossip. They serve more of it than pancakes."

"What does that have to do with anything?" She loved Marlo, but her point was something she had a hard time finding sometimes. "I just want to get some work done, and I apologize, but I don't want to talk anymore."

"I understand that, but you're going to listen. I heard from Gwen this morning because she knew I was close to you. Getting to the truth has everything to do with tipping the right person. Gwen loves Joe, and she listens to that gossip with an eye to truth instead of bile. Turns out the *wife* you met is Maybelle's niece, and she wants a relationship with Joe but doesn't have one. You can't force someone to love you, though, and Joe doesn't give that woman the time of day. Blanche—that's the niece—came down here in search of Joe and got the scoop on you and Joe from Maybelle, and she happened to be here when everything went down at Joe's place. Joe's no more married than you are, and Blanche managed to take advantage of the situation."

Hayley thought of the woman's declaration in the hospital. She'd certainly seemed to believe herself. "That can't be right. Are you sure?"

"Hayley." Marlo stood like she was leaving now that Hayley

wanted her to stay. "I've never met Joe, but she didn't lie to you. The woman you met played you, not Joe, and you believed her instead of your instincts. Try not to do that. It'll make you miserable."

"Oh Jesus," she said. Way to go out of her way to be a bitch just when Joe really needed her. "Could you excuse me a minute?"

"Sure, and I doubt she's going to answer the phone after your charm offensive, so get going. You need a Tippy in your life. I highly recommend it, and it sounds like you have one out there waiting for you." Marlo wandered out, shaking her head and muttering about stubborn women.

"Please pick up." She dialed Joe back, but Marlo was right. The phone rang until the message that the mailbox wasn't set up came on. "Of all times to be bitchy and race toward assumptions." She grabbed her purse and headed out, only to find their new author waiting outside. "Hey, did I forget a meeting?"

"I was headed to my favorite writing spot and had a few questions for you, but only if you have time." She smiled and pointed at Hayley's hand with the keys in it. "Are you late for something?"

The problem with being a responsible adult was being a responsible adult. This woman was important to their bottom line, and Joe was still an unknown. Gambling wasn't in her nature. From the time she was little, she'd made plans to get and exceed the goals she set for herself.

Being here with Marlo, working for her, was part of a plan, as was building the company to something bigger than when she'd joined it. It was the best way of saying *Hey, look what I did.* She'd need that if she was going to lead a team in New York. Meeting with this woman was part of the plan, and doing so meant putting her personal life on hold—again. The thing about goals and dreams, though, was they were no good if you didn't have someone to share them with.

Pining for Joe had made her realize that perhaps she needed someone to get under her skin and be underfoot. Learning to live with someone was the first step in learning to love them. She had to stop idealizing what she wanted and accept that she'd found the one person who might aggravate her on occasion but who would also be there to hold her when the world became a scary place.

She smiled back and nodded. "Actually, I have an appointment, but Marlo's inside. I'm sure she'd be glad to discuss whatever's on your mind." Fuck responsibility for the day. She thought about what her father had told her about having fun. Joe was fun, made her happy, and was about to blow her ordered life all to hell if she couldn't get her to talk to her. "If not, just give me a call."

She ran to her car and took the fastest route home. The guys were all there working on Joe's house, making progress on the rest of the outside. They paused when she parked and ran past them to the open door. "Joe," she yelled from the foyer. There was noise coming from upstairs, so that's where she headed and ran into DJ with a wrench in his hand.

"Hey, Miss Hayley." He lifted the wrench to the side of his head and saluted her with it. "Come for a tour?"

"I was looking for Joe. Her truck's outside, so where is she?" She started walking, glancing in each room as she went. "Joe!"

"I picked her up at the hospital this morning, but she had a doctor's appointment at the clinic, so she's not here." He slammed into her when she stopped short.

"You let her go alone?" She remembered how Joe sounded that morning.

"We all offered to take her." DJ sounded wounded. "Joe's good people and our friend. She was tired because of the concussion and all, so she took a cab."

"What clinic?" All the anger she felt that morning was giving way to the type of anxiety that made her want to peel her skin off. How could she have gotten this so wrong? She'd found everything she'd ever wanted, and she'd wadded it up and tossed it away.

"I'm not sure. She gave me a key and said she might take a few days off because of the noise. Do you need her number?"

"No, I have it, thanks. Would you tell her to call me if you hear from her?" Crying wasn't something she did often, but her tears fell to release the pressure. DJ appeared at a loss as to what to do, so he handed her his handkerchief and patted her shoulder in the most patronizing way possible.

"She'll be okay, and I'm sure she'll call when she's done. Me and the guys know she's really sweet on you, so it won't take long before she does."

"What makes you say that?"

"She called me for Daisy's number to send you flowers, and she's fixing this place so she can have you over. I guess it's for her comfort too, but she started on your side, and that should tell you something, since it would have made more sense to start on the other side. You want me to walk you home?" DJ was a little strange, but he was a nice guy.

"Thanks, DJ." She kissed his cheek and shook her head. "Hey," she said as she walked back to the stairs, "did she take anything?"

"She packed all the journals we found in the walls. You know how those doctors' offices are. She probably wanted something to read. That was it, though, so I'm sure she'll be back."

"I'm sure she will." Somehow, though, she couldn't help but feel the sunshine Joe had brought into her life beginning to fade.

❖

She'd been completely wrong about Joe coming back. It'd been an entire month of unanswered calls and ignored texts. She'd even sent a pleading email to the address Joe used for the sexy story submissions, but there'd been no reply. Joe hadn't come back, but the work had continued. The Fuller house had been completely restored outside and painted a light gray with white and black accents, which, according to JD the painter, was the original combination.

DJ had taken her on a couple of tours as the bathrooms were finished. They were now ripping out the kitchen and tearing down the old gazebo at the back of the yard. Joe was gone, but she communicated with DJ to keep the project going. That meant Joe's phone worked—she just didn't want to talk to her.

There were mistakes like forgetting to pay a utility bill, and then there were mistakes like telling the one woman who'd made her burn in the best possible way to fuck off. One took a check and an apology, the other took oodles of time and self-recrimination. A month wasn't long enough to get over the self-inflicted wounds. She was waiting for Lucy to arrive as she sat outside and watched the workman laying new sod. Her phone rang.

"Hey, Mom." Her mother called more often and had dropped

her quest to investigate Joe. Thankfully, she'd accepted Hayley's explanation and had avoided the lecture about what could happen if you jumped to conclusions.

"Hey, I saw on the national news that your weather is beautiful. Are you doing anything today?" That was her mom's way of dropping a hint and also suggested that her father's love of The Weather Channel was starting to rub off.

"Lucy's coming over, so we can go to lunch. How are you guys?" She always answered the phone but talking to anyone wasn't high on her priority list these days. Her mom gave her a rundown of her dad's activities that now included a home brewery where he was trying different blends of hops so he could decide what to plant.

She eyed George as he headed up the walk to her porch. "I'll call you later, Mom—George is here." Seeing him reminded her that she needed to take lessons in meditation, so she could zone out when he started talking.

"What in the world?" The truck that rolled by made her forget George.

It wasn't every day that you saw a large woman in pasties and a thong hanging on to a pole. The lifelike statue that looked like something usually found on Mardi Gras floats was strapped down on its back as a truck stopped in front of Joe's place. "What the hell is that?"

"That's something, huh?" George sat next to her and pointed next door where all Joe's buddies were cheering and high-fiving each other. "Wally told me he agreed to six months of meter maid duty, and his grandmother had to agree to a single golf hole. It'll be the only putt-putt hole going in, and it was the only way both the Waltons didn't end up homeless from the lawsuit their attorney assured them they were going to lose thanks to the video you took." George sighed. "That thing should pick up the traffic on our street."

"You have to admit, it's pretty funny." The thing was probably twelve feet tall, and it was already drawing a crowd.

"Yeah, DJ and the guys have been pretty excited about it, but they don't have to live here. It'll bring down property values, mark my word."

DJ and his crew were taking pictures of themselves in front of the thing once the woman was upright. "I can't be sure, but I doubt

Joe will keep it up forever. This is more of a warning not to trespass or tase her again. She's not someone you can bully. That she didn't have Wally fired and Roberta arrested was generous."

"Yeah, that's what Wally said even if he's having to bag groceries at the Magnolia Market after writing tickets all day."

Lucy joined them on the porch and laughed for ten minutes straight. It took a while before she noticed that Joe's new lawn ornament bore an uncanny resemblance to Maybelle, albeit with a much better body. It was proof Joe wasn't someone you wanted to take on, but instead of making her laugh, she started crying again.

"It's going to be fine. Fabio's grandmother told me to pass along that it won't be long now. It's in the tarot cards, and she also said not to forget to throw out some wishes." Lucy held her and let her cry.

If only that were true. She couldn't walk this one back, and it had cost her.

CHAPTER TWENTY-EIGHT

Wyatt glanced out the window of her office in her brownstone and thought back to her last conversation with Hayley. The only other times she'd been that mad were at the gas company for killing her parents, and at Blanche for fucking her over. There was little she hated more than being called a liar, and Hayley had not only blatantly done so, but she'd refused to hear her out when she'd tried to explain. She'd been tased, concussed, stitched, and had to deal with Blanche, and then Hayley had turned against her in the blink of an eye. She hadn't needed to hear anything else.

She probably hadn't been thinking straight, but instead of going to the clinic on that last day, she'd gone to the airport and taken the first flight home, risking the brain cells that had survived. All she'd taken were Lydia's journals, which she'd reread a few times. It was good to know there were in fact happily ever afters in the world.

Right now, after one of the worst and loneliest months of her life, she put all that aside and got dressed for her meeting with Virgil Billingsley. He'd agreed to come to her, and she was sure he'd be pissed when she didn't give him anything he wanted. Their conversation forty minutes later went about how she expected. Virgil was a man who was trying very hard to keep his cool when she wouldn't bend to his will.

"Wyatt, we've been good to you, so I'm asking you to reconsider."

"Staying isn't fair to you because I'm still not in a place to rejoin the grind. I'm going to try new things, and they won't fit what you want from me." She held her hand out. "Believe me, I appreciate everything you've done for me, but it's time to try new things."

He took her hand and shrugged, looking satisfied with that.

"Good luck and don't lose my number."

She put out a press release a week later so her phone would stop ringing with people who wanted desperately to know her next move. That was a mistake—they just wanted even more information. The manuscript she'd started in New Orleans was done, so she relaxed with Lydia and Sam and her favorite part of their story.

July 1913

Sam asked Lydia the night before if she wanted to change her mind. He told her he'd completely understand if she did. As Lydia's mother pinned the veil on her head, she remembered Sam almost coming to attention when she finished dressing him down for asking such an asinine question. It'd been a month since Sam had spoken to her father, and she was ready to start their lives together. Maybe if they were under the same roof, she could teach Sam to not be so muleheaded.

"You have any questions?" her mother asked.

Lydia smiled and shook her head. She doubted her mother could help her with the rather different wedding night ahead of her. The truth was her mother would croak on the spot had she really had any questions. The thing was, though, from the day Sam had told her the truth, any fear she had of marriage disappeared. Unlike most of her friends who had married the year or so before, she was getting a true partner in Sam. This wasn't going to be a marriage where she'd have no voice, and knowing Sam's truth paved the way to commit to Sam completely.

"Your father shared something with me about Sam." The hesitancy of her mother's words moved her to make eye contact in the mirror they were both facing. "He said Sam couldn't father children, but he's a man."

"He is," she said, curious as to where this was leading.

"That might be true, about his fertility, but he's still going to have expectations of you. All men do, and if you have any questions after you return from New Orleans, I'll be happy to talk to you. And don't let him get away with any rough stuff."

If her prayers were answered, Sam *would* have expectations of her as often as they could get away with. "Thank you, Mama, but Sam loves me too much to hurt me." On that she was willing to bet her life. If Sam's kisses and touch when they were truly alone were any indication of how good Sam made her feel, they might not make it to New Orleans. "I'm sure we'll figure it out, and I'm also sure you'll be a grandmother. You keep telling me about faith, and mine is firm in that I'll make Sam a father."

"I hope so, sweetheart. Motherhood is a truly blessed calling."

Their church wasn't a big place, so some of their guests were standing along the wall when her father walked her down the aisle. She'd told Sam not to waste money on a new suit that would only hang in the closet most days, and she smiled seeing him in his dress uniform.

Yes, sir, Sam Fuller could make you weep he was so easy on the eye. She shivered when Sam held her hand and said his vows before placing a ring on her finger. The day he'd proposed with a diamond ring, she'd been the envy of her friends because she was the only woman who had one. This new simple band added to that one made her feel complete.

A few folks laughed when Sam announced they were leaving early but that had cut through the tension created by Sam inviting Lester and his family, including his brother, who'd come in for the wedding. They'd not said anything ugly, but Lydia could tell they were thinking it. Some of their so-called family friends had chalked it up to Sam not being a local, so he didn't know any better. Had he announced he thought of Lester and his family like his own, the wedding reception would've ended way before it did.

"You can get mad at me now, but I got you a wedding present without talking to you about it first. I promised you we'd discuss all the big decisions, but I also promised your father I'd take good care of you." Sam shifted the delivery truck and drove to a section of town she'd never visited before. "Lester and his friends helped me fix it up, so it's like new. Hope you like it."

The house where they stopped was as amazing as it was massive. "You bought us a house?"

"Sweetheart, you'd be miserable in that shack I'm in now, and this will give us more privacy." Sam went around and opened her door. "It'll also give you more places to hide when I chase you around the house." He scooped her up and carried her inside. "Welcome home, my love, and thank you for giving me one."

That's about all the talking they did until the morning as Sam touched her in ways you didn't talk about in polite company. Suffice to say, Lydia was waiting naked on the bed most afternoons when she finished at the stand in the French Market. Sam and Lester worked out a deal where Lester ran the farm, and one of Lester's sons drove the produce into town. It'd taken a year for Sam to buy more land to keep up with the demands from restaurants that wanted anything they grew, and their large stand in the French Market always had a long line of people waiting too.

One day, a young woman came by the house, asking them to take her newborn baby. Seemed some of the girls in the red-light district had caught a glimpse of them and had seen how Sam treated Lydia when they were shopping for furniture on Royal Street, and word had gotten around that the couple had a big home and no children. The young woman explained that she had enough to deal with to add a baby to the mix. Once her friends found out about Sam's accident, offering them her baby seemed like maybe it could be a good option. Lydia and Sam had been ecstatic and welcomed the new baby with open arms. And then a few more girls came to the house over the years with the same need, until Sam and Lydia decided the house couldn't accommodate more than eleven.

"You think they'll eventually stop screaming?" Sam asked as he walked from one end of their room to the other, bouncing two baby boys. They were their only twins in their bunch and required a lot of care.

"Eventually, until the grandkids start showing up, but I promise it'll be fun." Lydia watched Sam and wondered if her heart could actually burst from being this happy. She'd taken a chance and married the person she loved, and now she had everything she'd ever wanted.

Wyatt had read about the chaos of raising a family that large when they were all fairly close in age. The years Lydia and Sam lived happily together throughout the chaos gave her hope for her own future, especially when she considered her own parents. The possibility of seeing Lydia and Sam's ghosts when she went back to New Orleans wasn't something she feared any longer.

"And you shouldn't," her mother said.

Wyatt put the journal down and laughed. "Don't worry, I'm going back to test the waters. Maybe she'll eventually get over being mad about the things I've lied about."

"You're too good-looking to stay mad at. It's what saved your father from an earlier demise."

She went upstairs with the last journal she had yet to read because Lydia hadn't included it as part of her novelization of her and Sam's life together. The fact that it was the last one made her sad since she'd come to enjoy getting to know the Fullers through Lydia's words, and she'd put this one off as long as she could. To her the journals belonged in the house where they'd lived and loved.

The quick flip through the pages showed the last journal was almost completely empty. She looked up Lydia's obituary and was amazed she'd written a week before her death. The handwriting still held traces of the beautiful script she'd come to love, but these last few paragraphs were a lot shakier.

February 1997
To the one who finds what I left,

It's my hope that you read the story with the intent I had in writing it. My life with Sam isn't such a strange thing nowadays. Today I'm only an old woman, missing the other half of my soul. Sam Fuller gave me a more complete life than I would've had with any man. He was mine, and I loved him with all I am.

Our children were wonderful additions to our lives, and as adults they've built the business Sam started on his own with Lester's help. I look back now, and the years have come in a rush, piling up before I was ready. You can't know how much I miss that young woman who ran through the house with every intention of being caught. As we grew older, I ran much slower and enjoyed Sam wrapping me up in his arms and taking me to bed.

Aren't I a rebel for talking like that? If you're one of my great-great-grandkids reading this, take it as a lesson to never settle, to not let anyone tell you who it'll be who makes you happy. I read something recently as folks fight for gay rights that struck a chord with me. Love is love.

Sam was my love, and I know he's waiting for me somewhere nice because what we shared was in no way a sin. It won't be long now, so treat each other kindly and search for whatever or whoever will make life worthwhile. You never know where that might happen, but don't ignore that first glance that'll grab you and won't shake loose. I didn't, and I had a wonderful life because of it.

—Lydia Fuller

❖

Hayley sighed when she found George waiting on her porch when she got home from work. She really needed to get a sturdy lock for the gate. "Hello, George."

"Hey, hope you don't mind, but I was chasing this guy down." He was holding a rabbit who wanted off his lap. Even the animals knew enough to get away from him. "DJ helped me and said they're almost done over there."

"Oh yeah." She stopped listening when the FedEx truck stopped in front of her house. She wasn't expecting anything, but sometimes Lucy had stuff mailed to her house. Work had been crazy after Cheryl had resigned to dedicate herself to mission work before the last of her soul was lost forever, so she'd been too busy to even shop online.

"Ms. Hayley Fox?" the guy asked, lugging a big box.

"That's me."

"I need to see some ID. It's in the directions." He finally handed the package over after she'd signed for it.

The box seemed to be something for work, which meant she shouldn't be receiving it at home. If this was Fabio's idea of a joke, she was stealing his lunch in retaliation. "Excuse me, George." She was curious enough that she opened it right away, with George trying unsuccessfully not to look nosy.

It contained a manuscript, a letter, and a Jumpdrive. Whoever this person was didn't follow directions well. The submissions protocol on their website was very specific, which made her want to send this back saying all that. She'd at least read the letter first, though.

Hayley,

For the longest time all I knew about you was your name. It took a bit of digging and asking around to find out more than that. From what I can tell, you've brought plenty to your job and have given the work the time and attention it deserves. That kind of respect is what I'm looking for with the enclosed manuscript.

Let me know what you think, so please be honest. I think I need more of that in my life, and you're the editor to do it. At least I'd like you to be, but only if you're interested. If it's not too late, send me a contract for the two short stories as well, but I was way late in my submission, so I'll understand if they can't be included.

I'd also like to apologize for the one thing I did lie about, but that's more story than can be told in a letter. So please give me the opportunity to explain before you write me off completely. I miss you.

Joe

She scanned the letter again, happy for the first time in weeks. Receiving it was a bigger shock than Joe being a writer, although she certainly knew she had a talent for it, thanks to the sensual short stories. It explained all the time Joe spent at home. It had nothing to do with snakes and train robberies or the development of putt-putt courses. She answered her phone without taking her eyes off the letter. "Hello."

"Did you read the literary news of the day?" Marlo spent a few minutes a day trying to figure out what big author was doing what and how that might give them an opportunity for the publishing house.

"No, George is over. Hold on a minute." She dropped her phone and bag to unlock the door, not wanting to put the manuscript down. "Thanks, George." He put all her stuff inside before waving in acknowledgment and heading back to his place when she held up the phone. "I owe you one for getting him to leave early," she told Marlo.

"Wyatt Whitlock is leaving her publisher." Marlo continued as if Hayley had never said a word. "We need someone who knows her to try to set up a meeting." Marlo stopped to cough up a lung, then wheezed for a minute. "You were in New York—do you have any ideas?"

"Are you talking about the mystery writer? I read all her books in college whenever I had free time. She can give you chills with some of the villains she writes."

"She is to mystery what Nora Roberts is to romance. It'll be a major win for whoever signs her, though I hear she hasn't been writing since the death of her parents."

"It'll be a loss if she stops. She's excellent." She placed Joe's manuscript on the kitchen counter and placed her hand over the leather cover it was bound with. "She's a very private person from what I remember, always saying the work is what should matter." She flipped the cover open and stopped moving. "Holy crap."

"What's wrong?" Marlo sounded hypervigilant. "Is it that Walton woman again? The stripper statue isn't that bad. People will be sad if it comes down."

"I got a manuscript delivered to the house today."

"Who the hell is mailing you stuff at home, and how'd they get your address?"

"Wyatt Whitlock." This was surreal. Butch—Joe—was really Wyatt Whitlock. That checked off the rest of her wish list. Not the fame or money, but the love of the written word. Lucy had been the only woman she'd met who loved books. Now she'd met another one who was perfect for her, and she'd told her to fuck off.

"Hayley," Marlo said loudly, "did you pass out or something?"

"Sorry, what?"

"How'd you come to get Whitlock's new book? And if you're kidding, I'm firing you and hiring Roberta Sue to picket your house."

"Joe is Wyatt Whitlock, which fits better than Joe, don't you think?" She realized she was talking to her phone. Marlo had hung up.

And Marlo was knocking on the door before she could get past Wyatt's title, *The Woman in the Window.*

Marlo read the letter and picked up Hayley's phone and shoved it in her hand. "Call her right now."

"I have called her, and she's not answering her phone. Believe me, I've tried numerous times." She caressed the book. "But obviously she'll be in touch with me soon, given what she said in the letter."

"Why oh why didn't you sleep with her?" Marlo said and laughed. "I'm kidding, before you sue me. Let's try to find out who her agent is. I don't want to wait until you two work out the personal shit. We can start the paperwork to lock this down. How about a round of miniature golf while we talk out the details?"

"I'll pass, and I think you have to have more than one hole to have a round of golf. Plus, George is on the prowl, and Belle isn't his favorite subject."

"Who's Belle?"

"DJ told me that's what Wyatt named the lady in the yard. Not a stretch if you imagine a younger Maybelle. Here"—she handed over the Jumpdrive—"you can't have the bound copy." She expected Marlo to run out, and she didn't disappoint. For the first time since Wyatt had left, she didn't feel lonely, so she took the manuscript and went up to her chair.

"Not a very imaginative title, honey."

She started reading and realized why the two short stories were familiar. She really had read all of Wyatt's books, and she had a distinctive voice. It was easy to get lost in the story, which really wasn't a mystery in the truest definition, but in her opinion it was the best book Wyatt had written so far.

The phone rang again a couple of hours later—Marlo—and she couldn't believe she had already finished. "I forgot to ask you one thing."

"What's that?" She stood and stretched, going down for a soft drink and to move her legs.

"The two short stories, fact or fiction?"

"I'd tell you, but why ruin all your rampant speculation with the truth." She laughed when Marlo made a rude noise before hanging up. The lights were on next door, and she stared at the house through her kitchen window. There were still plenty of people coming to take pictures of Belle, but like she'd told George, she doubted it'd be a permanent fixture.

The idea of hiring DJ's guys to finish her house was running through her head when she noticed the kitchen window across the way. Wyatt's back was to her, but she'd recognize that ass anywhere. She ducked when Wyatt turned around. It wasn't that she didn't want to see her, but not in sweats, not again.

She'd take a shower and then put something on that would give Wyatt no choice but to come over and pick up where they'd never started. There was no time like now to try new things. "Get ready for a welcome home you won't forget."

CHAPTER TWENTY-NINE

Wyatt moved the rest of her stuff in and finished setting up the office. DJ and his crew hadn't finished the kitchen, so they'd moved the coffeepot and microwave to the hallway, making it easy to smell the pot that was almost finished brewing. So far, she was happy with the work they had finished, and she'd moved into the main bedroom with the nice new bathroom, shower, and bed.

The clutter was also gone, taking the musty smell with it. Once she got her bearings, she was inviting Hayley over for a talk. She had some good news to celebrate. Gator had talked it over with her family, and they'd agreed to take a check for the journals if she made them a copy. It was sad—not all of them wanted to know Lydia and Sam's secrets, but Gator had been thrilled to hear what trailblazers her relatives had been. Gator's wife Patricia sounded pretty excited as well.

She was anxious to find out what Hayley thought of her new book since she was planning on making it into a new series set in the Fuller house. That was the only thing in the book taken from real life, but she figured her new main character would love solving crimes in the Big Easy.

The one person always on her mind, though, was Hayley. She'd never in her life considered herself a romantic, yet watching and sharing moments with Hayley without exchanging a word had soothed those parts of her that had been bleeding and sore for months. Her pain wasn't the first thing she thought of anymore whenever she had a moment of quiet.

Hayley was like a story that she'd started, and life had made her put it away. The thing about unfinished stories, though, was they had unlimited possibilities for an ending, none of which she had control over. So when it came to real life, maybe unfinished was the best kind of story. She'd always flown through her days without a plan when it came to her writing, but this was something completely different. Letting Hayley completely in was a chance she wanted to take, and the sense of anticipation made her hop the fence to save time.

"Thanks, guys," she said to the empty room. When she'd left home all those months ago, she'd thought she'd never find her footing, but the change of scenery, finding the journals, and meeting all the characters who stopped by the house on a daily basis had been the reboot she'd needed.

"See, you should listen to your mother, even in death." Her mom and dad were still talking to her, which had made the trip back interesting. She'd never gotten this much advice when they were alive. "And if you think you're going to live on coffee and cupcakes forever, that's not happening."

"It's been a long day, and I still have work to do, so don't give me shit about the coffee. I also don't know how to make cupcakes, so it'll be coffee and cookies."

"What you need to do is forget about the coffee and everything else and go upstairs. You'll like what you see."

"I agreed to come back, but I might have to work up to being social."

"Kid, don't make your mother call you an idiot this early," her father said.

"Okay already." She grabbed one of the books she'd bought at her favorite bookstore in the city before coming back. She'd have to find a new favorite if she was going to live here a majority of the time. The coffee came next, and she headed up to the chair she'd had shipped from her apartment.

It was dark outside, so she turned on the lamp and sat. Maybe it wasn't good for your health to get this hard this fast, but one glance out her window made her glad she was sitting down.

"Fuck me," she said as she placed her hands on the window frame and stared at Hayley, who was completely naked. "That's one way of signaling you're not mad that I've ignored you for weeks."

Hayley smiled, then spread her legs so she could touch herself in a way that made Wyatt glad she was alive and had the gift of sight. This was one seriously beautiful woman, and she wanted to open a bottle of champagne that they were neighbors again. She picked up her phone and punched her speed dial.

"I was thinking it's way past time to welcome you to the neighborhood," Hayley said when she answered. Thank God for hands-free. "But first I want to apologize for being such an idiot."

"And you think getting naked is going to make me forgive you?" She smiled to take any sting out of the comment and hoped Hayley could see her face clearly. "It might take more than that."

"I know what you're thinking right now." Hayley crossed her legs after she removed her hand and held her fingers up.

"What's that?" She gripped the chair arm hard enough that the leather creaked.

"Just how wet is she, and how forgiving can I be?" The need to get up and run next door was getting overwhelming, but she didn't want to rush this.

"I can be really forgiving, and you already know I'm friendly." She stood, and Hayley stayed in her seat. "Would you mind if I come over?"

"The door is unlocked, and you're about a month late. Why you're still standing there is a bigger mystery than the book you sent me."

Wyatt didn't bother with shoes or anything else as she ran down the stairs and locked up so she could head next door. There'd been nothing but writing and taking care of her responsibilities for weeks so she wouldn't have anything holding her back from her new life once she committed to this move.

"Finally," she said as she put her hand on the knob. It had to be a joke when her head snapped back from the blow to the side of her face. What the hell was with this place? She had a great sense of humor, but if this was someone's idea of a prank, it wasn't funny. The slap knocked her into the door more from surprise than pain, and she brought her arm up to block the next blow. Dealing with an angry George when she had plans for the rest of the night was not her idea of foreplay.

"She's not for you!" he said and swung again, missing this time.

She was about to hit back when the door opened, and she fell backward into Hayley's house. Thankfully, Hayley had put on a robe, which still showed plenty of cleavage when she leaned over her. "Are you all right?" She nodded at Hayley's question. "Hold that thought then," Hayley said as if reading her mind.

"George, if you step foot in my yard again, you're going to have to call your pals the Waltons to find out how best to navigate the legal system. Nod if you understand because if you open your mouth and say one word, I'm having you arrested." Hayley sounded serious, and George opened his mouth but seemed to consider what she'd said and nodded. "Good, get lost."

"What's with that guy?"

"Welcome home, baby. Eventually the neighbors will fall in love with you, but we don't have time to think about it right now."

She took a moment to appreciate Hayley's attire when she dropped the robe. The thong and push-up bra should be memorialized in poetry and were doing wonders to make her forget the pain at the back of her head from when it hit the door. At the moment all Wyatt could concentrate on was the swell of Hayley's breasts in the white lace bra, and she absolutely needed to touch all that skin. She thought she'd have preferred naked, but not so much.

"Do I need to take you to the emergency room?" Hayley leaned over her and smiled. "Hi."

"Hi," she said as she sat up and got on her feet. "I'm Wyatt." The part of her brain responsible for witty repartee was lost somewhere in the lustful haze Hayley's thong was creating. "I'm your new neighbor."

"Finally," Hayley said, taking a step toward her.

"Finally?" If she kept talking, then perhaps Hayley would come even closer.

"I've wanted you from that first day I saw you standing naked in the yard, and here you are."

"I would've been here sooner, but it was hell getting away from my wife and eleven kids. You know how it is." She arched her eyebrow, and Hayley's laugh went straight to her clit.

She'd always loved women—the sex, the building of desire, the first touch, the driving someone to crave her hands on them. Hayley was the first woman, though, who broke through all that control and had her on a hair trigger. She had to open and close her hands to keep from pouncing. *Pouncing no good*, the base Neanderthal part of her brain that went apeshit in situations like this screamed.

"Right now, I don't care if you really did have a dozen kids." Hayley stepped close enough to start unbuttoning her shirt. "You didn't come over here to leave me hanging again, did you?"

"I did not, but tell me something first." She smiled and wrapped her hand around Hayley's wrists, keeping them in place.

"What?" Hayley said pressing herself more firmly against her.

"You aren't hiding Wally and his Taser in the kitchen, are you?" Her question made Hayley laugh again and fall forward so she could bite her chest gently.

The move made Wyatt chew through her let's-be-polite-first leash, and she surprised Hayley when she picked her up and pressed her to the nearest wall. Hayley moaned and opened her mouth, inviting her in. The sound turned her on, and her memories of their ruined night seemed tame compared to how turned-on she was now.

Her clothes were constricting, but she couldn't tear herself away from Hayley's lips, so she put her hands on Hayley's ass to hold her up. The part of her that never really shut off made a mental note to include a long description of thongs in her next book. That kind of research would be fun. After all they were small, sexy, and gave you so much access to a woman's ass, they deserved their own chapter. Now wasn't the time to stop and take notes.

She squeezed, and Hayley moaned and bucked her hips as if trying to find relief. There was no need to touch her to know just how wet she was, so she broke the kiss and leaned back. She had to get another look at the bra Hayley was wearing. "Good God, you're beautiful."

"I'll take your word for it since your eyes aren't on my face," Hayley said and laughed again. "My eyes are up here." Hayley put her fingers under her chin and lifted her head.

She pressed Hayley harder to the wall and moved her hand under the pretty panties. They both exhaled loudly when she ran her finger along Hayley's sex. "Trust me, you have my complete attention."

"Shit," Hayley said.

"You're so wet," she said and felt like an idiot for stating the obvious.

"I read the stories you wrote for me, and I've been wet ever since," Hayley said, her hands anchored in her hair. "I need you to fuck me. Please don't make me wait anymore."

The direct request made Wyatt look Hayley in the eye, and for a split second she expected something cruel to happen, like her alarm going off, waking her from the best dream she'd ever had. She held Hayley close and walked up the stairs to the bedroom she'd only seen through the window and laid her down on the bed. Hayley lifted her ass so she could strip off her panties, then spread her legs in apparent invitation.

"Take your pants off, honey."

Wyatt stripped her jeans off like they were on fire.

"Have you thought about me?" Hayley asked as she sat up and pulled Wyatt's boxers down.

"You can't think otherwise," she said as her Neanderthal brain was rattling its bars and screaming, *No talk now.* "What happened made it clear I had a few things to wrap up in New York so that I could come back here permanently. Back to you."

Hayley lay back willingly when Wyatt pressed their lips together, moaning again when she got on the bed. The next round would be slow, or however Hayley liked it, but she couldn't wait anymore.

She lifted up enough to move her hand down Hayley's body and simply stared at how perfect Hayley was. She should've been able to come up with something better since she wrote for a living, but that's all she had. Hayley was captivating and had been from the first glimpse of her.

"You *are* going to leave me hanging, aren't you?" Hayley asked when she didn't move.

"Maybe I'm thinking of something romantic or intelligent to say." She bit her lip when her fingers glided through Hayley's wetness.

"Believe me, *not* the time for sappy, baby," Hayley said as she put her feet flat on the mattress and lifted her hips to make better contact with her hand. She smiled when Hayley wrapped her fingers around her wrist and pressed her more firmly against her. "Right now, instead of wasting time on that, I need you to fill me up and make me come."

She wanted to put her mouth on her, wanted to know how Hayley tasted, and she would satisfy her curiosity as soon as she satisfied Hayley. There were so many things she wanted to share with Hayley, but right now she did as Hayley asked and slid her fingers in and put her thumb over her clit.

"Baby, please," Hayley said, but all Wyatt could do was moan at the exquisiteness of the moment.

"Please what?" she asked, opening her eyes and looking at Hayley. The way Hayley intimately squeezed her fingers was sexy as fuck. "Tell me what you want."

Hayley smiled as if remembering the words she'd written. "Fuck me." Hayley played her part well, and she spread her legs farther apart and pulled her head down so she could kiss her. "I need you to fuck me." Hayley nipped her lip after she made her demand, and she could almost take her pulse by pressing her fingers to her own clit. "Don't make me wait any longer."

It was all she needed to pull out and slam her fingers back in. She didn't want to make Hayley beg, at least not this time, so she pumped her hand hard and fast while she stroked her thumb over Hayley's clit.

"Fuck," Hayley screamed as she wrapped her legs around her and pulled her hair so she could bring her mouth down on hers. "Don't stop. I need…God…I need…" She bucked up into her and pulled her hair harder. "That's it, like that, baby. Don't stop, don't stop."

She sucked on Hayley's neck as she lost complete control under her until she let out a scream that made Wyatt smile. "Come on, give me what I want." She wanted Hayley to come, wanted to hear her as she finished.

Hayley stiffened and trapped Wyatt's hand in place when she tightened her legs around her. "Yes…yes…yes," was all she could manage as she came. "Oh my God." Hayley's body relaxed, but she didn't let go of her. They were quiet for a few minutes as Hayley got her breathing back under control and she moved her hands from Wyatt's hair to her cheeks. "I see writing isn't your only talent. That was worth the wait, but let's make a pact we won't wait that long again. There's no way I can take it."

Hayley's sex gripped her fingers, making her smile. "Is that your idea of a handshake to seal that deal?"

"It's your fault for writing all that stuff and doing things like stripping in your room," Hayley said, kissing her. "I wanted you to come over here and put your head between my legs instead of having to touch myself I was so turned-on, but you're dense sometimes."

"You drove me insane, enough so I'm shocked I haven't fallen off a ladder or broken my fingers with my hammer." She pulled out and lifted up enough to paint the outside of Hayley's bra with her wetness. "All I could think about was what you tasted like." She lowered her head and sucked Hayley's nipple, feeling her moan when she gently bit down. "What you felt like." She moved down, kissing Hayley's abdomen as she made her way to where she wanted to be.

"Oh, honey, please," Hayley said, and Wyatt looked up. "I want you, but let me touch you."

"I want you to, but I want this more right now." She settled between Hayley's legs and kissed the top of her sex. "Do you want me to stop?"

Hayley smiled and brought her hands down her body until she reached her sex. "That's not a serious question, is it? I don't want to be selfish, but I need you to put your mouth right here."

She smiled up at Hayley, loving how she was holding herself open with her finger over her clit. Hayley dropped her head back when Wyatt lowered her head and flattened her tongue over where she wanted her most.

"Baby, please," Hayley said.

She wanted to assure Hayley she'd take care of her, but she didn't want to lift her head. The way Hayley pulled on the sides of her head was turning her on, but this was about Hayley. She sucked her in and went from sucking to flicking her tongue. That made Hayley flex her legs and buck her hips. They were going too fast again, but that didn't matter—they had all night to try everything they'd both thought and fantasized about. The frenzy would eventually die down, but hopefully not too much.

She placed her index and middle fingers at Hayley's opening

and waited. The situation was reaching frantic, and while she accepted the caveman part of herself, she wasn't a beast—she wanted Hayley's permission.

"God, yes." Hayley answered the unasked question, and she buried her fingers inside again.

They didn't stop until Hayley's body froze as she screamed. She pulsed around her fingers and it made Wyatt suck harder.

"Good Lord, honey," Hayley said in a voice that was soft and sexy. She laughed when Hayley whacked her in the head with her foot, which she took as a sign to lift her mouth off her. "Get up here." She did, glad when Hayley rolled into her and placed her leg and arm across her body to keep her in place.

"Thank you." She smiled again when Hayley moved to lie on top of her.

"I should be thanking you. That was a long time in coming but well worth the wait," Hayley said as she ran her finger around Wyatt's mouth. The contact did nothing to ease the pounding between her legs.

"I'm glad you liked it."

"Oh, I more than liked it," Hayley said, replacing her finger with her tongue. "Maybe you can put the jeans and tool belt on for my birthday." She smiled when Hayley laughed.

"Liked those, did you?" She laughed harder when Hayley slapped her hand when she tried to put it on her ass.

"You've had your fun, lover, so keep those to yourself and relax." Hayley sat up and straddled her.

"Ah, relaxing is going to be hard," she said as Hayley brought her hands up and cupped her breasts.

"Can I help you relax?" Hayley asked as she lowered the straps of the pretty bra.

"Don't be cruel."

"You have the nerve to say that after writing erotica and not delivering it in person? The second story should've come with a personal reading while you were naked, so that's my definition of cruel, baby." Hayley leaned down slowly, stopping to make Wyatt lift her head to reach her mouth. "Do you have any idea how wet those made me?"

"It made me wet, thinking of you reading them. I hope you didn't get a lot of shit from your boss."

"I don't want to talk about my boss or anyone else right now," Hayley said, kissing her and not stopping her when she put her hands back on her ass. "What I want is you."

"I want you too." She sounded like an idiot, but it was hard to think when Hayley sat back up and snapped her fingers to get her attention away from her chest.

"You seem to have a fascination with women's breasts." Hayley's hands went behind her back and it appeared she was undoing the bra, so she tried to keep eye contact as Hayley held up the garment before dropping it on the floor. "Is that a fair statement?"

Wyatt stopped breathing when Hayley put her hand between her legs to get her fingers wet. She groaned when Hayley painted one nipple, then the other.

"Is it?"

"I wouldn't call it a fascination with *women* so much as a blown-out obsession with *your* breasts."

Caveman brain was jumping up and down making grunting noises. It was amazing she was able to form words when all she wanted was to beg Hayley to touch her. To calm all her thoughts, she sat up and sucked Hayley's nipple in until Hayley pulled her hair to make her let go.

Wyatt released the nipple with a popping noise.

"Not so fast, it's my turn now."

"I'm only human, baby, not made of stone."

"You have to learn some patience," Hayley said, "so tell me— did you like watching me touch myself?"

"If that is in any way a serious question, the answer is yes." Okay, she'd just said she wasn't made of stone, but her clit was turning to stone as Hayley ground against her. "You're killing me."

"Sorry, you just feel good." Hayley pushed her down so she could lean over and kiss her again and took Wyatt's hands so she could put them over her head. "Keep them there and let me make you feel good."

Hayley's trip down her body could in no way be described as fast, quick, speedy, or any other adjective she could think of. The woman was a Sunday driver, but Wyatt felt so good she hated to complain.

"Are you hard, baby?" Hayley asked, finally between her legs, her mouth close to where Wyatt desperately needed it.

"Yes," she said, gripping the bars of Hayley's headboard, having to take a deep breath not to come instantly when Hayley sucked her clit in hard. "Fuck yeah," she was barely able to get out since Hayley's mouth was relentless. Wyatt was close to weeping with relief.

The way Hayley kept her tongue on her clit but still sucked was driving her to the point where the only way she could stop would be if someone tased her and knocked her out again. She had experience with that. When Hayley drove her fingers in, she lost all control and wrapped her hand in Hayley's hair. She felt the beginning of her orgasm and lay back to enjoy it.

Hayley didn't disappoint and didn't stop until Wyatt felt like overcooked pasta. "I'm an incredible idiot for not coming to introduce myself the first day I got to town."

"Maybe that's a good thing," Hayley said as she crawled back up. "If we'd met right off, we'd still be dancing around each other, trying to get where we are now. I'm the world's worst dater."

"Not your average romantic, huh?" She had to coax her arms off the bed to hold Hayley in place.

"I can be if I try real hard—you taught me I love getting flowers. Still, no, I'm not your average romantic." Hayley kissed her softly and less hurriedly. "I think we should take our time and see where we go next. You might decide I'm a workaholic who's not worth it."

"What a coincidence, I'm a workaholic who's known to lose track of time when I'm in the middle of a book. The cure for both of us might be to try this as a way to break us out of our bad habits."

"Is it going to be only about this?" Hayley asked, laying her head on her shoulder.

"I'll be happy to answer that, but let me ask you something. Do you have a lot of experience with relationships?"

"Not really. Will that be a problem?" Hayley finally looked at her with an indecipherable expression.

"I'm older than you, but we're in the same boat when it comes to that, and I think we should learn together. So don't worry," she said, putting her arms around Hayley. "It's going to be about this, as well as dinner dates, baking cookies, and playing strip putt-putt."

"You'll go a long way in getting George to like you if you get rid of Belle." Hayley smiled, and it made her want to spend the night holding her.

"I'd rather concentrate on making you like me, but Belle's finding a new home at the end of the week. Some woman got the idea for a whole course after getting a look at my yard, so there's one date night planned once Belle goes to her new home." She rolled them over and kissed the side of Hayley's neck. "There's a few other things I can promise you."

"Like what?" Hayley moved her head to the side, clearly liking what she was doing.

"I won't lie to you—I know that's all you asked of me. I also promise that I'll try my best to get to know you, so maybe one day we'll be more than neighbors. And the last thing is, I promise not to get lost in the work to the point you'll feel neglected. And if I start to, you have my permission to whack me upside the head and pull me in line." She kissed her again, liking the way Hayley hugged her with what seemed like all her strength.

"I'm going to hold you to all that." Hayley combed her hair off her forehead and kept her hand on the side of her head.

"I know you will," she said as she moved her hand down, and Hayley didn't stop her. This was hopefully the first of their nights together.

"Thank you for coming back." Hayley kissed her chest and moved back on top when she encouraged her.

"You gave me no choice, and there's so much I want to share with you."

"Like why you didn't tell me your real name when you moved in?"

Wyatt grinned sheepishly. "At first it was just a game, a way to preserve my anonymity and get the space I needed. Then it became a way to get to know you without the trappings of my job hanging around my neck."

"I might always think of you as Joe, to some degree." Hayley squeezed Wyatt's bicep. "Especially when you're wearing a tool belt."

Wyatt rolled on top of Hayley once again. "Baby, I don't care what you call me, as long as you call me yours."

EPILOGUE

A year later

Hayley sat on her side of the partner's desk they'd found at the Montbard Antiquities store on Magazine one Sunday. After three months of going between properties, they'd decided on Wyatt's house since it was completely renovated. She'd considered selling her place, but after meeting her mother, Wyatt had encouraged her to keep it so her mom wouldn't take out a hit on Wyatt for putting that thought in her head.

DJ and his guys had moved next door to finish all the renovations at Hayley's house, and the young couple who'd rented it were huge Wyatt Whitlock fans, but they tried not to bother Wyatt too much whenever she walked by. And somehow hiring DJ's crew again meant they showed up in their kitchen every morning for large amounts of sugar and cream to go with very little coffee.

The Woman in the Window had debuted at number one and was still going strong. The next one in the series was almost complete, and it'd been interesting to watch Wyatt go through her process. That she sometimes made arrangements to be dragged behind a boat with her hands and feet tied together, or to be hogtied in the back of a police car after promising Wally it wasn't a setup, made Hayley shake her head. You couldn't argue with Wyatt, though, because her attention to detail worked.

The greatest thing that had happened to her—aside from getting to not only edit Wyatt's work but to represent her—was the night Wyatt had taken her out for a round of miniature golf and admitted she loved her in Belle's shadow. It had been so Wyatt, and it was memorable. The other great thing was having a house between them and George. To discourage any impromptu visits, Wyatt had dipped her on the porch and kissed her until it was clear who she was with. George hadn't looked happy, but he'd stopped coming by.

"Hey," Wyatt called out after the door slammed shut, "I'm home. Are you naked somewhere?"

"You're only saying that because you know my parents are due in about an hour." Hayley walked out and leaned against the door of the office. "And if you do that in front of my mother, she's going to practice her sleeper hold on you. Don't accuse me of not warning you."

"She said it because I talked her into a swinging lifestyle at lunch," Lucy said, coming over to kiss her cheek. "We thought it would save time if you were already naked."

"I should warn both of you I have a gun." She laughed when Wyatt put her hands up as she bent to kiss her. "All you're safe doing is admiring her ass in these jeans, but not for too long." Her feet came off the floor when Wyatt put her arms around her and kissed her.

"What time do we have to leave to pick up Agent Fox?" Wyatt asked as she scooped Hayley into her arms.

"An hour, so forget about getting frisky." She didn't care how much time they spent together—being in Wyatt's arms still made her giddy.

"We can blame traffic." Wyatt jutted her chin at the small dish on the table in the foyer. "The keys are right there. Just lock the door when you leave," she told Lucy.

"Can I join in before I go?" Lucy asked with her hands pressed together in prayer and her lips in a pout.

"Not today," Wyatt said as she started up the stairs. "But call me later if you need help with any heavy stuff. I'm sure my girl will understand if I miss dinner."

"Your girl will not understand that. The only reason I love you is my mother's fixation with you, which makes her forget all about me and whatever she thinks is wrong with me." She waved at Lucy and blew her a kiss. "Let Sam know we'll both be over tomorrow."

One of the other people that came over often was Sam Fuller—

Gator's niece, the latest generation Sam Fuller—who'd bonded with Wyatt over the journals. Sam was a little younger than her and Lucy, but she reminded her a lot of Wyatt in personality. For all that Lucy pretended to want to join them in bed, she and Sam had been practically inseparable since their first meeting.

Lucy wasn't in a hurry to leave and kept talking from her place at the front door. "I'm trying to talk her out of inviting my mother to come live with us. Be careful what you throw out into the universe, my friends. I found a doctor who's crazy about me and wants her future mother-in-law to come live with us. That is some crazy shit."

Wyatt laughed as she kept climbing. Sam had proposed the month before, and Lucy had freaked out before saying yes. The move had totally shocked her old friend, and it made Hayley reconsider her own stance on marriage. Kids weren't in her plans, but then, Wyatt hadn't been planned either, and Hayley's reluctance when they'd talked about the future might've kept Wyatt from asking her.

"What's going on in that brilliant head?" Wyatt said when she sat on the bed with her on her lap. "If you're worried about Lucy, she only asked to touch my ass, and I was allowed to keep my pants on."

"Shut up," she said, pulling Wyatt's hair. "It's nothing. I missed you today." Marlo had been good about letting her work from home. She now had her staff meetings in the dining room when she could, and Fabio, like Lucy, was in love with Wyatt. She had to keep reminding him Wyatt was in fact female, but the tool belt had sent him into what could only be described as the vapors. The good thing about her lover was how she made a point of developing friendships with people like Marlo, Fabio, and Lucy.

"I missed you too, and I'm sorry I couldn't move my interview. I felt bad you had to get the guest house ready alone." Instead of rebuilding the gazebo in the yard, they'd decided on a guest house where her parents could stay as long as they wanted. She laughed when she admitted they needed the space because of her inability to have quiet sex, and DJ and his guys had gladly come back when they started building.

DJ and his crew dragged their feet, not to rip them off, but because they loved spending time with Wyatt. When Daisy stopped by every week, it was like a block party of guys in their yard. There was no more room to build anything, so Wyatt had put in an outdoor kitchen and a horseshoe setup, where they had everyone over once a month. George got to watch from his porch as payback for punching Wyatt the first night Wyatt had come back. DJ's guys had told him he could come over if he let Wyatt hit him back. It was still an open invitation he hadn't taken them up on.

"I should warn you about something before my mother makes your life miserable from the minute she gets in the car."

"What did I do now? I promise I've never killed anyone so I could write about it. The woman can't take a joke."

"Calm down, honey." She rubbed Wyatt's neck. "She found out about Sam and Lucy." Her mother had read the journals on one of her solo trips to visit and had fallen in love with Lydia and Sam, like all of them had. The journals were now in a bookshelf right under their picture on the stair landing, and her mom's favorite part was Sam proposing.

"Ah, I haven't proposed, so I'm an asshole. Am I right?"

"*I* don't think that. It was me who told you I might not want or need that." She stopped when Wyatt kissed her. "You know I love you, right? And I love that you're so nice to my parents even though my mother is probably sneaking in here at night to take hair and skin samples."

"I love you too, and I thought about what you said." Wyatt stood and set her on the bed. "I told your mother about that conversation when she called."

"My mother called you?" This couldn't be good, but Wyatt wasn't yelling. Granted, Wyatt never yelled unless she was watching the Yankees on a bad day. Aside from that, she was even-keeled.

"She did, after I called your father. My dad isn't here any longer, but he did teach me some manners before he died, and I was reminded of that when I read the journals. Your mom and Lydia have something in common." Wyatt leaned over and opened the drawer on her nightstand.

"What's that?" Her pulse raced when Wyatt got on one knee.

"They both think that when someone asks you to marry them, you should have a ring and mean it." The box creaked open. "One night, I found this place on the internet and had no idea what I was getting into. I started a reno, briefly owned a snake I never actually had, was picketed for a golf course I never had, and was tased for handcuffing a woman I'd never been near." Wyatt kissed her palm when she touched the scar that ran through her eyebrow. "The one thing that would make me do it all over and over again is you. I love you, I want to share my life with you, and I want the world to know it. Will you marry me?"

"Yes," she said, her eyes welling with happy tears. "Thank you for not listening to me when I said I wasn't sure I wanted to get married, and I love you too."

"Make sure you flash this when your mom walks into the airport," Wyatt said as she placed the ring on her finger. "And I plan to make some more promises and keep them, so you'll never have a doubt when it comes to us."

"I know that, but right now I need you to make love to me." She pulled her sweater off and laughed at Wyatt's expression. "Remember this?" She was wearing the white lace push-up bra.

"That bra is my favorite…especially when it's on the floor."

Wyatt was naked a moment later and helped her with her jeans. "If this outfit shows up in any book, we might have to have a serious talk."

"Uh-huh."

As always Wyatt undid her until she was desperate and begging. Whoever thought sex with the same person would be boring should give it a shot. Of course it was she who'd thought that, but it was hard to remember every dumb thing that had popped into her head when Wyatt's fingers were buried in her sex.

"You're so good at that." She pushed Wyatt onto her back and kissed right above her belly button.

"It's a gift." Wyatt loved to joke with her, and laughing made up big parts of their day.

"That it is, my love." She loved touching Wyatt, making her crazy, and bringing her over the edge with her name on her lips. "Do you think you'll be chasing me through the house until we're old like Lydia and Sam?" She loved the way Wyatt held her.

"I do, and I expect you to slow down when I'm ready for a walker." They talked a little more until it was time to leave for the airport.

"Do you still hear your parents?" Hayley asked. Wyatt had told her about her conversations that weren't one-sided, then swore she wasn't crazy.

"Not as often. They only pop in when they think it's important." Wyatt opened the door to the SUV she'd purchased to replace Hayley's small car. Lucy had borrowed the truck, and no matter how much Wyatt wanted to, Hayley had warned her they couldn't make her parents ride in the truck bed to keep them from giving her a hard time.

"Anything notable lately?" She waved to Karen, who was taking a pie to the couple who rented from them. God help them. "We might have to spot them a month's rent to cover the medical bills if they actually eat that."

"Don't worry, I sent DJ over there with our list of warnings, and those pies are number one. As for my parents, they stopped by to remind me what an idiot I was for taking so long to ask you to marry me. It seems my mother wanted to make sure I didn't do anything to make you leave. You're the best thing that's happened to me, and I totally agree." Wyatt leaned over and kissed her at a stoplight. "I'm totally crazy about you."

She laughed and nodded. "I think that about you too, honey, and that you're mine is what makes me the happiest. And in case you didn't pick up on my excitement, I'm thrilled you asked."

"The future isn't scary any longer because of you. I love you."

"I love you." She pressed her hand to Wyatt's chest and kissed her until the people behind them blew their horn. "And I promise I always will."

About the Author

Ali Vali is the author of the long-running Cain Casey "Devil" series, the newest being *The Devil Incarnate*, and the Genesis Clan "Forces" series, as well as numerous standalone romances including three Lambda Literary Award finalists: *Calling the Dead*, *Love Match*, and *One More Chance*. Ali's latest release is *Writer's Block*.

Originally from Cuba, Ali has retained much of her family's traditions and language and uses them frequently in her stories. Having her father read her stories and poetry before bed every night as a child infused her with a love of reading, which she carries till today. Ali currently lives outside New Orleans, where she enjoys cheering LSU and trying new restaurants.

Books Available From Bold Strokes Books

A Long Way to Fall by Elle Spencer. A ski lodge, two strong-willed women, and a family feud that brings them together, but will it also tear them apart? (978-1-63679-005-3)

Forever by Kris Bryant. When Savannah Edwards is invited to be the next bachelorette on the dating show *When Sparks Fly*, she'll show the world that finding true love on television can happen. (978-1-63679-029-9)

Ice on Wheels by Aurora Rey. All's fair in love and roller derby. That's Riley Fauchet's motto, until a new job lands her at the same company—and on the same team—as her rival Brooke Landry, the frosty jammer for the Big Easy Bruisers. (978-1-63679-179-1)

Perfect Rivalry by Radclyffe. Two women set out to win the same career-making goal, but it's love that may turn out to be the final prize. (978-1-63679-216-3)

Something to Talk About by Ronica Black. Can quiet ranch owner Corey Durand give up her peaceful life and allow her feisty new neighbor into her heart? Or will past loss, present suitors, and town gossip ruin a long-awaited chance at love? (978-1-63679-114-2)

With a Minor in Murder by Karis Walsh. In the world of academia, police officer Clare Sawyer and professor Libby Hart team up to solve a murder. (978-1-63679-186-9)

Writer's Block by Ali Vali. Wyatt and Hayley might be made for each other if only they can get through nosy neighbors, the historic society, at-odds future plans, and all the secrets hidden in Wyatt's walls. (978-1-63679-021-3)

The Business of Pleasure by Ronica Black. Editor in chief Valerie Raffield is quickly becoming smitten by Lennox, the graphic artist she's hired to work remotely. But when Lennox doesn't show for their first face-to-face meeting, Valerie's heart and her business may be in jeopardy. (978-1-63679-134-0)

Cold Blood by Genevieve McCluer. Maybe together, Kalila and Dorenia have a chance of taking down the vampires who have eluded them all these years. And maybe, in each other, they can find a love worth living for. (978-1-63679-195-1)

Greener Pastures by Aurora Rey. When city girl and CPA Audrey Adams finds herself tending her aunt's farm, will Rowan Marshall—the charming cider maker next door—turn out to be her saving grace or the bane of her existence? (978-1-63679-116-6)

Grounded by Amanda Radley. For a second chance, Olivia and Emily will need to accept their mistakes, learn to communicate properly, and with a little help from five-year-old Henry, fall madly in love all over again. Sequel to Flight SQA016. (978-1-63679-241-5)

The Hummingbird Sanctuary by Erin Zak. The Hummingbird Sanctuary, Colorado's hottest resort destination: Come for the mountains, stay for the charm, and enjoy the drama as Olive, Eleanor, and Harriet figure out the meaning of true friendship. (978-1-63679-163-0)

Journey's End by Amanda Radley. In this heartwarming conclusion to the Flight series, Olivia and Emily must finally decide what they want, what they need, and how to follow the dreams of their hearts. (978-1-63679-233-0)

Secret Agent by Michelle Larkin. CIA agent Peyton North embarks on a global chase to apprehend rogue agent Zoey Blackwood, but her commitment to the mission is tested as the sparks between them ignite and their sizzling attraction approaches a point of no return. (978-1-63555-753-4)

Something Between Us by Krystina Rivers. A decade after her heart was broken under Don't Ask, Don't Tell, Kirby runs into her first love and has to decide if what's still between them is enough to heal her broken heart. (978-1-63679-135-7)

Sugar Girl by Emma L McGeown. Having traded in traditional romance for the perks of Sugar Dating, Ciara Reilly not only enjoys the no-strings-attached arrangement, she's also a hit with her clients. That is, until she meets the beautiful entrepreneur Charlie Keller, who makes her want to go sugar-free. (978-1-63679-156-2)

With a Twist by Georgia Beers. Starting over isn't easy for Amelia Martini. When the irritatingly cheerful Kirby Dupress comes into her life, will Amelia be brave enough to go after the love she really wants? (978-1-63555-987-3)

The Witch Queen's Mate by Jennifer Karter. Barra and Silvi must overcome their ingrained hatred and prejudice to use Barra's magic and save both their peoples from not just slavery, but destruction. (978-1-63679-202-6)

Business of the Heart by Claire Forsythe. When a hopeless romantic meets a tough-as-nails cynic, they'll need to overcome the wounds of the past to discover that their hearts are the most important business of all. (978-1-63679-167-8)

Dying for You by Jenny Frame. Can Victorija Dred keep an age-old vow and fight the need to take blood from Daisy Macdougall? (978-1-63679-073-2)

Exclusive by Melissa Brayden. Skylar Ruiz lands the TV reporting job of a lifetime, but is she willing to sacrifice it all for the love of her longtime crush, anchorwoman Carolyn McNamara? (978-1-63679-112-8)

The Game by Jan Gayle. Ryan Gibbs is a talented golfer, but her guilt means she may never leave her small town, even if Katherine Reese tempts her with competition and passion. (978-1-63679-126-5)

Her Duchess to Desire by Jane Walsh. An up-and-coming interior designer seeks to create a happily ever after with an intriguing duchess, proving that love never goes out of fashion. (978-1-63679-065-7)

Take Her Down by Lauren Emily Whalen. Stakes are cutthroat, scheming is creative, and loyalty is ever-changing in this queer, female-driven YA retelling of Shakespeare's Julius Caesar. (978-1-63679-089-3)

Whereabouts Unknown by Meredith Doench. While homicide detective Theodora Madsen recovers from a potentially career-ending injury, she scrambles to solve the cases of two missing sixteen-year-old girls from Ohio. (978-1-63555-647-6)

Deadly Secrets by VK Powell. Corporate criminals want whistleblower Jana Elliott permanently silenced, but Rafe Silva will risk everything to keep the woman she loves safe. (978-1-63679-087-9)

Enchanted Autumn by Ursula Klein. When Elizabeth comes to Salem, Massachusetts, to study the witch trials, she never expects to find love—or an actual witch…and Hazel might just turn out to be both. (978-1-63679-104-3)

Escorted by Renee Roman. When fantasy meets reality, will escort Ryan Lewis be able to walk away from a chance at forever with her new client Dani? (978-1-63679-039-8)

Her Heart's Desire by Anne Shade. Two women. One choice. Will Eve and Lynette be able to overcome their doubts and fears to embrace their deepest desire? (978-1-63679-102-9)

My Secret Valentine by Julie Cannon, Erin Dutton & Anne Shade. Winning the heart of your secret Valentine? These award-winning authors agree, there is no better way to fall in love. (978-1-63679-071-8)

Perilous Obsession by Carsen Taite. When reporter Macy Moran becomes consumed with solving a cold case, will her quest for the truth bring her closer to Detective Beck Ramsey or will her obsession with finding a murderer rob her of a chance at true love? (978-1-63679-009-1)

Reading Her by Amanda Radley. Lauren and Allegra learn love and happiness are right where they least expect it. There's just one problem: Lauren has a secret she cannot tell anyone, and Allegra knows she's hiding something. (978-1-63679-075-6)

The Willing by Lyn Hemphill. Kitty Wilson doesn't know how, but she can bring people back from the dead as long as someone is willing to take their place and keep the universe in balance. (978-1-63679-083-1)

Watching Over Her by Ronica Black. As they face the snowstorm of the century, and the looming threat of a stalker, Riley and Zoey just might find love in the most unexpected of places. (978-1-63679-100-5)